Orola
Warrior Priestess

Herbert Grosshans

THE KIIR

They sat unmoving among the branches of a giant *Scrip-tree*, the foliage hiding them from anyone looking up. There were five of them. Scruffy looking men with stoic, brutal faces. Only their black eyes seemed alive as they watched the river below.

The object of their attention stood looking at the briskly flowing water.

A naked young woman. She had arrived some time earlier. After tethering her steed, she shed her rather skimpy clothing, which consisted only of a short kilt, a strip of cloth to cover her pubic area, and a pair of metal breast cups, hardly large enough to cover much of her ample breasts.

Testing the water with one foot, she seemed to hesitate, but then with a shrug, she dove into the water, her naked body glistening white in the midday sun.

When she hit the water, one of the watchers grunted. His lips parted to reveal brown, rotten teeth. The others nodded, and silently, they began to move through the branches.

Climbing down on the hidden side of the thick tree trunk, they reached the soft forest floor and, without making a sound, two of them moved toward the girl's steed. One took her clothing, and the other one tried to untie the animal.

When the black-coated beast snorted, the girl looked toward the commotion and called out sharply. Then she began swimming toward shore.

Letting go of the beast's rope, the man looked at her and grinned. His companion had already disappeared.

She climbed ashore and looked at the spot where she had left her clothing and her sword, realizing they were gone. "What do you want?" she demanded.

The man grinned, his eyes raking her naked form. They rested momentarily on the thick black triangle below her smooth flat belly then moved up to her large breasts, his attention suddenly on the red glowing object nestled in the deep cleft between them.

"Well?" she said, staring defiantly at him.

"I want you," he said, his voice thickly accented and his words slurred.

The girl laughed, shaking her long black hair. "You want me?" she taunted. "You and how many other men?"

Still grinning, he said, "Four."

Hearing the breaking of a twig behind her, she turned and looked at the two men approaching her. She stepped to the side and watched them coming closer, her body suddenly falling into a fighting stance.

Noticing her position, the two men slowed but didn't stop. "Don't try to fight us," one of them said. "We are five…you are just one helpless girl."

She took one step backward. The jewel between her breasts pulsed with a steady rhythm that she could feel. "I may be just a girl, but I'm not helpless." She whirled with a sudden movement, her knee came up and rammed into the belly of the man who tried to sneak up on her. He howled and dropped to the ground, his hands clutching his middle.

The other two rushed her and tried to grab her arms. She hit one of them in the face with her right fist, while the ball of her foot smashed into the chest of the other one. Rolling away from them, she came up, but collapsed, as a thrown club hit the side of her head.

———

Before the blackness engulfed her, she was pinned to the ground, and the heavy weight of a body bore down on her.

How long she was out, she couldn't tell. In the first moments of returning consciousness, she became aware of a weight still on top of her. She lay on her back, spread-eagled, her arms and legs tied to stakes driven into the ground. Between her legs, one of her attackers. She knew exactly what was going to happen to her. And there were five of them. Concentrating on the jewel between her breasts, she encountered only emptiness.

Silently crying out, she realized the *Holy Communicator* was gone. They must have taken it from her while she lay unconscious.

There was nothing left for her to do but suffer through the ordeal.

She drifted in and out of consciousness as the brutes satisfied their insatiable lust. Darkness had descended before they left her.

She heard them as they moved away, toward the stream. Listening to their splashing and subdued laughter, she wondered if it was really over now or if they would come back to her in a while.

To carry on. Or maybe to kill her.

Aware of nothing else but a deep painful throbbing in her entire body, but mostly in her private area, she didn't really care what they did. She was beyond further pain.

She opened her eyes again and turned her head slowly to look at them. They were clearly visible in the setting sun and the image of their faces burned into her memory. If she lived, she would hunt them down, one by one. They would pay for what they had done to her.

While she watched, one looked in her direction, grinned and came swaggering toward her. Fondling himself into an erection, he fell between her legs.

She looked into his black eyes.

"I will kill you for this," she whispered.

He just laughed. "If you live," he said hoarsely, clamping his mouth over hers. His breath stank of badly fermented wine and something rotten.

She ignored it; let him have his way. She could have bitten him, but she didn't.

Maybe they'd let her live. Just maybe.

She lost consciousness for a second time and when she became aware of her surroundings again, she knew she was alone.

Solar flooded the darkness with its pale light.

Looking up at the bright disk, she began to pray, but without her *Holy Communicator* her god could not hear her.

She willed her body to be calm, tried to ignore the dull pain, succeeding only partially. The bonds on her ankles and wrists were tight, but fortunately not so tight to cut off circulation.

She slept a little, waking up at irregular intervals. Each time she woke, she listened to the noises of the forest. Only once, she heard something large slinking through the underbrush, but then it was gone.

Daylight hit her eyes when she woke again.

She struggled to pull the stakes out of the ground, but they were driven deep and she was so weak. Closing her eyes against the glare of the bright morning sun, she tried again to pray, but it proved useless. There was no answer.

The sound of voices made her open her eyes, and she lifted her head to watch the approaching figures. A young man and a girl.

They stopped when they saw her. The girl put her hand to her mouth. "Look, Elto. A body!" she exclaimed.

Her companion took another step and looked closer. "It's a woman, and she's naked."

Grabbing his arm, she whispered, "Don't go closer, Elto. Maybe it's a *Forrest-Nhim*. They appear in the form of naked women, beautiful naked women. They promise pleasure beyond your dreams, but they will ensnare you in their own sexual fantasies and give you nothing but unbearable pain."

The young man snorted. "Who told you that?"

"The old Healer-woman. She knows everything," the girl said and squinted her eyes to get a better look. "She looks dead." Then she gasped and cried out, "She's tied to the ground."

"I am alive," the bound girl called, her voice coming out in a hoarse whisper. "Please, help me."

The pair came closer until they stood beside her.

"I'm not a *Forest-Nhim*," she said. "My name is Orola. I'm a stranger to this part of the world and just passing through. I mean no harm." She kept her lids half-closed, finding no need to let them see her eyes...not yet.

"Who did this to you?" the other girl asked.

"Five men," Orola answered. "Five ugly hairy men. More beast than man."

"*Kellos*," the young man spat. "They were *Kellos*." He produced a small knife from a sheath strapped to his upper arm, and he cut Orola's bonds. "Come on, Neltie," he said to the girl who stood watching. "Help me get her up."

Orola sat up and rubbed her wrists. "Thank you, but I can manage." She stood up carefully, swaying a bit, and smiled when the young man put an arm around her naked waist. "Thank you again, Elto. You are a kind man."

She saw the slight bulge in his thin pants but pretended not to notice. Neltie saw it, too, and giggled, staring at the bulge. Coloring, the boy dropped his arm. Then he pulled off his shirt and handed it to Orola. "Here, put this on."

"I'd like to wash the grime off my body first," Orola said, and then she walked to the water's edge.

———————

Elto swallowed hard and tried not to be too obvious as he watched Orola's plump naked buttocks moving enticingly as she walked toward the water. "She's beautiful," he blurted out.

Neltie slapped his arm. "How can you even think these thoughts? The last thing she'd want right now is someone like you sticking his *stinger* into her. After what those beasts did to her!"

Elto nodded, embarrassed, trying to hide his erection. "It's just...I have these strong urges, and you won't let me anymore," he said with an accusing stare.

"I let it happen that one time, and I'm sorry I did. It's not right, you know. We are cousins."

"Second cousins," he said, watching Orola as she washed off her full breasts.

"Besides," Neltie said, "you are much too young for her."

———————

Orola came out of the water and rubbed herself dry with her hands. She stood shivering for a moment and reached for the shirt, which the young man held out to her. Her nipples were pink and stiff, and she quickly slipped into the shirt. Because of her height, the shirt reached only to her navel, leaving her bottom bare.

She looked down and smiled weakly. "I guess you wouldn't want to give me your pants, too?"

"I...I...don't..." Elto stuttered and blushed.

"I'm only jesting," Orola said and leaned against a tree. "My knees feel a little weak. I need some rest and maybe some food. Would you mind if I accompany you to your village?"

"Oh no, we wouldn't mind at all," the young man said eagerly. "Our place is not far from here."

"You are welcome to stay with us," Neltie agreed. She touched Orola's elbow. "You can lean on me."

Orola smiled and put an arm around the younger girl's shoulder. "Thank you."

They walked slowly. Orola winced as dull pain spread from her womb to the rest of her body.

"You are hurting?" Neltie asked, concerned.

"I'll heal," Orola said, "but the ones who did this to me will pay. This I swear."

———

"You live fairly well," Orola remarked as they entered the immaculately kept yard and looked at the dwelling. Two stories high and entirely built with bricks. Red clay-tiles covered the roof.

She saw fowl running around free and heard the bawling and trumpeting of large food animals from another building.

"My dad raises *Sagos*," Elto said proudly. "He's very good at it, and he takes good care of them. The animals love him, and they grow large and fat."

"I'm impressed," Orola said. "*Sagos* are mean and unpredictable. They can gore a man to death with their long-curved horns. Any man who can handle them is to be respected."

The interior of the house looked as immaculate and clean as the outside. Rugs and furs covered the tiled floor. Curtains on the windows created a cozy and comfortable atmosphere.

A woman stood at a counter in the kitchen. She turned around when the door opened. Smiling, she came around the counter to greet them. Her smile vanished, and her eyes grew large when she looked at Orola.

"Who is this young woman, and why is she half-naked?" she demanded.

"This is Orola," Neltie answered. "She's been violated by a pack of *Kellos*. They took her clothes."

"Oh, you poor girl." The older woman came closer and took Orola's hand into both of hers. "You must feel awful. Come, sit down. Dinner is almost ready. But first, we'll have to get you some decent clothes. Can't leave you running around naked. Not with the men coming in at any moment." She gave Elto a stare. "Go get your father and brother. No need for you to watch. You've seen more than is good for you, anyway, young man. That is your shirt she's wearing, isn't it?"

Elto grinned. "Since I'm not wearing one, I guess it is." He disappeared through the doorway.

"Men!" the woman exclaimed and shook her head. "He's growing up fast, this one. I see him looking at my daughter when she's bathing unclothed in the creek."

"Oh, Mother, Elto is my cousin," Neltie said, blushing.

"That he is," the woman agreed, "but he's becoming a man, and you are turning into a woman. I think it's time you start putting on some clothes when you go swimming." She took Orola's arm. "Come with me. I'll find you something to wear."

They climbed a set of stairs and entered a bedroom. After rummaging around in a closet, the woman produced a loose robe similar to the one she wore. "Here, this should fit you. I used to wear it when I was slimmer." She touched her hips and belly, chuckling good-humoredly. "As you get older, your weight shifts to different places."

Orola smiled and took off Elto's shirt. The woman looked her over with appreciating eyes. "You do have a magnificent body, girl. Any man would love to bury his face between your beautiful breasts and have your lovely thighs embrace him. I had better tend to you myself. Can't have my men staring at your naked nest. They'd lose their heads for sure." She laughed and grew serious. "My, you're bruised all over. Those beasts really mistreated you."

"They will pay for it, my lady," Orola said with a low voice.

She looked up, and the other woman took an involuntary step backward.

"I believe you," she said slowly and stared into Orola's face.

"Where are you from?" she asked with a slight tremble in her voice.

"From the island Antanakka," answered Orola.

"The *Island of Witches*." The woman nodded. "You are a *Moon Priestess*. Your eyes give you away. You have the eyes of a nighthunter."

Orola laid a hand on the older woman's arm. "I don't know what you have heard about us, but much of it is probably exaggerated. We are not evil, and you don't have to be afraid. Just let me rest here in your home for a couple of days, and I'll be on my way," she said soothingly.

"You can stay as long as it takes to get well," the woman said with a warm smile. "I know you're not evil. I have a feeling for that."

Both women turned at the sound of the opening door. A man stepped through and stopped when he saw Orola with the older woman.

He was tall and big, middle-aged and quite handsome.

"I'm sorry," he said, staring in surprise at Orola's naked body. "I didn't know anyone was in here."

"Stop drooling and close the door...from the outside," the woman said and laughed when the man hastily closed the door again. "Men," she chuckled. "You'd think they'd never seen a naked woman before."

Orola smiled at the older woman's good nature. "You are certainly very tolerant with your husband."

"He's not my husband." The woman sighed. "He was married to my cousin. After her and my husband's deaths, I moved in with Carth. He takes care of my daughter and me. He's a good man."

She watched Orola slip into the robe. Then she went to a drawer and took out a jar. "We'd better put some ointment on that nasty cut on the side of your head," she said and proceeded to smear some of the salve on a piece of cloth and gently, she rubbed it into the wound.

Orola winced, but she didn't say anything.

"I know it stings," the woman said, "but it'll promote healing."

Orola, who had some knowledge of herbal medicines, recognized the scent of the herb in the ointment. She knew the woman spoke the truth. "Thank you," she said. "You are kind."

"It's nothing," the woman said. "Anyone else would do the same thing. People around here are very helpful and friendly, except..." A frown crossed her face, and her bright eyes clouded over. "Except for the Kellos. But you've met them."

They left the bedroom and went downstairs. The man, who had been upstairs, sat at a table. Another, a younger man, and Elto sat beside him. They were eating from heaped plates, while Neltie served more food. She was just about to sit down when she heard Orola and the older woman coming. She smiled apologetically.

"We started without you, Mother. You know how the men are. They can never wait."

"That's fine, Neltie. I know what you mean," her mother laughed. She turned toward Orola. "Sit down, girl. I see Neltie already set a place for you."

She looked at the men. "By the way, this is Orola. She'll be staying with us for a while." Staring at Carth, she said, "But you've already seen her, haven't you." She winked, causing the older man to chuckle.

"I have, haven't I," he said with an embarrassed grin.

Orola sat down and smiled. Aware of the younger man's stare, she looked into his eyes. He appeared to be the same age as Orola, and she felt an instant attraction toward him. She liked his open face and wide smile.

"I am Rylic," he said, "and you are the most beautiful girl

I've ever seen. I love your eyes. You have the eyes of a night-hunter."

"I told her that already," said the older woman. "Orola is a Moon Priestess from the island Antanakka. Just so you know, young man."

"What happened to you?" Rylic asked, still staring at Orola.

Again, the older woman answered. "Kellos! Does that answer your question?"

Rylic stopped smiling and became serious. "It does. It certainly does. I am sorry. What's a Moon Priestess?"

"We worship the moon Solar," Orola explained.

"What makes that moon so special?"

"Our god resides there."

"I don't believe in any gods. Not since my mother was murdered. The gods are dead. They never answer."

Orola detected bitterness in the young man's voice.

He stared at her. "How about your god? Does he ever answer you?"

Orola smiled. "All the time. I am in direct communication with him, but I need my *Holy Communicator*, which the Kellos stole from me."

"So how is it that your god did not save you from the Kellos?" Rylic challenged.

Orola shrugged. "Solar never interferes without our permission. We have to take the initiative, and then he will lend help. I cannot tell you more, because I am bound by an oath never to reveal our secrets, but believe me, Solar is a powerful and very real god."

The young man shrank back from the fire blazing in Orola's eyes. "These Kellos made a fatal mistake when they violated the body of a Moon Priestess, *my* body, and when the time comes, Solar will give me the strength to revenge the wrong that was done!" she said fiercely.

"I almost believe you," Rylic whispered hoarsely and shuddered. "But I don't believe you need a god to help you. Something tells me that you are quite capable of avenging yourself. It's not only your eyes that are strange." He looked at her for a moment, and then he lowered his eyes to his plate and started to eat.

Orola tasted her own food and found she was quite hungry.

Nobody spoke for a while, and Orola was grateful. The dull pain from her insides diminished the enjoyment of the food somewhat, and the cut at the side of her head gave her a headache. She looked up at the older woman. "Thank you for the food, but I am not feeling well. Is there a place where I might rest?"

The woman wiped her hand on her apron. "Of course, dear girl. You can sleep in Rylic's room. He can bunk with Elto."

"No, no, Aunt Firma," Elto protested. "Rylic snores. Why can't she sleep in your bed? It's big enough for three people."

"Oh, all right. She can sleep in my bed." The woman smiled and looked at Carth. The older man grinned but said nothing.

Firma accompanied Orola back into the bedroom. Elto had been right; the bed was huge. A strong iron frame supported a thick, soft mattress. A heavy curtain could be drawn for privacy or against drafts.

Orola removed her robe and, naked, she climbed under the covers. Firma brought another jar and pulled back the covers.

"This is good for aching muscles and joints." She proceeded to put little dabs of the ointment all over Orola's body, and then she rubbed it in.

Her hands were gentle and Orola closed her eyes, enjoying the massage.

"You have lovely, soft skin," Firma remarked, and her hands lingered on Orola's full breasts. "Beautiful breasts, too," she murmured, rolling the pink nipples between her fingers.

Orola opened her eyes. The older woman smiled and moved her hands down to Orola's belly. "You've been hurt inside, girl. Open your legs," she said softly and dipped her finger into another jar. "This will heal you."

Orola sensed no malice in the woman and spread her thighs. Very gently, Firma inserted her finger into Orola's sex-organ and rubbed slightly stinging cream into the walls of her sheath. When she was done, she said, "Turn over onto your stomach. I'll do your back."

Orola obeyed and closed her eyes again. The gentle massage and the ointment soothed her aching body, and the dull pain seemed less severe. Aware of Firma's hands lingering longer than necessary on her round buttocks and of the finger that softly stroked the cleft between them, she didn't care. She felt good and dropped into a deep slumber.

When she awoke, she was alone. A sheet covered her body, and the curtain had been drawn around the bed.

She stretched and yawned. Then she sat up, opened the curtain and slipped out of bed. She padded to the window and pulled open the blinds. Bright light lit up the room, and she realized it was morning.

A noise from the door made her turn. Firma stood there, a friendly smile on her face. "Good morning, my dear. I trust you slept well."

Orola rubbed the sleep from her eyes. "I never woke up once." She touched her body. "And I feel fine. Hardly any aches."

Firma laughed. "It's the ointment. The old Healer-woman from the village makes it. She is knowledgeable when it comes to medicine." She bent down and picked Orola's robe off the floor. "Here, put this on and come down for breakfast. There is a room downstairs where you can wash up and make yourself presentable."

Orola slipped into the robe and followed the woman downstairs.

Everybody had already eaten, it appeared, by the time she sat down at the table.

"We start the day early," Firma remarked. "The Sagos demand a lot of attention, and Carth gives it to them. A couple of heifers are calving today, so Neltie and Elto are helping, too. Maybe when you've had your breakfast you might want to go and watch. It is very interesting."

Orola wiped out her bowl with a piece of bread and emptied her cup. "That was great," she said. "I didn't realize how hungry I was." She got up. "I'll help you clean up," she offered, but Firma waved her off. "No, thank you. I'm fine by myself."

Orola went into the yard. She was barefoot, but the ground was soft and sandy, easy to walk on. She headed for the outbuilding. Reaching for the doorknob, she was almost knocked down when someone flung open the door. Neltie came charging out.

"We need some help in there," the girl panted. "Both heifers are calving at the same time, and Elto decided to go down to the pond for a swim."

Orola followed the girl into the building. Outside, she had smelled the Sagos, but inside the stench hit her nostrils, and she gasped for air momentarily.

"You get used to it." Neltie pointed to the far end of the barn. "They're in there."

The animals eyed her suspiciously as she hurried past them. They had black, shaggy coats, but shimmering scales covered their muscular short necks and large heads. Each animal was kept in its own pen, separated from the others by solid walls. A strong iron gate held the animal safely inside the pen.

"Don't go too close," Neltie warned over her shoulder. "Watch their horns."

The horns did indeed look vicious. Two long curved ones on either side of the head and one short, straight one right above the nose.

"Those gates are quite low," Orola remarked.

"They can't jump very well," Neltie explained. "They're too heavy."

Some of the Sagos snorted and bellowed at the two girls.

"Hush," Neltie told them, but kept her distance.

They reached the end of the building and halted in front of one of the gates. A female Sagos lay on its side. Carth knelt behind the animal and seemed to be pulling at something. "It's coming out fine," he called when he saw the girls. "Neltie, come in here and give me a hand. Orola, go get Rylic."

"He's in the last stall." Neltie slipped through the gate to join Carth.

Orola hurried past the snorting animals and found Rylic in the same position as Carth. He looked up when Orola approached. His naked upper torso looked slick with perspiration. "This one is bad," he panted. "We might lose it. It seems to be stuck, and it's coming out the wrong way."

Orola saw what he meant. The calf's hind legs were out, but nothing else.

"It's taking too long." Rylic groaned and pulled with all this strength at the two exposed hind legs. "The mother will soon come out of sedation, and then we have troubles."

Orola moved to the front of the stretched-out animal and looked at the eyes. The lids were still half-closed, but they were beginning to twitch. She bent down and touched the wide, scaly forehead. Closing her own eyes, she entered into a semi-trance. She dealt well with animals, and even though she did not possess her *Holy Communicator*, she hoped her gift had not left her.

As she sank deeper into a trance, she sensed the animal's uneasiness and slow return to awareness. She began to send soothing thoughts, and after a while, the female Sagos seemed to respond and calmed down.

Orola lost all sense of time, aware only of the primitive thought tendrils of the animal mind. Deeper and deeper she sank into that state. She felt a pain in her womb, an awful pain. Even though she knew the pain was not hers, it hurt.

Suddenly, the pain was gone, and she heard a faraway voice calling her name.

The connection between her mind and the primitive entity snapped, and she surfaced back to reality.

Rylic had his arms around her from the back; in front of her, the female Sagos struggled to its feet. Unfortunately, they were in the back of the pen, the entrance blocked by the large body of the animal.

The Sagos snorted, bellowed and lowered its scaly head. Orola stared at the sharp long horn pointing at her chest. If the animal lurched ahead, it would run that long horn right through her and Rylic.

Without thinking, she reached out and touched the horn.

She heard Rylic take a deep breath and hold it.

Again, the Sagos snorted, but made no other threatening moves. Then it lowered its large head even further and turned sideways. Orola stepped closer and began stroking the smooth, scaly neck.

The animal rubbed its shaggy shoulder against her, almost knocking her over.

Carefully, Rylic eased out of the pen, pulling Orola with him. When he closed the gate behind them, he let out a sigh of relief. Giving Orola a strange look, he said, "You are full of surprises. Even my father, who understands the Sagos, could not have done what you did."

Orola smiled weakly. "I have always had a good relationship with animals. By the way, where is the calf?"

Rylic shook his head. "It suffocated. We lost it, but my father was lucky. He delivered a healthy bull Sagos."

"That's good," Orola said. "Now...I need to sit down. This has taken a lot out of me. If only I had my Holy Communicator."

"There is a bench back where the calves are kept," Rylic said and took Orola's arm.

They found Carth in the pen with the newborn Sagos, busy rubbing down the shaking calf.

Orola sat down and watched. "It's got no hair," she said, staring at the gray-skinned little animal.

Rylic laughed when he saw her puzzled expression. "That's why it is so important to take care of them. The hair will grow fast. Look at the others. They are only about half a season old."

Orola counted fourteen calves of various sizes; most of them displayed a thick coat of hair.

Looking up from his work, Carth gave her a friendly smile. Then he looked at Rylic and frowned. "You should have gotten her out of there sooner."

"I know." Rylic replied, looking sheepish. "I'm sorry, but she seemed to have things under control. Did you see what she did?"

"I saw," Carth said curtly. "Still, you should have been more careful."

"My father is very possessive when it comes to his Sagos," Rylic said under his breath. "And maybe a little jealous. He doesn't believe that anyone else can achieve a rapport with them."

"I heard that," Carth called. "But you have to agree, you've never met anyone who can."

"Until now," Rylic said, smiling triumphantly.

Carth unsuccessfully suppressed a chuckle. "Until now," he admitted and gave the little Sagos bull a gentle slap on the rump. "That should do it." He looked at Orola. "Why don't you and Neltie go down to the pond for a swim? You'll enjoy the cool water. Rylic can join you after he's helped me bury the other calf."

Neltie reached for Orola. "Come." She tugged Orola's hand. "Let's see if we can surprise Elto."

Orola followed the giggling girl. She still felt a little sluggish, but a dip into cool water sounded great.

They didn't see Elto in the pond or anywhere near it. The girls shed their clothes and gingerly entered the water.

"It's cold," Neltie said, shivering. "I have goose bumps all over." She looked at Orola. "Your breasts, they are so large, so solid." Touching her own breasts, she said, "Mine are small, underdeveloped. They make me look like a little girl, much younger than I really am. Do you think they'll ever be big?"

Orola chuckled and shrugged. "Breasts aren't everything. Big breasts don't make you a woman."

"But men like them. I've seen Elto and Rylic gawking at Lady Rhena when she comes swimming in the pond."

"Most men don't really care. They might look at a woman's breasts, but a nicely formed body and a pretty face gets their attention. And you possess both. Any man will find you attractive."

Neltie sighed and ducked her head under water. She came up, shaking her wet hair. "This is so nice. I never had a sister to play with. Come on, let's race."

The girls swam toward the other side of the pond. Orola could easily have won the race, but she let Neltie take the lead. Reaching the other side, they lay back on soft grass and stared up into the sky.

"Do you have any brothers and sisters, Orola?"

"Many brothers and lots of sisters."

"Really? How many?"

"Many. I don't actually know all of them."

"How can that be?"

"Because there are so many."

"How many?"

"I don't know. Hundreds."

Neltie snorted. "Now I know you're playing with my mind. How can you have hundreds of brothers and sisters? How many did your parents have at one time?"

Orola smiled. "We have many parents. I never knew my birth parents. After we are born, we are raised in the *Place of Learning*. Our place in society is determined during that time. I was trained to be a warrior and also a priestess."

"You don't look like a warrior."

Orola chuckled. "You mean fierce and menacing?"

"Yes, that's what I mean. You look so…so soft and curvy."

"You think so?" Orola stared at the moving clouds in the sky and made no further comment on Neltie's assessment of her. "My home, my island, is far away from here. I have no means of letting my sisters know where and how I am." She sat up. "Did you hear that?"

"What?"

"Listen. It sounds like someone in pain."

Neltie strained her ears. "I think it's coming from behind those bushes over there."

The girls rose and cautiously made their way toward a thick clump of high shrubs. Through an opening, they could see two people in the high grass.

"I think we found Elto," Orola whispered.

Under the wide branches of a *Barl-tree*, Elto lay in the embrace of a woman, his naked lean buttocks moving with a steady rhythm between her widespread thighs.

"I wondered what he's been doing these last few days, always going swimming by himself," Neltie whispered a little breathlessly. "I did have a suspicion, though." She giggled. "That looks like Lady Rhena. I knew she still had a nice body, but I didn't know about her appetite for younger men."

Though hidden, they had a clear view of the two lovers.

After a short time of watching, Neltie suddenly jumped up and cried out softly, "I can't bear to watch those two. This is not right. She should be doing this with her husband, not with someone half her age. Not with Elto!"

She turned and ran away.

Orola hardly paid any attention to her, watching fascinated, as Elto moved untiring on top of the older woman. She couldn't take her eyes off them, finding something hypnotic about the whole scene.

Gently, the woman pushed the young man away. Getting to

her knees, she presented her ample buttocks to her lover. He moved into position behind her, and with a forceful stroke, he entered her again. His hands clamped around the woman's smooth hips, and like an experienced lover, he rocked between her fleshy buttocks, leaving no doubt that this was not the first time the couple had done this.

Orola could see the rapture on Elto's face, his eyes glued to the spot that joined him to the woman.

Without realizing it, Orola assumed the same position as the woman. She shivered slightly when she felt the touch of hands on her hips and the probing of a warm, solid rod of flesh between her soft buttocks.

"Watching is no fun," a soft voice whispered into her ear. "You have to participate to really enjoy it."

Quivering with anticipation, she pushed back and cried out as the hot flesh entered her hungry sex-canal. Forgotten was the pain she endured while being forced just a few days past. This was different. This time wasn't forced. This felt right and good.

The man behind her moved gentle and lovingly and gave her almost unbearable pleasure. She cried out low as an orgasm shook her body. His lips brushed against the nape of her neck.

"Hush, my sweet," he murmured. "Take my gift as I take yours."

After giving her several orgasms, he pulled out and gently turned her onto her back. She spread her thighs wide, and he moved between them. Looking into Rylic's smiling face, she saw the love in his eyes.

He moved lower and again entered her thick bush of black hair. His fleshy rod felt even more swollen this time, and she gasped as he let her body swallow his hot sex-organ.

She moaned and writhed underneath him, and he closed her mouth with his kisses.

His saliva tasted sweet and fruity, and it seemed to give her the strength she needed to keep up with his virility.

He turned her onto her knees again, entered her tenderly

from behind. She gasped as his fat rod glided into her inflamed sheath.

Staring through the opening in the shrubs, she saw another person had joined the two lovers.

Neltie.

The older woman gave up her place on the soft moss and let Neltie lie down. The young girl smiled up at Elto and reached for him. Her slim legs bent sharply, and her knees touched the ground. Orola could see her swollen mound and noticed the sparse pubic hair.

Without hesitating, Elto knelt between the girl's inviting thighs and let her guide his stiff member into her pink cleft.

Smiling, the older woman watched the two young lovers for a while, then her eyes spied Orola. Still smiling, she walked toward where Orola and Rylic coupled behind the shrubbery.

Orola watched her coming closer, somewhat embarrassed about being discovered.

The woman was beautiful. Tall with slim legs, her breasts were still firm , while her hips flared below a narrow waist.

Reddish shoulder-length hair framed a lovely, oval face. She seemed more young than middle aged. Orola found it impossible to tell. Stepping through the opening, she knelt down beside Orola. Then she lay on her back and pulled Orola's face toward her own. Her lips were warm, soft and her saliva tasted like Rylic's, sweet and fruity.

Orola swallowed it eagerly.

Behind her, Rylic moved slowly and lazily. His lean belly flattened her soft buttocks with each forceful thrust. He didn't hurry, and it seemed as if time stood still. Orola rode the crest of wave after wave of pure pleasure.

Reluctantly, she came down to reality when she heard the voice of another man beside her. She recognized the voice.

Carth.

"What are you doing?" he asked.

Orola smiled up at him. "Sharing love with your son," she

said, and then she gasped as another wave of pleasure gripped her body.

The other woman stood up and swayed toward Carth.

"Lady Rhena," he exclaimed and drew a deep breath. "I never saw you unclothed before," he blurted out and stared at her voluptuous nude body. "You are so..." "Naked?" she laughed.

"Yes...yes..." he stammered. "So naked and so...beautiful, and much younger than I thought."

"Much, much younger," she agreed and took his face between her hands. Then she put her open red lips to his.

At first, he resisted, but then he sighed and eagerly returned her kisses. After a few moments, he pulled away and said, "Let's all go up to the house. We'll have more privacy there."

"Lovely idea," Lady Rhena said and took his hand. She turned toward Orola and Rylic. "Come," she said sweetly. "We have been invited."

When they arrived at the house, Firma stood in the kitchen, a knowing look on her face. Carth frowned when he saw her. "I thought you went to town," he said.

She came up to him and kissed him full on the mouth. "I decided to stay. I see you brought company." She gave Lady Rhena a hug. It didn't seem to bother her seeing Lady Rhena stark naked.

The women smiled at each other.

"Why don't we go up into the bedroom," Firma suggested. "It will be so much more comfortable."

"I'll go along with that," Carth agreed. Putting his arm around the women's waists, he walked between them up the wide stairs.

Orola watched them climb the stairs, saw Carth's hands move to grab the women's buttocks.

From one of the other rooms, she heard a girl giggling and then the sounds of a gasping little cry. "Wow," she heard Neltie's breathless voice. "You've grown."

Through the open door, Orola saw Neltie lying on her back on top of a narrow bed, her legs spread wide. Between them, a pair of naked buttocks moved up and down. In a mirror on the wall, she recognized the reflection of Elto.

Orola didn't get time to wonder how the pair got there so fast. Rylic pulled her down on top of him. He stretched out on the floor, his rigid pole jutting up between his legs. Orola straddled him, and with feverish fingers, she guided his sex-organ into her own.

She cried out as the pleasure spread again through her body and bucked uncontrollably above him, until he grabbed her thrusting hips and steadied her movements.

"There is no hurry," he said soothingly, and his eyes locked with hers.

After what seemed like an eternity, a multitude of orgasms and changes in positions, Orola sensed someone beside them. She opened her eyes, not remembering when she closed them and looked into Firma's smiling face.

The older woman seemed younger looking and more radiant. She kissed Orola, and the girl noticed the same sweet fruity flavor of her lips. Firma took Rylic's place between Orola's widespread thighs and rubbed her pubic area against the girl.

Orola opened her legs wider and became aware of a warm, snakelike thing entering her womb. It grew hard and solid inside her and moved with the rhythm of Firma's snapping hips in and out of her.

It felt good and Orola didn't ask what gave her this great pleasure. Looking into the other woman's wide-open eyes, she let the waves of ecstasy wash through her body.

For long periods, she seemed unaware of her surroundings, her whole being focused only on the thing filling her insides.

Nothing else existed.

Once, when she looked around, she saw Neltie bouncing in Rylic's lap. He gripped her slender hips, and with his strong arms, he lifted her up and down. Orola could see his erect organ appear and disappear in the girl's youthful vagina.

Even though small and slender of body, possessing small, underdeveloped breasts, her sexual appetite seemed quite large. She appeared to have no problem taking the full length of Relic's thick penis into her, because she sank deep into his lap every time he pushed her down.

Her wide-open eyes stared into Rylic's, her face an expression of pure rapture.

Orola's attention moved back to the woman between her legs and realized it wasn't Firma anymore rocking on top of her, but Lady Rhena. The living rod of flesh still moved inside her.

Lady Rhena offered her one of her ample breasts, and Orola began sucking on the long red nipple. It tasted like fresh picked fruit.

Suddenly, she was on her knees with Rylic behind her again. She recognized Rylic by the way he moved and the way his rod felt inside her.

In one of her sane moments, she saw Lady Rhena on the thick carpet in front of her. She lay on her back. Between her shapely, widespread thighs Carth moved with forceful plunges, his eyes locked with Lady Rhena's. With every deep thrust, the older man grunted like an angry *banter*.

Even in her foggy state of mind, Orola wondered, if only briefly, at the stamina the older man displayed. She also noticed that time after time, when Carth seemed to falter and slow down, Lady Rhena put her lips to his and kissed him deeply. Then she would present her large nipple to his searching mouth, and he would suckle eagerly, swallowing whatever came out of those beautiful breasts.

Behind Orola, Rylic moved untiring with a steady rhythm. Somehow, his rod seemed to have grown larger and stiffer, filling her completely.

Suddenly, his rod began to throb, and then she felt a gushing explosion inside her. The hot liquid burst with incredible power out of the pulsing, swollen head and entered her aching womb.

Pushing her fleshy buttocks higher, she tried to engulf him even more and cried out as the exquisite pleasure washed through her whole body and her own release joined his.

Rylic's rod still lay buried inside her, but it began to shrink in size. He pulled out and sluggishly moved away from her. Orola lay on her belly, watching Carth and Lady Rhena as Rhena offered him her nipple once more. "Take this gift," Lady Rhena whispered, "as I take yours."

Carth's buttocks began to quiver, and he lay shaking between Lady Rhena's clutching thighs.

"Now!" she cried out. "Now..." Her heels dug into his lower back as she opened herself wider to his deep thrusts. Her beautiful smile changed to an almost savage expression, and her eyes closed.

She shuddered and lay motionless beneath him. Carth rolled away, and gasping for breath, he looked at her still body. Her eyes were closed.

He shook her, but she didn't move.

"What happened to her?" he asked Firma who stretched down beside him. "Is she dead?"

Firma smiled. "No, not dead. She's just ...resting. You gave her what she craved and needed. You gave her life. Because of your gift, she will live."

Carth shook his head. "I don't understand."

"You will." She pulled him on top of her. "Now give me what you gave her."

"I don't think..." he started to say.

Her eyes locked with his. "You can," she whispered and pulled his head toward her breast. His mouth fastened on the rigid nipple, and Orola saw him swallow eagerly.

He gasped as Firma took his hardened rod between her hands. Opening her legs wide, she guided him into her fluffy triangle. Carth groaned loudly as his pole vanished inside Firma's smooth belly.

Orola had been watching, lying on her belly. Now someone touched her and gently turned her over onto her back. She looked up and saw Elto smiling down at her. She marveled at the size of his rigid pole strutting below his belly.

The young man moved into position. Without effort, he slipped into her welcoming sex-canal.

Just like Rylic's, his sex-organ seemed to swell inside her, and with it the pleasure.

He kissed her and some of his saliva trickled into her open mouth. She swallowed it eagerly as she tasted the sweet fruity flavor.

He rode her for a long time.

Then suddenly the throbbing, swollen head of his sex-organ burst open and flooded her interior. While he didn't make a sound, just quivered inside her tight embrace, Orola gave a long cry of pleasure.

When it was over, he collapsed on top of her, lying still.

Orola held him for a while, and then she gently pushed him off. He lay beside her, his eyes closed. His face looked slack, but his chest heaved slightly, like the chest of a person in deep sleep.

Her own breath came in great gasps. She looked at Carth and Firma. The woman writhed on top of Carth, who emitted a loud sigh each time Firma's sex-organ swallowed his rod of flesh.

"I'll take your gift now," the woman said softly. She seemed to clamp down hard on the man's penis. He grabbed her hips and pulled her deep into his lap while lunging upward.

With a rumbling cry, he emptied himself into Firma's clutching sheath. When he was finished, the woman smiled and whispered, "Thank you," and collapsed on top of him. Her large breasts flattened against Carth's deep chest.

He sighed and held her close. "It's never been this good before," he murmured, and turned to let her slide to his side. Her eyes were closed like Lady Rhena's. Carth studied her for a

26

while, a tender smile on his lips. Then his eyes fell on Orola. He saw her looking at his erect penis. He grinned and rolled over to her.

Still sexually stimulated, Orola needed no encouragement, and watching Carth and Firma had only fueled the flames of desire burning inside her. She opened her legs wide and watched Carth slide between them. Then she engulfed his rigid organ, cried out softly as he entered her.

"I never felt like this before." The older man grunted and pushed deep into Orola's hungry sex-canal.

At first, they clawed at each other like two animals in heat. Carth pounded furiously between Orola's clutching thighs and Orola lifted her hips off the floor to allow him deeper access.

After the girl experienced several orgasms, Carth came inside her with a loud roar. His warm fluid flooded her insides and she felt her own juices flow like a river. They lay in each other's arms, both of them breathing hard, but his penis felt still solid inside her. When their breathing slowed back to normal, he pulled out and turned her onto her stomach. Very slowly, he entered her and watched his rigid pole disappear inside her sheath.

"I don't know what's happening," he groaned, "but I feel so full of energy. I think I could go on for hours still."

"Then do." Orola moaned and cried out as another orgasm ripped through her. "I feel the same way," she gasped. "My body seems to be on fire and only you inside me can put it out."

"I'll try my best." His laugh came out as a hoarse, gagging sound. "You are very beautiful," he moaned, "and so young. I feel lucky and young today."

Outside, the sun had disappeared and two of the moons shone their reflected light through the windows.

"Here I come again," Carth called out and grabbed Orola's long black hair. He lunged once more and released his sperm into her clutching organ.

Orola's ecstatic screams blended with his hoarse shouts as they both rode the crest of pure rapture.

She giggled and let her inner muscles ripple over his shaft. "You are still hard," she said.

"I know," he murmured into her ear. "And you seem to want more."

He pulled out and rose to his feet. "Let's go upstairs into the bedroom," he suggested. "We'll have more privacy there."

Upstairs, he opened the curtains to let the light of the moons flood into the room. Solar, the largest moon, had risen and Orola looked at the great green disk, shuddering. "I wish I could contact you," she whispered and turned away to join Carth on the wide bed.

He lay on his back, his sex-organ standing straight up. Orola straddled him and guiding it into her black fluffy triangle below her belly, she took the big stiff organ into her lubricated sheath.

The eerie green light of Solar bathed her face and Carth looked into her strange eyes. "Like a demon-beast," he murmured. "Like a wild, beautiful demon-beast."

She laughed, shaking her long black hair. "If I only had my *Holy Communicator,*" she panted, "then I could make you feel the way you've never felt before."

"How can it be better than this?" His swollen organ pumped its creamy liquid into her womb and her own fluid gushed out freely. "This is impossible," he groaned, when his body calmed down, his penis still hard inside her demanding vagina. They changed positions. And still the loving went on.

When the first rays of the rising sun entered the room, they finally collapsed exhausted on the wide bed.

When Orola heard voices, she sat up and yawned. She knew it must be close to evening, even though daylight lit up the room.

She looked down at her nude body and ran her fingers through her disheveled hair.

Getting up, she searched for a robe. When she didn't find one, she walked naked through the open door.

Carth stood at the bottom of the stairs, as naked as she. Then she saw Rylic and Elto standing in the middle of the room. They looked up, and Orola noticed the widening of their eyes when they saw her.

"I had a strange dream," Orola heard Neltie say. The young girl stepped into Orola's field of vision. She wore a coarse robe, slightly open in the front. When she saw Elto staring at her partially exposed body, she blushed and pulled the robe closer around her slender form.

Rylic stood staring at Orola. When she looked him in the eyes, he dropped his gaze and looked away.

Then Orola saw them. Four naked bodies on the floor.

She walked down the stairs.. Memory flooded back as she stood beside Carth. The older man seemed embarrassed by her closeness and put one of his hands down to cover his groin.

"Something happened here last night," Carth said with a shaky voice. "And it is best we forget about it."

The bodies of Firma and Lady Rhena looked as if they were chiseled from stone. Their skin had turned completely white.

Orola gasped when she looked at the other bodies on the floor.

Rylic and Elto.

"How...?" she started and stared at the two standing in front of her.

"Kiir-nymphs," explained Rylic, and sank into one of the chairs. "Watch," he said. "They're almost ready."

Suddenly, the body of Lady Rhena split open with a sharp crack. From between her breasts emerged a small head, a pair of slim arms, and then a fragile body followed.

The creature was pure white, almost translucent. About half the size of its host-body.

Large, green eyes looked out of a small, beautiful elfin face.

The other three bodies split open, and three more of the creatures emerged. Long, transparent wings unfolded from their backs and trailed behind them as they walked across the carpet.

All four looked at the watching humans. Then they emitted highpitched, twittering sounds. One of them walked up to Carth, reached out and gently touched his hand.

Never speaking, they walked out of the door.

Orola heard their twittering voices as they took to the sky.

Kiir. The beautiful creatures of the clouds. She had heard of them, but never seen them before. Never knew how they came into being.

Until now.

"There are two more down by the pond," Rylic said, looking again at Orola, desperately trying not to stare at her strutting breasts or her fluffy black triangle. "One looks like Neltie, the other one like you."

"The nymphs take on the shape of people they see in the minds of those they meet. Once they take a person's form, their own mind draws from the mind pattern of the one they mimic. Even if that other person is far away. It doesn't make any difference," Carth explained.

"They have the ability to cloud your thoughts. You'll never know the one you're with is not the real one. They need us humans to enter the next stage in their lifecycle. Once they have you in their power, you are helpless. You do what they want."

"But they are not evil," Rylic interrupted his father. "They don't just take. They also give."

"What do they give?" Elto asked, his eyes traveling unashamedly across Orola's body. She didn't care. He had seen her naked before.

She noticed the bulge in his pants.

She also saw Rylic's.

"They give incredible pleasure," Rylic said, his gaze flicking toward Orola's pubic area. "They also give healing and vitality."

"I know about that," Elto said proudly. "Lady Rhena and I..." He stopped and looked at Neltie, who blushed under his scrutinizing eyes.

"It wasn't real," she gasped. "They were fakes."

"They were real enough," Carth said and looked at Orola. "Some things were too real, but they happened. There is no denying that." He turned and walked up the stairs.

Orola could not miss his half-erect penis, which he tried to cover up. Looking back at the split bodies on the floor, she noticed something peculiar. They were beginning to shrink and lose their shape.

As she watched, they dissolved, leaving only a handful of fine crystalline powder behind.

Orola looked at Neltie. "Will you come down to the pond with me? I left my clothes there, and I'd like to pick them up." Neltie nodded and followed Orola outside.

"I still feel kind of strange inside," Neltie said after a while. "I feel so..."

"Sexually aroused?" Orola smiled. "So do I."

"But you're older and more mature," Neltie protested. "I shouldn't have feelings like that though I am a woman. Especially toward Rylic and Elto."

"They are males. Young and virile males with raging hormones. You are female. Young, attractive, with your own raging hormones." Orola laughed. "It is only natural."

"But they are my cousins. Second cousins, as Elto likes to point out, but still cousins." Neltie put her hands over her face. "Things will never be the same again. Even though I know it wasn't really them, and it wasn't me they did it with. "She gave Orola a sidelong glance. "Elto, I mean the real Elto, and I, we did it once. Only because he was pestering me, and I admit, I was curious, but I never did it with Rylic. He's too old for me."

"Not that old." Orola smiled, thinking of Carth, who had to be twice her own age.

Neltie sighed. "You know, if Rylic would ask me now, I would let him. Would that be wrong?"

Orola put an arm around the girl's shoulder. "I've been to places where it's acceptable for a brother and sister to have sexual relations. But then again, there are places where they would stone to death a mother who taught her son about sex, but not the father who seduces his daughter. I cannot tell you what is right or wrong. That is up to you."

They had arrived at the pond, and Orola found her garment under a clump of shrubs. "You want to take that swim now?"

"Okay." Neltie stripped, and both jumped into the water.

"It's cold," Neltie shrieked and, laughing, she began splashing Orola.

After splashing each other, they began swimming back to shore, when someone called from the other side of the pond.

"How's the water?"

Orola saw two young men standing under a tall tree.

"That looks like Garron," Neltie gasped. "From the village. He's the blacksmith's son, and he is so good-looking." "May we join you?" Garron called.

"If you can stand the cold water," Orola answered. "Come on in."

Within moments, the young men were out of their clothes. They dove into the frigid water. When they came up for air, they had traveled half the distance to the girls under water.

"You're right. It is cold." Garron laughed and came closer with powerful strokes. He stopped in front of Neltie. "Nice to see you again." He smiled at her and let his eyes rest on her nubile breasts.

Both girls stood in waist deep water, their upper bodies exposed.

Neltie blushed and sank up to her neck into the water.

Orola watched the other youth. He was tall and muscular, with a tanned, handsome face. She let him look at her naked upper body and smiled back at him. "I am Orola," she said.

32

"I am Erton, and you are the most desirable creature I have ever seen."

Orola lowered her long lashes. "Thank you," she said, putting a husky tone into her voice. "And you are one of the boldest young men I've ever met."

He laughed and came closer. Orola could see his erection in the clear water.

"You are right. I am bold," he said and put one of his hands over her breast.

She didn't pull away, knowing what he wanted. She also knew that she would give it to him. It didn't take long before she experienced her first orgasm. Crying out, she slammed against him.

He lost his balance, and they both tumbled under water. He released her and they came up spitting.

"I think we should go on land where it is not so dangerous." He grinned.

"I agree." She laughed and walked toward the shore.

He didn't follow her immediately, just watched her walk. She deliberately put a little more sway into her hips and smiled when she heard his breath catch in his throat.

Later, recovering from another powerful climax, Orola heard ecstatic cries beside her. She looked and saw Neltie and Garron locked in a deep embrace.

Erton lay on his back, his stiff pole sticking up between his legs. Orola straddled him.

Very slowly, her body swallowed him, savoring the sensation as the swollen fleshy mast slid into her lubricated sheath.

Then she began a slow grind in his lap.

After a while, she stretched out on top of him, flattening her breasts against his deep chest.

Then she kissed him.

He moaned and bucked underneath him.

She rode the crest of her own climax and sucked the last drop of his squirting member into her womb. Something seemed to be missing, and when she came down from her high, she knew what.

There had not been any sweet fruity flavor on his lips.

He looked at her with a slight frown, then he sat up. "You are real," he blurted out.

"And so are you. Seems we all made a mistake."

They both looked at Garron and Neltie, his fingers digging into her slim hips, trying to steady her as she bucked wildly under him.

"He'll be surprised," Erton chuckled.

Orola giggled. "And so will she."

When Garron was finished, he collapsed on top of Neltie. "That was the best," he said after a while, his chest still heaving. "You nymphs sure can give a man pleasure."

Neltie pushed him off. "What do you mean by *nymphs*?" she demanded, her eyes wide and blazing angrily.

Garron smiled lazily. "Don't pretend," he said. "I know what you are. But it doesn't matter to me."

"I am no nymph," Neltie protested. "You are."

"What?" Garron sat up and looked over to Erton and Orola, who sat with silly grins, watching the two.

"We are no nymphs," they said, almost in unison.

At first Garron looked angry, but then he flung himself back and burst out laughing. Neltie looked embarrassed and sat up, her body in a fetal position.

"But it was so beautiful," she whispered, looking at Orola for comfort. "I feel so ashamed and stupid."

Orola got up and walked over to her. Putting her arms around Neltie, she said, "I never knew, and neither did they. Don't blame yourself. Besides," she smiled, "we did it willingly, and we all enjoyed it. Blame it on the after-effects of what happened yesterday."

"What's worse?" Neltie whispered. She stared in the direction of Erton. "I am still turned on. And I want Erton."

The young man saw her looking at him and grinned. He didn't even bother hiding his erection.

"I believe the same thing is on his mind," Orola chuckled. "Take my advice. Follow your desire. He's a handsome young man and quite virile."

Neltie pressed Orola's hand. "I can't help myself," she whispered fiercely as she headed toward Erton.

———

Orola and Garron had recovered sufficiently. They lay in the soft grass, watching the young couple.

"Oh, this is so good," Neltie cried, arching her back and pushing backward. "So awfully good. I think I'll die."

"Young lovers, they say such foolish things," Garron's voice whispered into Orola's ear.

"Are you ready again?" she asked teasingly, her breath coming faster.

His probing member found what he looked for, and as he slid deep into her, an almost unbearable feeling of pleasure surged through her body.

Her mind became hazy, unable to think clear thoughts.

Time stood still.

Only pleasure existed.

She lay on her back, her unfocused eyes staring into Garron's smiling face. Her arms reached for him, pulled his face toward hers.

She kissed him.

He tasted of fresh fruit and sweet honey.

When she looked around, she saw a familiar looking dark-haired young woman, not far away beside her, mounting a young man who looked remarkably like Garron, except Garron lay in her own arms.

The dark-haired young woman guided Garron's erect penis

into her thick triangle, swallowed it into her sex-canal. She turned her head to look at Orola and smiled.

Orola recognized *herself*!

Her double shook her long black hair, let it spill over her creamy shoulders. Staring into Garron's eyes, she rocked back and forth with slow, steady movements.

When Orola looked to her other side, she saw Erton and Neltie. Orola tried to focus her eyes when she saw another young couple, just beyond the first one.

The second Erton was on his back. Neltie's double sat above him. Her breasts seemed fuller, more bouncy, her figure still slim, but more fleshed-out. Her white, round buttocks moved up and down.

"Life," Garron said above her. "It is a precious gift. It must be cherished." His penis throbbed inside Orola's clutching canal, gushing more fluid into her.

"Receive my gift," he said, "as I take yours."

Her body seemed aflame and, staring into Garron's wide-open eyes, she slipped into an altered state.

Her mind seemed befuddled and clear at the same time.

She was Orola, the girl, gasping for breath beneath Garron's tirelessly moving body. She was Garron.

No…she was not Garron, only a simulacrum. A form *It* had assumed out of necessity. The real Garron lay nearby, giving life to another of his kind.

Life. It would have Life.

Exhilarated, it continued giving pleasure to the life form beneath it, continued feeding her life-giving fluid, which flowed freely from the orifice between her lower extremities, her *flower*, as she called it. It drank the nectar from her lips when they tasted each other.

But it did not just take. It gave back. It gave of its own fluid, which was laced with elements of healing, elements that gave endurance, vitality and youth.

Through the thoughts of the life form whose body it copied,

it knew that coupling with a female was not only used for the continued existence of their species. They coupled also for the experience of pleasure.

And pleasure it gave, while taking pleasure in return.

It had no memories of a life before this. Only fragments of a life as a formless blob suspended in water.

Waiting.

Then it became aware of another life form close by. On the land.

It felt joy and ecstasy.

It would have *Life*.

It crawled on land.

One entity was close. No...there were two. Two minds, one body.

After the ecstasy came separation. One body became two.

One, the female, she called herself Orola, lay watching another body/two minds.

The other, the male, Garron, lay on his back, eyes closed.

Instinctively, it knew what it must do.

It took Garron's thoughts, his memories. It became Garron. Its gelatin body became solid and warm. It formed the feeding tube between its legs, shaped it into the likeness of a male penis.

Then, as Garron, it moved on top of the female Orola, pushed its feeding tube/penis into her sex-organ. It created strands of pleasure inside its new body, and the moment the simulated penis entered Orola vagina, it experienced extreme pleasure.

So did Orola.

The fluid the creature exuded acted like an aphrodisiac to her. As she absorbed it into her body, she slipped into an immediate trance, totally under the creature's control.

As it joined with Orola, it became aware of three others of its kind, shaping themselves into the likeness of the other three life forms.

It was jubilant.

It would not be alone.

Joyfully, it moved its lower body with a steady rhythm, pushing its feeding tube deep into the female's clutching orifice. The creature's source of life.

Coupled with intense pleasure, the creature released a spray of fluid into Orola's womb. The seeds inside searched and found the ova, melded, fertilized. Then it sucked the life-givers back into its own body, where the growing process began.

Another life formed. A superior life form would emerge.

There would be no offspring in Orola's womb; all she received was pleasure, vitality and health for a long time after.

A fair exchange.

Orola didn't feel appalled by this. Sharing the creature's thoughts and memories, she understood the need.

Her consciousness shifted back to her own body.

Opening her eyes, she stared into Garron's face and eyes, but she knew it wasn't Garron.

As if reading her thoughts, the creature said, "You know me now as I know you, *Moon Priestess*. The joining of our minds has given me as much joy as the joining of our bodies. From your memories, I received glimpses of my own future. I hope I will somehow remember you. It would make me very glad. Take this last offering."

Once more, it released a gush of warm fluid and once more, their minds joined.

Orola gasped and cried out as she reached another orgasm.

Experiencing it with two minds created the ultimate ecstasy.

When it was over, the creature slumped into her arms.

Very gently, she turned over until she lay on top, then she lifted off, letting the limp organ slide out of her. She looked around and saw the other Garron, the real one, and her own double, still locked together.

From the other side of her, Orola heard the ecstatic cries of Neltie and Erton. Almost simultaneously, their Kiir-nymphs sagged in their tight embrace.

Orola found it curious that all nymphs had been in the top position before they released their gift.

Garron looked at the quiet body of the Orola-nymph beside him and then at Orola.

"This is incredible," he said, shaking his head. "I should be totally exhausted, but I feel so alive, so full of vitality.

"I don't know about you, but I'm far from satisfied." Orola received him into her over-stimulated hungry sex-organ.

Beside them, Neltie and Erton watched silently before they began clawing at each. They never saw their duplicates metamorphose, never saw the hardening bodies break open to release the emerging fairy-bodies of the Kiir.

Twittering, the frail beautiful creatures lifted into the air on gossamer wings. Below them, the two young human couples, the *Givers of Life*, were lost in a world of ecstasy and pleasure.

The Kiir circled above them and then took off into the clouds.

Orola swung her bundle of extra clothes and food across her shoulder. "How can I ever thank you for your hospitality?"

"Be kind to others." Firma squeezed the girl's hand. "I hope you'll find your belongings again, but I must advise you against this foolish venture. It can only lead to trouble."

"She is right," Carth said. "I wish you'd just forget this notion of revenge. Be happy you're alive and well again. Leave it at that."

"I wish I could," Orola said, "but they took my *Holy Communicator* and my *Transmuter*. Without them, I am lost." She looked at the green disk of Solar, partially visible above the far mountains. "They are part of what I am."

"And what exactly are you, my child?" Firma asked softly.

"I am Orola, the Warrior Priestess."

"That you may be," the older woman said, "but these last

few days ,you have proven that you can exist without those things the Kellos stole from you. Are they really that important?"

Orola smiled. "They are. Like the Kiir, I cannot help being what I am. I must spread my own wings and let them carry me where my god wants me to go."

THE GREAT MUKOR

"That one. The tall black-haired one. The one with the strange eyes and big breasts."

The man who spoke was short and stocky, almost plump, but he possessed a deep, commanding voice. "She promises a satisfactory addition to my entertainment."

One of the slave girls snickered, which earned her a reprimanding look from her master. It was obvious that she knew of his peculiar tastes and desires.

"You want to take her place?" he demanded, staring at her.

"Oh, no," she stammered, lowering her lids in a demur gesture, but in reality hiding her hatred and fear. "I would not be worthy of your attention, Great Mukor."

He threw back his head and laughed. "You are a sly one, girl, and foolish. You might even like my attention. Maybe another time, but not tonight. Now I want that newly captured one. I'm told she is strong and wild, ready to be tamed."

Two burly guards dragged the struggling naked girl before their master. They forced her to her knees. One of them grabbed her long black hair and pulled back her head. She stared defiantly at the man they called *Great Mukor*.

He held a long, wicked-looking sword in his hand. Sliding its tip gently between the girl's ample breasts, he said in a low voice, "You have two choices. Submit to me, and you will not regret it. The reward will be high and pleasurable. Defy me, and you will be sliced open like a *gurruch*."

He chuckled. "In fact, my loyal troops would be grateful for a tasty treat like you. I might let you live, let them still their animal lust first and then have them cut you apart to be feasted upon. It is your choice. Just say *I want to live, Great Mukor*."

The girl's eyes narrowed, then opened wide. She did not hide her feelings. Her green, strange green eyes blazed with cold fire as she answered. "I want to live, Great Mukor."

He laughed deeply. "That's a smart girl. I know you are already scheming how you can get away but be warned. My guards will cut you to pieces at the slightest chance of betrayal." He sheathed his sword. "Let her go."

The guards stepped back but kept their hands on their weapons. The Great Mukor turned and walked toward a wall of heavy curtains. Before he parted them to step through, he called back over his shoulder, "Follow me." Then he was gone.

The girl got up and followed him slowly.

As the curtain closed behind her, she looked around. Her new master had seated himself among a pile of thick cushions. Behind him knelt a young woman who brushed his hair. She was naked and petite, almost elfin-like.

The man patted the cushion beside him. "Come, sit down." Reluctantly, she obeyed.

"What is your name?" Mukor asked her as she seated herself.

"I am Orola," the girl answered, giving him a sidelong glance. "From the island Antanakka. Perhaps you have heard of it and my people?"

Mukor chuckled. "No, I haven't, but whatever you were and

did before doesn't matter. From now on, you will serve me and do whatever I ask." He glared at her. "Do you understand this?"

Orola lowered her head. "I understand, Great Mukor." She let her long black hair fall over her face to hide the fierceness in her gaze.

Mukor clapped his hands. "We shall have entertainment," he shouted.

From another set of curtains stepped three figures, one a tall, big woman with a coarse face but a well-formed strong body. She was naked. The other two were males.

Orola sucked in her breath when she saw their naked, hairy bodies. Mukor, who misread her reaction, laughed and gripped her knee. "Aren't they magnificent creatures? Wait until you see them in action."

Orola forced herself to stay calm. Ugly memories flooded up inside her. Again, she saw the brutish faces above her, felt the pain in her belly as she lay spread-eagled tied to stakes in the ground, assaulted until her mind mercifully slipped into unconsciousness.

She had burned the faces of the ones who had done that to her into her memory forever, but these two were not the ones, even though they looked like them.

The woman began undulating her body, and Orola admired her graceful movements. Turning and twisting, she eluded the clumsy hands of the two males when they reached for her.

However, it was all a calculated performance. She pretended to stumble, landed on her back, her legs spread. Before she managed to rise again, one of the males fell between her open thighs.

Orola had seen his tremendous erection. With a grunt, he stabbed it into woman's welcoming sex-organ. She cried out and arched her back as he entered her.

The other male squatted above her head and pushed his stiff organ into her mouth.

Orola sensed movement beside her and turned her head.

The young woman who had been stroking the Great Mukor's hair had slipped in front of him. Her head dipped between his bare legs. Orola heard his sharp intake of breath as the young woman took his penis into her mouth. Then the Mukor's hand reached for her breast and grabbed it. His fingers dug painfully into the soft flesh.

The threesome in front of them had changed positions. Now the woman was on her knees. It became evident that this woman was an expert, and, under other circumstances, Orola might even have been turned on by the performance.

She looked into the Mukor's glazed eyes and felt his fingers digging into her breast. She wanted to slap his hand away but knew it would be unwise.

He groped her for a while, and then he stretched out on his back, his head propped up by a pillow so he could watch the woman and the two males. Orola glanced over at Mukor and watched the young woman free his penis. She had to suppress a fit of laughter when she noted its small size. A young boy was better endowed. Small wonder he liked petite women.

Climbing on top of Mukor, the girl-woman squatted above him, her pink clit hovering above the thin but erect penis. She grabbed it with one of her small hands and expertly guided it toward her hairless vagina.

Slowly, she sank down and soon her lower body was just a blur of movement.

Her eyes were wide open but unseeing. From her open mouth came little shrieks and her elfin face showed an expression of pure rapture. It was obvious she enjoyed what she did.

The Great Mukor was staring at the two men and the woman. Orola felt his hand fumbling between her thighs, and then he pushed one finger into her vagina. He knew what stimulated a woman. His finger stroked her sensitive spot with gentle motions, and against her will, she felt a climax approaching. Clamping down hard on the caressing finger, she erupted with a series of loud gasps.

The Great Mukor laughed and pulled out his finger. He put it into his mouth and looked at her with shiny eyes, "You did not disappoint me." He let out a loud gasp and emitted a drawn-out groan. And it was over.

Breathing hard, he relaxed into his pillows. After a while, he opened his eyes and clapped his hands.

The three performers stopped their activity and, reluctantly, it seemed, they separated. The Great Mukor motioned to Orola. "Join them!" he commanded.

Knowing that resistance was futile, she obeyed. She accepted the moment and gave up all her inhibitions. There seemed to be no end to the prowess and stamina of these males.

Orola's species had abilities that normal humans did not possess. Her vagina-lips were powerful muscles and she tightened them around the base of the last male's penis, making the knobby head swell with engorged blood.

Then she relaxed her grip again.

Before long, he doused her insides with another burst of spermatic fluid. When he was finished, she clamped her labia around his withdrawing penis, keeping the swelling head trapped inside her.

Orola laughed at his frantic efforts to free himself and gasped as another powerful climax gripped her body.

When it subsided, she let him go and was surprised to find him hard again. He came back down, his penis slid smoothly into her welcoming vagina.

When he began furiously to move in and out of her, she looked into his eyes and commanded, "Slow!"

She smiled when he obeyed, and then she directed his movements. Slow or fast, whichever way she felt inclined. She knew from now on, this male would be devoted to her. He was her sexual slave.

After a few more enjoyable orgasms, she let him reach his own. His discharge was strong and long lasting, but when she released him, he was completely exhausted.

No female had ever done that to him, of that she was certain. As far as he was concerned, she was a goddess…a love-goddess. He would do anything to experience again the incredible pleasure she had given him. Even die, if necessary.

Orola turned lazily over onto her stomach. Her eyes half-closed, she looked at the Great Mukor. "Did I please my master?" she asked coyly. "Would you like to sample my meager abilities in the art of love?"

He smiled, stood up, and walked toward her. There was something in his smile that should have forewarned her, but she was still turned on too much.

Between his short legs, his pitiful, small penis stood erect. Orola spread her legs wide and watched him as he knelt between them. He leaned forward and she took him into her embrace. The head of his thin, snakelike rod touched her vulva, entered her sex-canal and slid into her.

She cried out in surprise and then in pain as the thin piece of flesh began to swell and change into a hard, knobby phallus. The swollen glands scraped along her inside walls, the giant organ filling her as completely as nothing ever had.

The two beast-men had been well endowed, but they had been small to what was inside her now. After a moment of shocked panic, she calmed down and adjusted to the intruder.

The Great Mukor grinned down hat her. "Now you may please me," he said, his eyes glinting with malicious humor. "Let's see what you're made of, Moon Priestess." He knew who and what she was. He also knew that she was helpless.

The Great Mukor's sexual prowess was unbelievable.

Orola managed to enjoy it for a while. Most of the time, she was only half-aware of what he did.

She lost consciousness, because when she became aware of

her surroundings again, she was on her back, her legs wrapped around the torso of the man laboring above her.

He had the Great Mukor's face, but the body was not the same. Long and thin, it was almost skeletal, yet he seemed quite muscular and powerful. She could see the pronounced muscles rippling as he pushed his thick organ forcefully into her aching vagina.

"You are pleasing me, Moon Priestess," the Great Mukor said, his voice gravelly and resonant. His eyes blazed yellow. "You wonder," he growled, and then he laughed with a hollow sound, never missing a stroke. "You wonder what I am, don't you? My species has been called *Demons* by some. *Gods* by others. We are neither, but here, I am a god. Remember that!"

His yellow eyes bored into hers. "You could be my equal, but you are not. In this backward place, you are a helpless primitive. Your heritage forgotten. In a way, it is a shame." Blackness descended mercifully upon her. When she regained consciousness, she was lying on her side, alone.

A loud moaning from nearby made her open her eyes. When she looked around in the semi-darkness of the room, she saw shadows moving in a corner.

Then her eyes adjusted to night vision and the shadows became two figures locked together in a deep embrace. She recognized the slave girl who earlier had been reprimanded by the Great Mukor.

The girl lay on a pile of furs; between her widespread legs moved a handsome young man. Orola watched them through half-closed eyes, but they never noticed that they had an audience.

The girl gasped suddenly and whispered fiercely, "Don't wait too long. I'm getting tired."

The man gave a choking laugh. "You are a tireless sex-starved Kiir-nymph, girl."

"Now, now...come now!" she cried and sat quivering in his lap. He clamped his hands around her shapely hips and lunged upward. Letting out a hoarse, suppressed gasping sound, he erupted inside her.

A wail came from the girl's lips, and then she collapsed into his arms, breathing fast and loud.

Covering his face with kisses, she whispered, "I love you. I hope you love me, too, and don't you ever put that beautiful stick of yours into another female…unless I permit it."

He chuckled and held her close. "You suck me dry every night. There is nothing left for another girl."

"Good," she said, and then she sighed. "I just wish we were at some other place, very far from here. Every day I fear Mukor will choose me for his sick pleasures." She glanced at Orola. "Poor girl. They brought her here unconscious and delirious. I am surprised she lives."

"He is not human. He is a beast," spat the young man.

"Hush," the girl warned. "Speak softly. Someone might hear. The walls have ears." She slid off him and lay on her back beside him. "Kirba told me that she heard him call her *Moon Priestess*. I wonder what that means."

"That she is some kind of priestess, what else?" The young man shrugged and moved on top of the girl.

Orola closed her eyes and listened to the sounds of their lovemaking. Her pain was just a dull throb now. Relaxing, she concentrated on techniques she had learned to will the hurt away. How she longed for her *Holy Communicator*. Her god Solar would give her the strength she so desperately needed now.

She must have fallen asleep. Someone touched her shoulder lightly, and she recognized the slave girl. "I am alive, and I believe I'll live for another day."

The girl returned her smile. "I am glad. You wouldn't be the first corpse they dumped in my quarters. The last girl didn't survive her encounter with the Great Mukor."

"Someday I'll kill him," Orola said softly, but her eyes burned as she spoke those words.

"There are many who think what you just blurted out," the

slave girl said, "but unless you have greater powers than you've displayed so far, I fear it is only brave talk...and dangerous."

Orola sat up. "Where is your friend?" she asked.

"My friend? Oh, you mean Trito." The girl blushed. "Did you watch us?"

"A little," Orola admitted and put a hand on the girl's arm. "No need to be embarrassed, because I am not. I have played the role of performer countless times." She smiled. "He is a handsome male. You are very lucky."

The girl chuckled. "You are right. He is handsome, and I am lucky to have him. At least for a while."

"What do you mean?"

The girl sighed. "We are not allowed to mate for life. I am a slave, and so is Trito."

Suddenly, she clung to Orola. "I live in constant fear. So do all of the other slaves. The Great Mukor, our supreme ruler, sees to it that we are not happy. He is a night-demon come to us from the sky and sows terror among my people."

"How long has he ruled?" Orola asked.

"About three cycles. He appeared maybe four or five cycles ago. Our former ruler, Lord Rylar, took him in like a son, made him a trusted advisor. One day, Lord Rylar fell into a coma from which he never awoke. There were rumors, but nobody dared voice them. When Lord Rylar died, Mukor proclaimed himself Lord and Ruler. We've lived in terror ever since."

Orola stroked the girl's soft black hair. "Do you have a name?" she asked.

The girl smiled and wiped her cheek. "I am Rhesa."

"I am called Orola."

The girl nodded. "I know. I was there when they brought you. Are you a priestess?"

Orola stood and stretched her lithe body Muscles rippling beneath her smooth, ivory skin.

Shaking her luxurious black hair, Orola stared at the green

disk of one of the moons visible through the small window. She knew her green eyes glowed softly.

"I am Orola, Warrior Priestess of God Solar," she said proudly.

Rhesa shivered. "You are an imposing figure bathed by the green light of the moon. A warrior priestess, indeed. Maybe even a goddess." She paused, as if giving thought to some insane idea. "But you are a slave, like me."

Orola slumped her shoulders and looked down, the glow in her eyes gone. "Without my *Holy Communicator*, I am nothing," she said, despair in her voice. "My god will not respond to my pleas for help."

Orola sank down again beside Rhesa and put her head into her hands. "If I only knew where to look, so I could find it again." She lifted her head. "The Kellos took it from me after they left me to die. If I could find those ugly brutes, I would make them talk."

"They are not very smart," Rhesa said. "The Kellos are closer to the animals than to us. I doubt they'd even remember you."

"I remember them," Orola said fiercely, recalling in her mind's eye each savage face.

Rhesa put her slim hand on Orola's arm. "Maybe I can help. I have many friends among the other slaves. If you describe this object to me, I could tell my friends to keep their eyes open. Who knows?" She lifted her shoulders. "Someone may have heard of it."

"There are actually two articles I have lost." Orola pursed her lips and nodded. "You're right. There might be a chance. The Communicator is a long, red jewel, and my sword has the same type of jewel in its hilt."

"Perhaps you should talk to the Weapons Master then," Rhesa said. "He might know."

"Where can I find him?" Orola asked, a glimmer of hope in her eyes.

"I'll introduce you to him, but you have to be careful." She looked at Orola's nude body. "You are very beautiful. Any information he'll give you may be costly."

Orola shrugged. "It won't matter. As long as I get back what belongs to me."

Rhesa patted her hand. "I wish you luck, but now we have to get back to our duties." She got up, began to walk away. Looking back at Orola, who still sat on the floor, she said, "Come on, we are late already."

"I don't even know what I'm supposed to be doing," Orola said, rising to her feet.

"All the new slaves usually work in the kitchen. I'll take you there."

The cook turned out to be a little, skinny man with big ears, a flat nose and only one eye.

"You're late," he said accusingly, with a shrill, whiny voice. His one good eye focused on Orola. "A new one," he observed. "I hope you last longer than the last one they sent me."

Rhesa grabbed Orola's hand and pulled her away. "Come and help me check on the vegetables."

"Not so fast!" The cook's fingers dug into Orola's upper arm. "Forget about the vegetables. You two go and find some fungus. And make sure you're back before the sun sets. I need time to prepare it."

While Rhesa went to get a couple of baskets from the back, Orola looked around in the kitchen. She counted nine girls and three men performing various tasks. All of them were naked, except for the cook and one older woman. Two of the girls were still young, their breasts just small bumps on their skinny chests. The men were old. She noticed one of them walking with a limp.

"Come on," Rhesa called, interrupting Orola's survey.

She hastened after the girl, not wanting to fall into the cook's ill graces.

***

They descended a flight of roughly hewn steps and followed a dark underground tunnel that finally ended in a large cavern. Glowing strips of lichen on the damp walls and ceiling illuminated the cavern.

Orola saw black patches of thick, knobby growth around cracks in the walls and watched Rhesa approaching it. "Take only from the outside rim," she instructed Orola. "The inside is still soft and sticky. It doesn't taste very good. The flavor only develops once the fungus dries up."

Orola began breaking off chunks of the dark stuff and putting them into her basket.

"Oh, I forgot, watch out for the trems!" the girl called back over her shoulder.

"What are trems?" Orola asked.

"They hide in the cracks, small six-legged monstrosities that can give you a nasty sting."

Orola wiped the sweat from her forehead and almost slipped on the greasy floor as she reached for a piece of fungus above her head. The air was hot and humid and smelled unpleasant, but they were lucky. Most of the fungus they found was ripe and ready to be picked.

Their baskets were filled in no time.

"We don't have to rush back," Rhesa said. "There is something I want to show you. You will understand our situation better after you've seen it."

They walked through a maze of long tunnels, until they came out into another cavern, smaller than the last one, but it was brightly lit.

Orola stared curiously at the source of the light. Small,

miniature suns seemed to be buried in the ceiling of the cavern. Rhesa noticed her stare and chuckled.

"One of the wonders our Lord Mukor brought with him, but there is more," she whispered, putting a finger on her lips. "Don't draw any attention to yourself. Act as if you belong."

They entered a short, narrow tunnel that ended at a thick wooden door. Rhesa cautiously pushed it open, and then she slipped through. Orola followed her slowly and with apprehension.

Another cavern, also brightly lit. However, this one was not empty. She saw rows upon rows of transparent cylinders. Inside each one of them, something moved.

Orola put her hand to her mouth when she recognized the shapes inside. "Kellos," she whispered. "Immature Kellos."

Rhesa touched Orola's shoulder. "They are grown inside those tubes. They grow very fast."

"But why? There must be thousands of them."

"Our lord is building an army. The Kellos can be trained to be fierce fighters, and they have no fear of death. Once his army is large enough, he will invade Skuras, our neighbors to the north. We've had border skirmishes already. Lord Mukor blames it on Skuras, but we've never had problems with them before, and we know he's not telling the truth."

Orola gave Rhesa a long look. "For a simple, slave girl you seem quite informed."

Rhesa gave her a quick smile. "My father used to be an advisor to Lord Rylar."

"I see. Where is your father now?"

"Dead. Killed in a hunting accident shortly after Lord Mukor was made an advisor." Her features darkened. "It was not an accident. Of that I am certain."

The creaking of hinges behind them made both girls turn to face the opening door. Two Kellos appeared in the doorway. They stopped when they saw the girls.

"What you do here?" one of them asked, stumbling over the words.

"We have business here," Rhesa said haughtily and drew her body erect. "What are *you* doing here?"

"Clean up here," the other one said, eying them from under heavy eyebrows. "You no belong."

"Maybe we have fun," the first one said, grinning. His big teeth showed yellow below his scruffy mustache.

When he approached Orola, she whirled and kicked him in the chest with her right foot. He went sprawling backward, right into the arms of another Kellos. This one looked different from the other two. He stood taller and straighter, and his face was free of hair.

He pushed the one who had fallen against him out of the way, and then he looked at the baskets the girls carried. "There is no fungus here," he stated. "This place is forbidden to you."

"We got lost," Rhesa said, trying to brush past him.

The Kellos grabbed her arm and pulled her back. "You come with me. You must be punished."

Rhesa struggled in his grip, but he was strong. When the other two reached for Orola, she shook off their hands and followed Rhesa and her captor. They were taken down a well-lit tunnel until they came to another door.

One of the Kellos opened it. Rhesa and Orola were pushed through the opening.

The room they entered was not large, but it was brightly lit. Orola saw benches and tables. A number of young Kellos were sitting on the benches, listening to an older man, who seemed to be lecturing them.

When the girls entered the room, the old man stopped talking and looked at the tall Kellos who came in after them.

"It is time to teach these young ones things they need to do when they encounter females," the Kellos said, grinning.

"Aren't they still a little young for that?" protested the old man.

"Put them to the test and find out." The Kellos spoke to one of the other two, and then he pointed at Rhesa.

Rhesa submitted with no word of protest, almost as if she wanted the young Kellos to take from her.

When ordered to excite one of the youngsters, Orola bent over him. She touched his penis and began stroking it.

He reacted almost immediately.

"That was very good," said the Kellos without the facial hair, "but that is not the way we want them to learn." He turned toward the other watching youngsters. "Watch, this is how it is done."

She told herself again that there was no use to fight it. She did not enjoy the actions of the Kellos but it was not bad.

"You look different from the other slaves," the instructor said. "You have strange eyes. Where are you from?"

"I am from the island Antanakka, the Island of Witches," Orola answered, looking into his eyes.

"So you are a witch." He grinned. "You may look different, but you feel the same. You're good and tight, like all the other females."

By the time the old teacher put a stop to it, she felt some discomfort, but it was bearable.

She wondered about Rhesa, but the girl seemed unharmed. Standing uncertainly beside the table, she looked at the old teacher. "We have to get back with our fungus. The Kitchen Master will be angry," she said, her voice pleading.

The teacher looked at the tall Kellos, who nodded.

"You can go," he told the girls. "Next time I'll take you to the barracks."

The girls picked up their baskets and slipped by the Kellos who partially blocked the entrance.

Outside, in the tunnel, Rhesa stumbled a little. "Someday," she whispered, "We will kill them all." She touched Orola's hand. Orola could feel the fire burning in her eyes. "Someday we both will get our revenge," she said fiercely.

Work in the kitchen wasn't hard. Troller, the Kitchen Master, was always whining and complaining, but Orola soon realized that he was a man with a gentle heart. Pretending to punish the girls, he would send them on errands that took them away from the kitchen. That gave Orola a chance to visit the Weapons Master.

When she asked Rhesa about Master Troller, the girl smiled. "He is a distant uncle from my mother's side. We have nothing to fear from him."

The Weapons Master turned out to be a big, ugly brute of a man. Ugly on the outside and ugly on the inside. His eyes were barely visible between thick folds of skin.

He let his gaze travel down Orola's naked body. Grunting, he reached out with one huge hairy hand and cupped her soft breast.

She didn't flinch and let him paw her. "Have you seen such a weapon?" she asked him again.

He grinned. "My information is not free," he rumbled, squeezing her breast.

"I have nothing to give you. I am a slave." Orola lowered her head, letting her long black hair fall over her eyes to hide their soft glow.

The Weapons Master licked his thick lips, and then he grinned, displaying his big yellow teeth. "Come to my quarters tonight. We will discuss payment then." He looked at Rhesa. "Bring your friend here with you also."

Giving Orola's nipple one more twist, he dropped his hand to his crotch and scratched himself.

Orola saw the big bulge under the leather kilt and suppressed a shudder.

"Tonight," she said, smiling. "Perhaps you should also bring a friend. Are you sure you can handle us?"

He gave her a surprised look, and then a wide, ugly grin split his face. "You are a bold one and full of fire. I can see it in your strange eyes. Those are not the eyes of a gentle creature. Maybe I should be careful."

Orola smiled sweetly and turned away, again hiding the blaze in her eyes. "Tonight," she said over her shoulder, "but I expect information for my services."

When they were far enough away and they were certain the Weapons Master couldn't hear them, Rhesa stepped in front of Orola. "You mustn't play with him," she said seriously. "He is a dangerous man. He wouldn't think twice about slitting your throat."

Orola touched the girl's flushed cheek. "I am not as foolish as you might think, nor as helpless. I can defend myself, even if I lack the strength my Communicator lends me. You cannot show fear in front of a man like that."

Rhesa shuddered. "I don't like him, and tonight he will paw my breasts and violate my body. His man-pole is thick and hard and he possesses great virility."

"I'm sorry I dragged you into this," Orola said, "but maybe he'll leave you alone if I wear him down. I can endure much."

Smiling, the slave girl touched Orola's hand. "Thank you, I am grateful, but you won't have to do that for me."

"But it is my fault."

"Not really. Master Rellus has cornered me countless times and taken me as many. I have felt his giant rod inside my belly much too often, but this time I go to him freely. Perhaps I will even enjoy it."

Orola gave her a hug and kissed her on the forehead. "I have coupled with men who have taken me by force more times than I care to remember. Most gave me pain, but I have learned to take pleasure from them, even though they never meant for me to experience it. That is one way to get back at them." She sighed. "Some paid with their lives for what they did to me, but I took no pleasure in that."

She looked into Rhesa's dark eyes. "When a man takes you

against your will, he means to hurt you, and not just physically. If you let him, he wins and you lose, but if you turn the pain he means to inflict into pleasure for you, he cannot hurt you, and you win. Remember that."

After finishing their chores, the girls bathed and went to see the Weapons Master.

He didn't live in the palace. His dwelling was nestled among a small grove of trees outside the palace grounds. Two human guards were stationed beside the entrance. They gave the girls curious looks as they came walking down the gravel walkway.

"Master Rellus is expecting us," Rhesa told them.

The guards grinned at each other and crossed their spears in front of the girls, blocking the entrance. "We know nothing about that," one of them said. "Besides, the Weapons Master is occupied at the moment."

Rhesa took a step backward. "Then we'll be back later," she said haughtily.

"Not so fast." The guard's hand shot out, strong fingers circled around the girl's arm. She struggled to get free, but he was strong and pulled her into the nearby bushes.

Orola watched him throw the slave girl to the ground. She moved to interfere, but a sharp object against her ribcage stopped her.

"You move, and I'll run you through!" rasped the other guard.

Orola watched helplessly as Rhesa was made to lie on her back, watched as the guard moved between her spread legs, saw him pull aside the loincloth he wore under his kilt to free his manhood. "Touch me," she heard him say to Rhesa."

The girl obeyed, and he entered her. After a while, she began to move with the guard, gasped loudly when his buttocks clenched and his body stiffened. Then he pulled out.

"That was very good," Rhesa said bravely, "but I'm far from finished."

The guard grinned. "I am, but I must say, you're a lot tighter and much more helpful than the one Rellus is with now." He turned to the other guard. "Hey, Rold, don't you want to stick your worm into this one's flower? Her nectar is sweet and flowing."

Rold shook his head. "If the Weapons Master finds out you've been taking samples, he'll have your head, or most likely he'll cut off your worm. Heed my warning, Mirkas."

Mirkas laughed and came back to take his place by the entrance to the house. "The Weapons Master is my mother's brother. I am just warming them up for him." He looked at Orola, and then he put his hand on her breast. "Tell me, slave, did Master Rellus really send for you, or are you just begging for favors?"

"I have business with him," Orola said, her head held high.

"Business? The Weapons Master has no business with slaves." He backhanded her. "Don't lie to me, slave." Suddenly, he held a dagger in his hand. He held it against Orola's throat. "Move over into the bushes!"

Orola walked toward the shrubs where Rhesa still lay.

"On your knees!"

She obeyed. The pressure of the dagger was gone. Orola knew this was her chance to fight back, but she dismissed it. She'd have to kill him and the other one also. Where would she hide?

She felt the guard's hand between her buttocks, felt his probing finger. Then a large, hard object slid between her thighs, found her sex-canal, entered and slid inside.

She took him into her, adjusted herself to his size, found he was not overly large.

She closed her eyes, inhaled deeply, savoring the fresh crispness of the evening air. Her senses became aware of the fragrance of the flowers in the tall grass, the chirping of a bird in the tree above her.

Her anger vanished.

She pretended to be in a meadow with her lover, who brought her pleasure as a token of his love. If she pleased him, her own pleasure would be so much greater. His organ-of-love moved inside her, caressing the sensitive walls of her love-sheath. She began to move her body, arched her back, pushed up her buttocks to take him deeper into her. Her inside walls tightened around his shaft, squeezed gently, released him again.

He responded by slamming into her soft buttocks with forceful thrusts. His hands reached around her, took hold of her breasts. Strong fingers dug into their soft flesh.

She bucked beneath him, milked his driving rod.

He exploded inside her with a loud roar. She kept milking him until he was dry.

Orola sank to the ground; Mirkas lay on top of her, his organ inside her.

"You liked it," he whispered into her ear. Parting her long, black hair with one hand, he pressed his lips to her neck.

A flame of anger flickered inside her, but she doused it. She was still lying in the meadow, a cool breeze caressing her naked skin. Her body still glowed from the pleasure she had shared with her lover.

"I liked it," she said. "You know how to make a woman feel good, but you are heavy and your sword belt is digging into my back."

He laughed and rolled onto his back.

Orola pushed herself into a kneeling position, then she stood up.

She looked down at the guard who lay with his eyes half-closed.

How easy it would be to crush his throat with one blow of her foot!

She held out a hand to Rhesa, who had been watching in

silence. "Come," she said, "we mustn't let Master Rellus wait any longer."

Rold moved aside when the girls approached him. Orola opened the door unmolested and stepped through.

They entered a small room with a wooden table and a couple of benches. On the table stood a jug and a few clay cups.

The door in the back stood half open. Orola heard grunting and soft cries coming from the next room. Pushing open the door, she walked boldly into the other room.

The room was large. Thick rugs and animal skins were strewn across the floor, covering the cold stones.

They found the Weapons Master on his back, a naked female straddling his fat body. "I guess he couldn't wait," Orola said to Rhesa.

At the sound of Orola's voice, the girl who sat astride the Weapons Master twisted her head around to look at the girls. When she saw the two, she stopped moving for a short moment, and then she shrugged and carried on.

Orola walked over to the copulating pair's side and noticed the closed eyes of the Weapons Master. She smiled wickedly and gestured to the girl, then she moved behind her and matched her movements with her own. She squeezed the slave girl's arm and when they both lifted up, Orola pushed her pelvis forward, moving the other girl out of the way.

Then she plunged down and impaled herself on the Weapons Master's thick pole. She was still greased up from the guard and the big phallus slid into her with relative ease.

The other girl was quite agile and managed to move away without touching the fat man. Orola began to rotate her pelvis. Every time her buttocks touched the man underneath her, she constricted the walls of her vagina. Lifting up, she relaxed them again, but even then her sheath was still tightly wrapped around the hard rigid piece of flesh.

She had to admit Master Rellus was endowed and quite virile.

Orola moved with feverish haste on top of the big man; her pelvis snapped back and forth with ever increasing speed, but she couldn't bring his fat organ to release its load. She had lost all inhibitions and took full advantage of the situation. Since she had taken the Weapons Master's organ into her by her own choice, she saw no reason not to enjoy the occasion.

Her own juices were flowing freely and twice she experienced a tremendous orgasm. Throwing back her head, she whimpered and dug her fingers into her breasts as she felt another climax approaching. When it hit her with full force, she let out a suppressed cry.

This time, Master Rellus opened his eyes. As he focused on Orola, they widened, and then his mouth formed a huge grin.

"You are quite a surprise," he rumbled, putting his big meaty hands around her quivering hips. Lunging upward, he pulled her into his lap and held her there.

Orola squeezed her inner muscles tightly around his fat organ, and with great satisfaction, she watched a tremor going through the big body of the man. With a triumphant cry, she released her grip and sucked up the seeds of his first eruption.

A deep-throated sound escaped his open mouth, and his small eyes focused on Orola's ample breasts as he emptied his load into her quivering sheath. His strong hands never lost their tight grip around her hips. Only after he was spent did he let go, and his large body relaxed.

His breath came in ragged gasps, and his chest heaved with the effort to suck more air into his lungs.

Sitting in his lap, his penis still inside her, Orola chuckled and wiggled her bottom. "This is what's it's like when a woman comes to you out of her free will," she said. "Perhaps you should think about that the next time you force yourself on some young slave girl."

The big man grunted. "Which young girl would come to me freely?"

Orola shrugged. "I don't know, but if word should get

around of your kindness and generosity, and most of all your virility as a man, not to mention the size of your man-weapon, you might just be surprised."

Rellus heaved upward and dislodged her from his lap. She rolled onto her side and, lying unmoving, she watched the Weapons Master get to his knees. Below his fat belly, his mast strutted proudly. He waved to Rhesa, who had stood there, just watching. "Come here!" he growled.

Hesitantly, Rhesa walked forward.

"On your knees," the man commanded.

Orola knelt beside him, however, and reached under Weapons Master's fat belly. Her hand cupped his scrotum, then she moved it to encircle the root of his penis. Orola's fondling aroused him. "Get on your back," he told her.

Adjusting her inner muscles to accommodate the large intruder, she relaxed and concentrated on the sensation the moving thick pole created, and it didn't take long before she experienced her first orgasm.

Her body was agile and supple. She wrapped her long legs around his wide hips and rested her heels on the fat, quivering buttocks.

He moved on top of her for a surprisingly long time. When he finally came, he surprised her again with the force of his eruption. She managed to have her own orgasm at the same time and was quite satisfied. "You are no mortal woman," Master Rellus gasped, as he lay panting beside her. "I saw your eyes glow when I spilled my seed into you, and I felt hot liquid gushing from your insides to mingle with my discharge. That is not the way of a mortal woman."

Orola chuckled. "It is when she gives herself freely. Of course, it helps when the man she is with is as virile as you, Master Rellus."

"I never heard of it," he growled, and then he looked at the slave girl he had been coupling with when Orola and Rhesa came into his room. "Have you heard of that, Malese?" he almost bellowed.

Malese shook her head. "No, Master, I haven't," she stammered.

"You always come to me of your own free will, don't you?" His small eyes squinted at the girl.

"Oh, yes," Malese said eagerly. "I look forward to our time together." She lowered her lids demurely. "Today I missed the excitement of feeling your mighty weapon jump inside me as it delivers your gift." Her eyes moved to Orola. "Perhaps you can teach me this thing you do so I can please my master the way you did?"

Orola smiled sadly. "It cannot be taught, not really, but then again, there are always ways to stimulate yourself to achieve this state of excitement. It does take some practice. Of course, a gentle lover is of great help."

"I see." The girl sighed.

Orola turned to the Weapons Master. "What about the information you promised me?"

"What was it again you wanted to know?" His eyes were barely visible between the thick rolls of skin around them.

"A slender sword with a red jewel in its hilt."

Master Rellus shrugged his massive shoulders. "I haven't seen or heard of it."

"Then you lied to me!" Orola snapped angrily and took a step toward the fat man. "My services are not free. I expect something in return."

The Weapons Master glared at her. Then his hand moved with surprising speed, and he backhanded Orola. "You dare to speak to me in such manner, slave?" he roared. "Are you forgetting your position? Let me remind you. You are a slave, and you demand nothing. Ever. I can take you any time I choose to do so, and should I be displeased with your performance, I can let the Kellos have their way with you, and nobody would care."

His thick lips quivered. "You are nothing! You have no rights and no desires. You don't feel anything unless I say so. Do you understand? Now, get on your back, spread your legs wide."

Orola's eyes narrowed, and then they opened wide. "You touch me again like that and you'll be dead before your fat body hits the ground," she said with a low voice.

Behind her, the loud gasp of one of the girls sounded like a thunderclap in the sudden silence. The silence lasted only moments, then a pair of hairy hands shot forward and steely fingers clamped around Orola's neck.

She lashed out with her foot and kicked the fat man below the belly.

Master Rellus howled but didn't let go.

Orola jumped up, wrapped her long legs around the man's waist, and squeezed hard. Her fingers dug into his muscular arms, and she tried to break their hold, but she felt herself go weak from lack of oxygen and blood to her brain.

In desperation, she unwrapped her legs, put her feet against the Weapons Master's massive thighs and pushed hard.

His grip loosened, and she was free. Falling backward, she twisted in the air and kicked up with one foot. She felt it connect. Hitting the floor, she rolled, turned, and stood facing the angry Weapons Master.

He was holding his belly. Pointing a finger at her, he rasped, "You will pay for this. All of you!"

"But Master, I didn't..." Malese protested.

Rellus cut her off in mid-sentence. "You watched, saw me humiliated by this...this...thing. Word will get out and spread. I will make you an example." Then he bellowed, "Guards!"

The two guards came rushing into the room with bared swords in their hands. They stared at the fat naked body of their master.

"Take these three into the deepest dungeon you can find. Let them rot there," he roared.

"As you command," the guard Rold said.

"Are they fair game?" Mirkas asked.

Rellus waved a hand. "Do whatever you wish. Just get them out of my sight."

As the guards dragged the three girls across the courtyard, a small figure stepped into their path.

Orola recognized the elfin girl who had been with the Great Mukor.

"Where are you taking these slaves?" the girl asked with a sharp voice.

The two guards stopped. "Into the dungeons," Rold told her.

"By whose orders?"

"Master Rellus gave the order," Mirkas said.

"Master Rellus should be very careful with his orders," the girl commented. "Of late, he has been taking too much liberty upon himself. You'd better remind him that only the Great Mukor, his master, decides the fate of any slave." She smiled suddenly, but it didn't make her face look any kinder. "Even the fate of Master Rellus."

Orola shuddered when she looked at the girl's elfin face. It seemed suddenly very ugly and her eyes were as black and cold as a demon's pit.

"What would you want us to do, then?" Rold asked.

Orola sensed the sudden fear in his voice.

"I want these two to come with me." She pointed at Orola and Rhesa. "The other one will go back to her assigned chores."

The girl grabbed Orola's arm. "Come with me. I need your services."

They entered the palace through a side door, walked down a series of narrow corridors until they came to a large, wooden door.

"In here," the girl said. She pushed open the door and told Orola and Rhesa to enter.

The room lay in semidarkness. Through small windows high

up in the rough walls, meager streaks of light illuminated a large pool in the middle of the room.

Orola heard the bubbling sound of water and searched for its source. She spied an opening in one of the walls. A stream of water emerged from it. Running over a bed of natural rocks, it tumbled into the pool.

She couldn't see the other end of the pool; it was too dark in the room. She sensed more than saw something move, but before her eyes adjusted to night vision, her attention was brought back to the small girl.

"We're going to take a bath," the girl said, and then she pulled the loose robe she wore over her head.

Orola stared at the red crystal suspended from a thin rope around the girl's neck.

The girl noticed her staring. "Pretty, isn't it?"

"Very," Orola said, her breath suddenly coming a little faster.

The girl put a hand around it as if to protect it from spying eyes. "I found it among the loot a group of runaway Kellos had in their possession. It's a mystery where it came from. This is a communicator, you know." She smiled a little. "Of course, you don't know what I'm talking about. Let's say it's a device that should not exist in a primitive place like this. You people don't have the technology to build this." She shrugged. "It is useless here. Just another pretty bauble, that's all."

She pulled it over her head and turned to walk away.

"May I see it?" Orola asked, trying to keep her voice from betraying her anxiety.

"Why?" The girl's eyes narrowed.

"I've never seen anything so pretty. Maybe it has magic." Orola smiled sweetly.

"Magic?" The girl laughed and shook her head. "You know, sometimes I hate this awful place where people believe in magic and demons. I wish I could just leave and be myself again."

Her eyes bored into Orola's. "I hear you are a Moon Priestess. You pray to the moon Solar?"

"Yes I do. It is my god," Orola said.

The girl nodded. "So it is. If you only knew about your species." She was still staring at Orola. "I should fear you, but I don't, and I'll tell you why. Here, you are just a superstitious and ignorant primitive.

A slave. I can do with you whatever I choose. I could kill you without any fear of reprisal." She suddenly laughed. "Here, I am a goddess. Maybe you should pray to me instead of some dead rock, Moon Priestess."

She opened her hand and studied the oblong red object. A ray of light from the setting sun fell through an opening in the wall, caught on one of the facets of the crystal, and for a short moment, the seemingly dead trinket was a brilliant flash on the girl's palm.

With an angry gesture, the girl swung out her arm, flinging the crystal into the air. It bounced off the wall and came to rest on a natural shelf too high to reach.

The girl shrugged. "Let it rest there. It reminds me too much of home."

A splash in the pool made Orola turn her head. Someone came out of the pool. Another girl. She seemed a little taller and older than the girl with them. Orola studied her naked body. Small breasts jutted sharply from her thin ribcage. Between her legs, her genitals were without hair.

"Dyvori," the new girl said. "I didn't hear you come in."

Dyvori smiled. "I need some company. I thought you might feel the same, Dirma."

Dirma looked at Orola and then Rhesa. Orola thought she detected a hungry look in her cold, black eyes.

"I do," Dirma said. Her voice sounded cruel and somewhat hollow, not at all like that of a young girl. She went over to Rhesa.

"Come, you can wash my body." She pulled Rhesa toward the pool.

"You can do the same for me," Dyvori said to Orola.

The pool was shallow at one end, and the girls waded into the water until it came up to their knees. Orola scooped up some water and splashed it over Dyvori's body.

"Rub me," the girl told her.

Orola let her hands run over the girl's smooth skin.

"That feels nice," Dyvori murmured. "Rub a little harder."

After a while, she turned and stared at Orola. "Kneel down. I'll wash you off."

Orola knelt in the water. Her body was half submerged; the water felt cool and refreshing on her skin. She closed her eyes and enjoyed the girl's small hands on her body.

"You know," Dyvori said, "we are different from you. Our bodies have certain cravings that must be stilled. I want you to relax and not fight me. No harm will come to you, I promise you. I'll be careful. Do you understand?"

There was a hypnotic quality to the girl's voice, and it seemed as if it came from far away.

"I understand," Orola said, shaking her head to clear the wisp of fog that had enveloped her brain. She suddenly felt relaxed and drowsy.

Cool, scaly skin touched her back, her buttocks. She felt something wet snake between her legs, probe the entrance to her sexorgan. Then a knobby, warm, semi-hard appendix slid into her canal, expanded to fill her out completely.

Orola cried out in surprise, and then she moaned as a wave of pleasure began spreading through her body.

She arched her back, tried to take more of that strange, wonderful thing into her. Bucking, she clenched her buttocks, snapped her pelvis back and forth.

Strong, scaly legs wrapped around her hips; long, thin arms encircled her chest, bony fingers dug into her breasts.

"Don't move, please," a voice hissed into her ear.

The thing that filled her womb moved inside her. She felt a sensation, like tiny needles pricking the walls of her sex-canal. After a moment of pain, incredible pleasure rushed through her.

"I won't take much," the voice whispered. "Just enough to still my needs."

Orola lifted her head.

On the rough tiles beside the pool, Rhesa lay on her back; between her legs crouched a creature straight from the deepest pits of hell. Black and scaly, it writhed on top of the girl's naked body. It its open mouth gleamed two needle thin fangs. The scaly crest that ran along its spine, ended in a long, knobby tentacle.

Dripping saliva, the creature hissed and lowered its snout. It was about to sink its teeth into the girl's neck.

Only half conscious and feeling faint, Orola was aware of a great danger. She called out, "No, don't!"

The creature stopped, turned its fearsome head. Orola stared into two red glowing eyes. "I have a need," came the utterance from the creature's snout.

Behind Orola, a gravelly voice hissed, "So have I, but we must not!"

The phallus-like appendix seemed to shrink inside Orola, and then it was pulled out of her. It left her feeling empty.

With the weight on her gone, she sank beneath the water. She listened to the sounds of something swimming away. When she looked at Rhesa, she saw the monstrous creature getting off the girl; its red eyes boring into Orola's then it dove into the pool, disappeared below the surface.

Orola slowly rose out of the water. On unsteady feet, she walked toward the edge of the pool and climbed out.

Rhesa seemed to come out of her trance. Still on her back, her eyes focused on Orola. "What happened?" she asked. "I feel so drained and tired."

"You didn't see or feel anything?" Orola squatted down beside her and searched her neck, but she didn't find any blood.

"I felt pleasure." Rhesa closed her eyes, took a deep breath. "I hurt inside." Her eyes fluttered open and she looked at Orola. "Was I violated? I don't remember anything. Where is Dyvori?"

Orola shrugged. "Gone." She got up and reached for Rhesa's hand. "Come, we must leave this vile place." She also felt drained and fatigued, but her pain was fading. When she looked to the other side of the pool, she saw movement in the shadows.

"Leave now!" a gravelly voice drifted across the pool.

Orola didn't need any encouragement. Pulling Rhesa forcefully to her feet, she dragged the girl toward the door, then out into the corridor.

"I think we're lucky to be alive," she said to Rhesa, who finally seemed to come out of her stupor.

Her eyes were large when she stared at Orola. "I remember two glowing eyes," she whispered. "I remember a body between my open legs. I remember the feeling of lust coming over me, and I remember pleasure spreading through my body as something warm and slippery slid inside me and filled me completely. Trito never gave me such pleasure."

"Bloodsuckers," Orola said. "They drank our blood. The pleasure you experienced is false, not at all what you feel when you're with your friend Trito or any other man. This pleasure can kill you."

Rhesa wiped a hand over her eyes, and then she touched her belly. "I crave it. I feel empty."

"So do I," Orola said fiercely, "but this craving is wrong and deadly." She pulled the girl with her.

"Come on, let's get away from this place."

That night Rhesa slept alone. When her friend Trito came to her, she sent him away. Then she padded over to Orola's sleeping corner, crawled under the covers, and pressed her body against Orola.

"I am afraid," she whispered. "I've heard rumors of people disappearing. This slave I know, he found his sister dead in the woods, her body without a drop of blood, but there wasn't a mark on her." She shivered. "What kind of horror is this?"

Orola stroked the girl's hair. "I don't know," she said. "I've seen many strange things. This is just another one."

"The creature that violated me, you said you saw it clearly. Where did it come from?"

"I'm not certain." Orola hesitated. "Perhaps it was hiding in the water. There were two." Remembering the touch of the cool, scaly body on her skin, Orola shuddered. "They are not animals. They talk."

"The Kellos talk, and they're more animal than human. Maybe these creatures are Dyvori's trained pets. She is a strange one, you know. She may be a little girl, but she couples with Lord Mukor."

"I know," Orola said. "She is not a little girl, just appears like one because of her immature looking body. I sensed strangeness in her. She is evil."

Rhesa shivered in Orola's embrace. Her skin felt cold and clammy against Orola's. "That other girl, Dirma, I've seen her a few times in Lord Mukor's chambers. I think she is Dyvori's sister."

The girls fell asleep in each other's arms, physically and emotionally exhausted from the ordeal. Orola wasn't surprised when she awoke and found it to be daylight. She shook Rhesa, who was moaning softly in her sleep.

"Wake up, Rhesa. We are late for our chores."

Rhesa opened her eyes, smiled, and stretched lazily. Then she stared at Orola. "Why am I not in my own bed?" She touched her naked breasts, and then she moved her hand down to her belly. "I had a strange dream. I coupled with a horrible looking creature. I can still feel its large worm inside me."

Orola stayed silent. Then she smiled. "I've had strange dreams like that. Come on, we must get ready."

They rushed to the communal bath hall and took a quick dip

into the pool, and then they rubbed their bodies dry with the coarse towels that hung on hooks beside the entrance.

"I feel much better now," Rhesa said. She threw her towel into the heap of wet towels on the floor.

They ran to the kitchen, where a fuming Kitchen Master met them.

"If you weren't my cousin's daughter, I'd have you flogged." Master Troller fixed his good eye on Rhesa, who gave him a sweet smile. She rushed up to him and planted a quick kiss on his cheek.

"I'm sorry," she said. "It won't happen again."

"You said that the last time." His voice sounded even more whiny than usual. Then he sighed and gave Rhesa a slap on her bare buttock. "Go, take your friend here and help Silsie with the vegetables. Lord Mukor is giving a feast tonight. You'll both be expected to serve the food."

"I hope that's all we're expected to do," Rhesa whispered to Orola.

"I heard that." Master Troller lifted a bony finger. "Take some advice, girl. Bide your tongue and be careful what you say. The walls have ears."

Rhesa nodded and bit her lip. "The walls have ears. I know," she said soberly. Then she looked around as if searching for unseen listeners. Grabbing Orola's hand, she said, "Let's go and prepare the vegetables."

Silsie was a tall, thin girl with a pair of oversized breasts. Her hair was tied loosely with a piece of colored cord. It was long enough to touch her round buttocks. Her dark eyes gave her face a haunted expression.

She smiled at Rhesa and gave Orola a searching look.

"This is Orola," Rhesa said.

"I saw you as the guards dragged you in," Silsie said to Orola. "Did our lord the Great Mukor bed you?" she asked.

Orola looked into the girl's large, dark eyes and shrugged. "If that's what you call it, then the answer is yes."

Silsie put her hand to her mouth. "Speak softly or not at all. The walls have ears."

"So I've heard." Orola smiled. "I'll say it again. Your Great Mukor is a beast, and he forced his ugly body on me."

Rhesa put a hand on Orola's arm. "Silsie is right, Orola, be silent." She grabbed a basket full of black, long tubers and handed it to Orola. "Here, you can scrub these."

Orola took the basket, walked over to a basin, and began cleaning the tubers. Her thoughts wandered back to the events of the previous night.

The meeting with the Weapons Master had been fruitless. Either he really knew nothing about the sword or he was lying. Then she suddenly remembered the strange happenings in the room with the pool.

The star-crystal!

How could she have forgotten!

Dyvori had flung it against the ceiling. It was resting on a ledge high up on the wall, too high to be reached without help. If she could get someone to stand on her shoulder, she might be able to get it down.

A light slap against her bare rump made her turn to find the old man with the limp standing behind her.

He gave her a toothless grin. "Don't daydream, girl. Those tubers still have to be boiled today." Staring at her ample naked breasts, he sighed. "You have the kind of body that makes an old man like me wish he were young again. If I had teeth, I'd like to take a bite out of your deliciously plump buttocks."

"It you had teeth, I'd probably kick them in, old man," Orola said fiercely, but her smile took the sting out of her words.

"My name is Brakkus," the old man said. "In my younger days I used to bed wenches the whole night long and sometimes all day, but I don't believe I ever had one with fire like yours. Where are you from?"

"I am from the island Antanakka."

"The *Island of Witches*. I've heard of it. I wondered about your eyes. You have the eyes of a swamp-tiger."

"She's a priestess," Rhesa said. "A Warrior Priestess. She prays to the moon Solar."

The old man chuckled, and then he stared at Orola with narrow eyes. "I've heard strange tales about your people. Tales of awesome powers and unbelievable weapons, like swords that change into whips. Are they true? If they are, why are you a slave?"

Orola flashed him a smile. "Some tales grow taller with the telling but let me tell you this. Nobody ever held a Moon Priestess captive for very long, and there was always a terrible price extracted."

Brakkus kept silent, but she could feel his eyes on her as he watched her scrub the black tubers.

"Maybe you are the one," he whispered, more to himself than to her, but though she pretended not to listen, her keen hearing didn't miss the words. "Perhaps my wife was right when she told me about the visions she suffered just before she died."

"Stop telling stories, you old fool!" Silsie said from the other side of the trough. "It'll get you killed. Your wife was mad. She always had these prophetic dreams. Tell me one that came true."

Orola gave Brakkus a sidelong glance. "What did your wife see?" she asked.

"She saw the death of Lord Mukor." His voice was barely audible, and he leaned closer to whisper into her ear. "In her vision, he was killed by a tall warrior woman with the flaming eyes of a night hunter...eyes like yours."

Orola shook her thick, black hair out of her eyes and looked at Silsie, who had been watching. She noticed the trembling hands of the other girl. "Sometimes dreams become real," she said.

"We will all get punished if you don't stop this insane talk," Silsie almost shouted. "I won't listen anymore. The walls have ears." Orola sighed. "I am a slave already. I've been stripped naked. Abused repeatedly. What else is left? I'm not scared."

Brakkus went back to his table where he busied himself chopping vegetables. He kept glancing at Orola and chuckled merrily.

Orola scrubbed her tubers with greater vigor, humming as she threw the clean ones into a big basket. Across from her, Silsie was cutting the purple tops from the tubers. Once in a while, she looked around, a gloomy, haunting expression on her face.

Rhesa came over from one of the other tables and touched Orola's arm. "Don't pay too much attention to Brakkus. He's old, and his mind isn't what it used to be. If it weren't for that limp, he'd have been chosen a long time ago for the hunt, and his head would have decorated the walls of the Great Mukor's trophy room. He is lucky, for it is not sport to hunt a cripple."

"Mukor hunts humans for sport?"

Rhesa shrugged. "Most of them are criminals or runaway slaves."

"My father was not a criminal!" Silsie protested vehemently.

"Your father?" Orola gave Silsie a questioning look.

"Her father talked openly against our lord," Rhesa answered for Silsie. "He was selected for the hunt."

Orola nodded, suddenly understanding why Silsie was so afraid.

"It's a barbaric custom," she said, "and not always just."

"Will you girls stop your jabbering or do I have to use the whip on you?" Master Troller stood in the entrance to the kitchen, his one eye glaring at the girls. "I can't leave you alone for a moment. What am I going to do with you?"

Rhesa rushed back to her table. "It was kitchen talk," she said. "I showed Orola how to scrub the tubers in the correct fashion. She's never done this kind of work before."

The Kitchen Master threw up his hands and took the lid off one of the pots. "Why is this water boiling with nothing in it?" he complained. "Do I have to do everything myself?"

Orola carried a platter of steaming food when Master Troller stopped her. "You...I have different orders for you. Go with her." He pointed to a young girl who was standing beside him.

Orola put the platter back onto the table and followed the little girl.

"Where are we going?" she asked.

The young girl lifted her narrow, naked shoulders. "I don't really know. I was told to bring you to the Entertainment Master.

The Entertainment Master was short and fat. He was dressed in a bright, colorful outfit. "Come, come, girl," he said, wringing his pudgy hands. "Our guests are already seated and waiting for their entertainment. Here...put these on."

Orola held her breath when she saw the items another girl handed her. A halter with two metal breast cups and a short kilt woven from soft metal mesh.

"Where did you get these?" she asked.

"Never mind that!" the Entertainment Master snapped. "Just put them on."

Orola slipped into the kilt, closed the familiar metal buckle of the wide belt. Then she covered her breasts with the metal cups. They were small, left much uncovered, but they were a perfect fit. She tied the leather straps behind her back.

Then the girl handed her a wooden sword.

"What should I do with this?" she asked.

"I'm told you're a Warrior Priestess. Go. Show off your skills. The guests are waiting."

Orola stepped through the curtains, looked around. Lord Mukor was seated on a thick, wide cushion. She spied Dyvori on one side of him and Dirma on the other.

The guests were lounging on pillows on the other side of the room.

When they saw the tall girl, a momentary hush went through the room.

"This is Orola. She claims to hail from the island Antanakka, the Island of Witches. Of course, we have only her word." Lord Mukor chuckled. "Doesn't she look splendid in that warrior's outfit?"

"I'll pay you a hundred gilds if she comes to my bed tonight," one of the male guests called loudly. "She'll have no trouble bewitching my warrior."

Some of the other guests laughed.

Lord Mukor lifted his hand. "I might just consider your offer, Councilor Framor, but for now, let's see how she can defend herself against my own warrior."

The curtain parted. The man who came into the room was a giant. He wore skimpy leather armor, and his bare arms bulged with corded muscles. The skimpy breechcloth couldn't hide the huge bulge between his legs.

Grinning, he stepped toward Orola and reached for her. She stepped back, fell into a fighting stance, the wooden sword she held in front of her.

"Put that stick away," the giant growled. "This is only a mock fight. You know what we're supposed to do."

"Fight," Orola said, pretending not to understand, and hit him on one of his padded shoulders.

The giant was quicker than he appeared. His right hand shot out, grabbed the wooden sword, and wrenched it out of her grip. With a grunt of contempt, he threw it to the floor. Then he ripped off his breechcloth to reveal a huge erection.

"Now let's play," he rumbled, reaching again for her.

Orola's foot lashed out, connected with the big man's crotch.

He howled, grabbed his scrotum and then he launched himself again at her.

She evaded him easily, rammed her knee into his belly, and then she brought both of her fists down on his corded neck. He went down, lay stunned. Before he could regain his senses, Orola pulled both of his arms behind his back and sat on him.

The guests laughed. Orola looked defiantly at Mukor.

78

He did not look pleased.

Beside him, the two girls joined in the laughter, which seemed to infuriate him even more. He clapped his hands.

The fat Entertainment Master came waddling into the room and rushed to Lord Mukor's side. Mukor whispered something into his ear. The Entertainment Master nodded then he disappeared through the curtains.

Lord Mukor clapped his hands again and lifted a pewter cup. "Drink up, honored guests and sample some of my fine foods. More entertainment in a moment."

The giant under Orola moved. "Let me up!" he growled. "Leave me some dignity."

Orola let go of his wrists, stood up and watched the big man come to his feet.

Shaking his bald head and holding his belly, he left the room.

Orola looked around, studied the guests sprawled on their huge cushions. Some of them were local citizens, most likely important businessmen and men in high government positions.

Some were obviously dignitaries from neighboring provinces.

Her eyes fell upon a woman who was openly studying her. She was a beautiful woman, her face narrow and her eyes gray like polished steel. Her long auburn hair fell in small curls around her bare shoulders.

She nodded when she noticed Orola's eyes on her.

Beside her sat a figure dressed in a plain gray robe. Orola couldn't see his face. It was hidden inside a large hood.

A rustling sound made her turn her head. The curtains behind her had parted again. Five naked hairy men came rushing into the room—Kellos. Two of them dragged a naked girl between them.

Orola recognized Silsie. Her long hair was disheveled, and her dark eyes blazed with hidden anger.

Four of the Kellos held her pinned to the ground, the other one knelt between her spread legs. It was obvious that the group intended to rape her.

Enraged, Orola scanned the room. Most of the guests seemed to enjoy the show. She saw a couple of naked slave girls sitting astride two of the watching men. Their lower bodies moved lazily in the men's laps.

Three other slave girls stalked between the guests, obviously looking for a willing partner.

When she searched for the Great Mukor, she saw him leaning back into his pillows. Dirma, the older one of the girls, sat in his lap, her slim hips gyrating with slow motions. She saw Orola looking and winked at her.

With an angry shout, Orola stepped toward the group on the floor and delivered a vicious kick into the body of the Kellos on top of Silsie. The man-beast let out a loud cry and fell to the side, but before Orola could make another move, a hard object smashed against the side of her head and sent her spinning.

Momentarily senseless, she stumbled and fell. Rough hands grabbed her, pulled her down, and held her in a kneeling position.

She stared at the giant she had humiliated standing above her.

"Now we play." He grinned and sank to his knees, began fondling his half-erect member. The giant grunted, bent close to her ear. "You made me look bad and I should be angry, but I am not an animal, just a slave...like you. Don't worry, I'll try not to hurt you."

"You are hurting me already," Orola said.

"Maybe if you'd help a little, I won't last very long."

She smelled the foulness from his open mouth and tried to take shallow breaths. Her mind began to drift. She was barely aware of the body on top of her. She heard a girl crying beside her, assumed it was Silsie, but didn't care anymore.

When she regained consciousness, she was back in the room she shared with Rhesa. The girl bent over her, a concerned look on her face.

"Are you all right?" Rhesa asked.

Orola lay silent for a moment. "I think I'll be fine," she said, her voice hoarse from her parched throat. "I need something to drink." Rhesa got a small pitcher. She lifted it to Orola's lips.

Smiling gratefully, Orola emptied half its contents. The water tasted a little brackish, but it went down like a delicious elixir. "Thank you," she said, licking her lips. They felt rough and dry.

"You should rest," Rhesa said.

It was dark in the room, only the rays from one of the moons illuminated the interior with a pale light. Orola's eyes adjusted to the darkness. She could see the tears in the girl's eyes. Lifting a hand, she patted Rhesa's cheek. "Don't worry about me. I'll survive."

She sat up, winced when a sharp pain shot through her. "I need your help, Rhesa."

"Anything." The girl didn't hesitate. "What do you need?"

"Remember the room with the pool? I want you to go there with me. There is something that I have to recover. Something that belongs to me."

Rhesa lifted her hands. "Oh, no, Orola, not that. Anything but that. I know I promised, but I can't go there."

"It is important that I get back what was stolen from me. My life and my future may depend on it."

Rhesa stared into the darkness. Orola could feel her tremble. She touched the girl's hand. "I wouldn't ask you, but you're the only one I can trust."

A shudder went through Rhesa. She turned and looked into Orola's eyes. "I'll come with you," she said softly. "When?"

"Now."

The two girls walked silently down the dark, empty corridor.

Flickering torches set into rings in the wall at irregular intervals made it possible to see where they were going.

Rhesa knew the way, but Orola was certain that even without the girl, she could have found the room. The wooden door was closed. It swung open when Orola pushed against it.

Even though the room lay in near-darkness, Orola's night vision let her see quite clearly.

"This room gives me the shivers," Rhesa whispered. "Something may be hiding in the darkness."

Tiny slivers of light fell through the small windows high above, enough to illuminate the upper part of the wall Orola was seeking. "Up there on the shelf." The room seemed empty, but she kept her voice low just in case she was wrong.

They moved toward the wall. "Stand on my shoulder," Orola instructed the girl. She squatted down and let Rhesa step onto her shoulders. Holding on to Rhesa's legs, Orola stood up.

"I can't reach it," Rhesa said.

"Hold on to the wall. I'll lift you higher." Orola grabbed the girl's ankles and pushed up. She could hear the soft scraping sounds as Rhesa's fingers searched for the Amulet.

"I got it," the girl said triumphantly.

Orola let her down. When Rhesa's feet touched the ground, she turned to give the crystal to Orola. As Orola reached for it, a splashing sound made her turn her head.

All she saw was a moving shadow, then she was pushed aside by strong hands. She stumbled, regained her balance, and fell into a fighting stance.

Mocking laughter and the sight of a creature with red, glowing eyes and gleaming fangs made her blood run cold. Beside the creature stood Dyvori. She held Orola's pendant in her hands.

"You seem to go to a lot of trouble to get this," Dyvori said. "It makes me wonder why you want it so much."

Orola shrugged her shoulders. "It's a beautiful crystal. I like beautiful things."

Dyvori's laughter sent a chill down Orola's spine. "You are a slave. It doesn't matter what you like. Slaves are not allowed to own anything. Remember that."

"I just would like to touch it," Orola said, putting a pleading note into her voice. "I think it has magic."

"Of course it has magic, you ignorant fool. But none you could make use of. Now get back to your quarters!" Dyvori said sharply.

Trembling with anger and frustration, Orola obeyed.

"I'm sorry," Rhesa said as they walked down the damp corridor.

"It's not your fault," Orola said. "I should have been more on guard."

When they got back to their sleeping quarters, Trito was waiting for them. "Where have you been?" he asked anxiously. "I was worried."

Rhesa put her arms around his neck and kissed him hungrily. "I need you tonight, Trito. Badly," she whispered into his ear.

Orola smiled, went to her cot and sank into a pile of blankets. Her hearing was keener than that of normal people. Even now, she could hear their whispered conversation.

"Maybe we should wait until she's asleep," she heard Trito whisper.

Rhesa giggled. "She's my friend. Let her listen." "Listen and watch," Trito said.

"She won't see. It is dark."

Orola lay on her side, watched as Rhesa lay back on her cot, her legs apart. Trito moved on top of her, fumbled between her spread thighs.

The faint moonlight falling through the small window was enough to make everything bright for Orola. She saw Trito's erection quite clearly, heard him sigh as he entered Rhesa's welcoming love channel. The girl moaned quietly as she took Trito into her. Their movements were steady and without hurry.

Two lovers who had done this many times before and were comfortable with each other.

Orola felt a stab of envy. That was one thing she never had…a man who truly loved her.

Sexual intercourse, the joining of two bodies, she had experienced too many times, freely and by force, but love was denied her. She loved her sisters and brothers, and they loved her in return, but that was not the same.

This moment she longed for the warm, loving touch of a man; she longed to feel his hands stroking her body, to have his fingers caress her breasts, feel his lips press on hers in a passionate kiss, take his manhood freely into her body and reach an orgasm together not for the sake of lust but out of love.

She heard Rhesa crying out softly, heard Trito's loud moans as his body shuddered between the clutching thighs of Rhesa.

They lay still for a moment, embracing and kissing then Trito rolled onto his side. Between his legs, his penis stood still rigid.

Aroused, Orola touched herself, moaned as her fingers found her tender spot.

"Are you ill?" Rhesa called.

"No, just lonely," Orola answered truthfully.

"Come, join us then. We could use another warm body."

Orola padded over to them, crawled under the covers. The feel of Trito's naked skin against hers sent small shivers through her body. "Hold me," she said in a small voice.

Trito looked at Rhesa who lay on his other side. She nodded. "She needs you, Trito. She is my friend."

Trito put his arm around Orola, his erect member pressed hard against her thigh. Her hand moved down, touched him. He moaned, pulled back a little.

Orola heard Rhesa giggle. The girl was fully aware of what was happening. She whispered into Trito's ear. "I permit it." Trito chuckled and slid on top of Orola.

Sighing with anticipation, she pulled up her legs, opened her thighs wide. She had recovered from her ordeal and experienced no pain when Trito entered her.

He was gentle, took his time, moved with steady but forceful strokes.

Trito called out harshly, "I'm coming." He crushed her to him, erupted inside her.

Orola pulled his face down, kissed him with passion, moaned into his mouth as her own floodgates broke and a powerful orgasm pulsed through her body.

She milked his seed giver with her pulsing sheath and accepted his gift.

When they were both spent, he lay breathing hard between her cradling thighs, his pole still rigid, still deep inside her. She knew he was still aroused and so was Rhesa.

She pushed him off. "Go to Rhesa," she said softly. She had forced herself to hold back. She couldn't afford to have him experience the ecstatic pleasure she could have given him. He didn't belong to her. His gift of love had been enough.

He fell between Rhesa's welcoming thighs, almost shouted when Rhesa lifted up to take his stiff organ into her.

With a roar of raw emotion, Trito exploded. He grabbed Rhesa's quivering hips and pulled her deep into his lap. Whimpering and clawing, Rhesa went suddenly limp and collapsed on top of Trito.

Orola put her arms around both of them, happy and satisfied.

Orola had just started to scrub a basket full of tubers, when Kitchen Master Troller walked up to her. His usual sour expression was even more pronounced. Looking at Orola out of his one good eye, he patted her arm. "Take care," he said solemnly, and then he turned and walked away.

Moments later, two guards stalked into the kitchen. One carried a small bundle.

"Come with us!"

"Why?" she asked.

"Don't ask questions, slave. Just follow us."

When they were in the corridor, the one who carried the bundle threw it to the floor. It opened up and spilled its contents onto the tiles.

Orola recognized her kilt and breast cups.

"Put these on," the guard ordered.

She did so gladly. She felt better when she wore her familiar clothing.

The guards led her outside, took her to a fenced-in corral and shoved her inside. A group of naked slaves cowered in one corner. They looked at her without expression, but she saw the desperate fear in their eyes. She spotted Silsie among them. The tall girl was covered with grime, her hair hung knotted and disheveled.

The clanking of metal made Orola turn around. A number of guards came through the gate and into the corral. They grabbed and shackled half the slaves, Orola one of them. Lying on the filthy ground with her hands tied behind her back and her feet bound tightly together, she watched as the guards teamed up the unbound slaves with the bound ones.

They assigned Silsie to Orola.

"What is going on?" Orola asked the tall girl.

Silsie stared at her out of dark, haunted eyes. She looked even paler than usual. "We've been chosen for the hunt," she said sullenly.

"Now listen up," one of the guards called out loudly. "You slaves who are not tied, you have two choices. You can either leave now and gain some time before the hunt begins, or you can untie your assigned partner, lose precious time, but perhaps have a better chance to escape later with the help of your partner. Anyone left behind will be executed immediately. Now…go!"

Orola noticed some of the slaves running out of the corral, others bent down to help the ones on the ground to get free.

Silsie fell to her knees and began to pull on Orola's bound feet.

"Leave me, Silsie. Go, and maybe you'll get away."

Silsie laughed shrilly. "What's the point? Nobody ever escapes."

She used her teeth to gnaw through the tough leather straps, and soon Orola was free. Bolting after the tall girl who had run away as soon as Orola's bonds fell, she saw that some of the other slaves had also been freed.

All of them headed toward the wooded area that surrounded the palace.

Silsie was a fast runner, but Orola caught up with her before she reached the forest.

"Do you know where we are going?" she asked the running girl.

"Anywhere," Silsie said breathlessly. "It really doesn't make any difference, but the forest is our best bet. My father used to be a forester. I know some places where we can hide."

Silsie found a trail, and they followed it for a while. Orola heard the footsteps of other slaves who had chosen to take the same trail. "We have to lose them," Silsie called back over her shoulder. Her long hair trailed behind her and was getting caught in branches that had grown across the trail. While running, she grabbed her hair and tied it into a loose knot.

Another trail intercepted the one they were on. Silsie turned to the right without slowing down. Bursting into a large clearing, Orola noticed a number of narrow trails on the other side. Silsie hesitated for a moment, and then she said, "That one."

Before they reached the trail, Orola heard the sound of a trumpet.

"The hunt begins," Silsie said. "We don't have much time."

The new trail was narrow, overgrown. Sharp thorns scratched their legs and snaking vines and branches tripped them continuously. Once, Silsie stumbled, fell to the ground. Getting up, she brushed off the dirt and leaves. There was an angry red streak across one of her breasts and plenty of scratches on her legs and belly.

Orola saw a number of red marks and slightly bleeding wounds on her own body.

"There is an old cabin not far from here," Silsie said. "We can hide in there and rest for a while."

"Wouldn't we have a better chance if we kept moving?" Orola asked.

Silsie shook her head. "In the end, it doesn't really matter. We'll be found eventually."

"We'll fight," Orola said grimly.

"I'm not a fighter." Silsie sounded resigned.

"Let's go." Orola smiled encouraging. "Not everything is lost. We are free."

The cabin was there, as Silsie had said, but now it wasn't much of a hiding place. The roof had holes in it, the walls were rotting and the door lay inside, ripped off its hinges.

Silsie threw herself on top of a pile of leaves that had gathered in the corners. Sweat covered her skin, and her breath came in great gasps. "My feet are sore, and they are bleeding," she complained.

Slightly winded, but ready to go on, Orola squatted against a wall. She was still angry at herself for being so careless. With the *Holy Communicator* in her possession, things would be different. She wouldn't be hiding and cowering like a frightened animal. Her god Solar would lend her strength to defeat her enemies.

The snorting of an animal outside brought her to her feet. Moving silently, she looked out of the small window.

"What is it?" Silsie whispered.

"Seems they didn't lose much time following our trail," Orola whispered back. She didn't want to be cornered inside the cabin, and knowing that running wouldn't do any good, she decided to face their pursuers.

Stepping through the door, she walked into the open.

To see the two girls didn't surprise her, but she did not expect to see that one of their riding beasts was her black-coated steed *Shadow*.

When Silsie, who had followed Orola, recognized the girls, she bolted away, toward the trees, but she didn't get very far.

Crying out, she faltered, fell to the ground. Tugging on the arrow that had pierced her thigh, she tried to get up.

"Stay where you are!" Dirma commanded, aiming her crossbow at Silsie. "The next arrow goes straight through your heart."

Orola stared at the girl who sat astride Shadow. Orola's *Holy Communicator* hung between her small breasts.

"Hello Moon Priestess," Dyvori said with a honey-sweet voice. "We have some unfinished business." Beside her squatted a creature that could only have been spawned in someone's sick mind. Red eyes glowed above a snout filled with long, razor-sharp teeth. Yellow saliva dripped from drooling black lips.

The girls dismounted. Dirma walked over to Silsie, tied the whimpering girl's hands behind her back and then to her good leg. Then she strolled back toward Orola. "Take off your clothes and lie down on your back," she said.

Orola obeyed. The loaded crossbow aimed at her throat didn't leave her much choice.

Dyvory stepped on Orola's outstretched hands. "Spread your legs wide!"

When Dyvory bent over Orola, the red crystal that hung from a leather strap around her neck touched Orola's naked belly.

A shockwave of pure ecstasy flooded her body. The *Holy Communicator* began to glow and throb like a searing iron, but only Orola was aware of it.

She closed her eyes, let the familiar pattern enter her mind. Strength returned to her limbs, damaged tissue was repaired throughout her body.

Orola's view was blocked by Dyvori's thigh, but she sensed the presence of Dirma to one side and the creature on her other.

They were confident that Orola was helpless, and that would be her advantage.

Sending a silent prayer to her god Solar, Orola grabbed the crystal, pushed Dyvori into Dirma, and somersaulted backward away from them.

She heard shrill screams from someone. Crouching, she faced her enemies.

Dyvori lay face down on the ground, her hands clawing at an arrow protruding from her back. Dirma stood staring dumbfounded at Dyvori, the crossbow hanging from her limp hands.

She looked up, her eyes blazing.

Suddenly her eyes glowed red, the contours of her face began to change, her jaw moved forward, became a snout. When she opened her mouth, Orola saw long, thin fangs.

"You!" Dirma roared with a voice that did not sound human.

The creature beside her howled and leaped. Orola moved aside with lightning speed, and when the creature landed on the ground, she jumped on its back, threw one arm around the scaly throat and grabbed the snout with her free hand.

The beast bucked, tried to dislodge her. Twisting the thick neck, Orola heard bones cracking. The creature collapsed; its body convulsed, and then it lay still.

Orola rolled onto her back, the dead beast on top of her like a shield. She heard the impact as the arrow that was meant for her hit the lifeless carcass. Freeing herself from the dead body, she rose to her feet with smooth movements, sped toward Dirma. She was on top of the girl before she could successfully load another arrow onto her crossbow.

Kicking the weapon out of Dirma's hands, Orola grabbed her, twisted her around, and held her arms behind her back. The girl struggled, kicked back viciously. From her beastly throat came ear-piercing howls. Orola threw her to the ground, pinned her down.

"I don't want to kill you," Orola said, "but I will."

"We underestimated you."

"So you did. Now tell me, do you want to live?"

Dirma laughed hollowly. "What do you think? Let me go. I promise I'll behave."

Orola set her free, rose to her feet. While watching Dirma, she tied the leather straps of the amulet, which she still held clutched in her hand, behind her neck, let the star-crystal nestle in the cleavage between her breasts. It radiated brilliant red fire.

Rising, Dirma eyed Orola. Her face had changed back, but her eyes still glowed red. "I should have known. The *Communicator*. That is where your power comes from. Dyvori was careless."

"What manner of creature are you?" Orola asked. "You appear to be human, but you are not."

"No, I am a shape shifter."

"What is your true form?"

Dirma looked at the dead creature. "You've slain my brother, and I've killed my own sister."

"You are evil," Orola said slowly. "Are there many of your kind?"

"Just the three of us and the Great Mukor." She stared at Orola.

"We are not evil, just different."

"Where do you come from?"

"From far away. Our...carriage crushed, many died. Only the four of us survived."

"What about the Kellos?"

Dirma shrugged. "We keep them as pets and for other needs. They have minimal intelligence."

"Intelligence enough to rape and kill."

"They have their uses."

Orola turned away from Dirma and walked over to the blackcoated beast. "This belongs to me," she said, whirling when she heard Silsie scream.

Dirma was almost upon her. Long fangs gleamed in her open snout. Her hands were scaly claws tipped with razor-sharp curved nails.

Orola jumped sideways but was not fast enough. Sharp nails raked across her back. Without conscious thought, she dampened the pain, closed bleeding blood vessels.

Dirma faced her, crouching like an animal. "Never turn your back on me," she said with voice filled with gravel.

"I'll remember that. You are a creature without honor," Orola said sharply. "I will kill you if you attack again."

Without warning, Dirma leaped on top of her own riding beast and dug her heels into the animal's flanks. Orola watched her disappear into the forest. When the creature was gone, she walked over to Silsie.

Silsie's white face looked even paler from loss of blood. Orola ripped apart her bonds then bent to examine the wound in her thigh.

"I'll have to push the arrow through," she told the girl.

"It hurts," Silsie whimpered, her face a mask of pain.

Orola smiled, put her hand on Silsie's thigh and closed her eyes. When she opened them again, Silsie had stopped whimpering and shaking.

"What did you do?" she asked.

"Shh, lie still." Orola broke off the feathered end of the arrow, and then, with a quick move, she pushed the remaining stub all the way through Silsie's thigh.

Silsie cried out. Blood began to flow from the exit wound, but Orola laid her hand over it and stopped the flow. Closing her eyes again, she initiated the healing process, and after a while the other girl breathed easier.

"That is all I can do for you. The rest is up to your body," she told Silsie. Then she added with a saucy grin, "If you were a man, I could heal you completely."

She didn't go into details, and Silsie didn't ask.

Shadow neighed, and moments later, two riders burst into the small clearing. Recognizing them from the night before, Orola drew herself erect and watched them come closer.

The Lady and her hooded escort.

Sliding off her steed, the Lady walked slowly toward Orola. Stepping in front of her, she nodded.

"Greetings, Moon Priestess. I see you've managed to defeat your pursuers. I have something that belongs to you." She waved to her hooded companion.

The broad shoulders could not hide the fact that he was a man. He walked his horse closer, then jumped from his riding beast. In his hands, he carried a long object wrapped in cloth. He handed it to Orola with one hand; with the other, he pushed back his cowl.

Bowing slightly, he looked at Orola out of blue eyes. She noticed the slit pupils. He was not young anymore; his handsome face was beginning to show fine lines. The sun reflected from his polished skull.

There was no doubt what he was.

"I am Arkos," he said and made the sign with his right hand.

"I am Orola." She lifted her hand, touched her thumb to her small finger, while her other fingers stayed erect. Only members of her species were capable of doing that. "Why is a Warrior Priest taking part in this barbaric and cruel sport?" she asked.

He smiled. "I am not. I came to observe and to rescue you." She unwrapped the bundle he had given her.

"My sword," she said. "Where did you get it?"

"I traded for it," the Lady said. "My gift to you."

"A gift? Nothing is free, my Lady."

The woman laughed. "You are correct. There is a small favor I ask. The Great Mukor is becoming a threat. He must be eliminated. I want you to take care of that."

"I am not an assassin." Orola stared into the woman's steel-gray and unflinching eyes.

"You want revenge for what he did to you?" the woman asked.

Orola nodded. "I do."

"Then there is no problem." The woman held up one slim hand. "My people call me Lady Aleena."

"This is what you were trained for," Arkos said. "You are a Warrior Priestess. It is your duty."

Orola watched Lady Aleena and her escort ride away, her mind uneasy. Arkos was right.

She had no choice.

Soft footsteps made her turn. Silsie had come up behind her, her dark eyes shining brightly in her pale face. "Perhaps Brakkus was right. Perhaps you are *The One*."

Orola shrugged. "I know who and what I am, and I know what must be done." She swung onto her steed and helped Silsie up to sit behind her.

"Now we are the hunters," Orola said.

They entered the trail that Dirma had taken. It was not the same one Orola and Silsie had come from when they sought protection in the cabin. This one was wider and less overgrown. The riding animal's hoof prints were easily seen in the soft soil.

"Where are we going?" Silsie asked.

"She will lead us straight to Mukor," Orola explained. Then she added, "I hope."

She felt a tremor running through Silsie's body, and Orola knew it wasn't because the girl was cold, even though she was naked.

"I am scared," Silsie said with a small voice.

"I won't let anyone harm you," Orola assured her. She felt whole again. Alive. The power of her god Solar vibrated through her body. Her senses were aware of everything around her; her eyes saw things she hadn't before.

She heard the exploding rush of fluttering wings as a flock of *triacs* took to the air, and then she saw the small creatures above the treetops not far ahead.

The scream of a human being in agony told Orola what she had suspected already. "Hold on tight," she said. Digging her heels into her steed's flanks, she raced down the trail, unmindful of the branches that raked her body. Bursting into a clearing, she pulled hard on the reins and brought her steed to an abrupt halt.

The gross body of Lord Mukor sprawled on the ground, nearly covering up the naked body of a slave underneath him.

Dirma knelt not far away from him. She lifted her head to look at Orola. Blood and saliva dripped from her bestial snout and her eyes glowed red.

It front of her lay the blood covered body of a young girl.

Emitting a bloodcurdling cry, Orola dug her heels into *Shadow's* flanks. The animal neighed and raced toward Dirma. Before Dirma could react, Orola was upon her. Kicked in the head by *Shadow's* powerful hoof, the beast-girl fell sideways, shuddered and lay still.

The Great Mukor rose to his feet, moved with a speed belying his bulky body. Picking up a crossbow, he lifted it.

Orola had pulled her sword from its scabbard. It changed as she raised it into the air, became a long, thin whip. Before Mukor could bring up his weapon completely, the bow was ripped from his grasp.

Orola slid off her steed, stood wide-legged in front of her enemy.

"You will pay for this, slave!" Mukor hissed.

"I am not a slave. I am Orola, a Moon Priestess," Orola said, standing tall. "It is you who will pay."

Lord Mukor laughed. "A Moon Priestess," he said mockingly. "You're a savage playing with powers you don't understand. That god you're praying to, it is nothing but a dead rock."

"I am not the savage," Orola said quietly. "I don't rip apart human beings to eat their flesh and drink their blood. Only a beast does that."

"Your reaction does not surprise me. You kind has always pretended to be noble and superior," Lord Mukor sneered. "You know nothing about my species and our needs." His body outlines wavered, began to change. He ripped off his clothing with hands that had become claws.

Orola watched in fascination as the Great Mukor changed from a human being into a demon.

Shimmering blue scales covered a long, sleek body with rippling muscles. A red crest rose from the elongated skull, ran along the backbone in a row of sharp spikes.

With a hissing sound, the beast-man rushed Orola, who barely managed to roll out of his way. Coming up, she cracked her whip; the sharp tip of the leash raked across Mukor's soft belly, leaving an angry red streak.

Roaring again, he snapped at the withdrawing leash with long, sharp teeth. Then, propelled by powerful hind legs, he leaped into the air, heading straight for Orola.

The whip in her hand shortened, changed into a short stout sword. As Mukor came down, she drove the sword into his soft exposed belly. Pulling it out, she had barely time to roll free. As she did so, she drew her weapon across the beast-man's throat in a backhanded slash.

Silsie, who still sat on the back of Shadow, watched the short battle with horror. Everything happened with incredible speed. Before she realized it, she saw the beastly body of what once had been the Great Mukor shudder violently on the ground, while his blood painted the grass red.

Orola stood over him, her sword touching his severed throat. Her strange eyes blazed with brilliant fire, and the jewel between her breasts pulsed brightly. When the body of the Great Mukor stopped convulsing, she took a deep breath and stepped away from the still form.

The sword was still in her hand as she walked over to where Dirma lay on the ground, her head in a pool of blood. Orola rolled her over with one foot, then she sheathed her sword.

When she walked toward Silsi, her strange blue eyes were still cold, but the fire was gone.

"You are *The One*," Silsie whispered with awe. "Crazy old Brakkus was right after all."

Orola nodded as she surveyed the carnage. "It is over."

PIRA

A gust of cool wind blew into the room, causing the small flames to flicker and spit in their earthen containers. The innkeeper looked up as a hooded figure entered the open door.

Rain was still falling heavily from the darkened sky, and water dripped from the stranger's cape onto the wooden floor. He watched the visitor walk over to one of the corner tables and shook his head in disgust when he saw the muddy footprints.

Filling a pitcher with ale, he waddled across the stained floor and set the pitcher in front of the silent figure.

"Half a gilding," he demanded and caught the coin when the stranger flipped it into the air. Glaring angrily, he turned and shuffled back to his counter. "I'm an old man," he complained. "Why do I have to take this?"

Forgetting about the newcomer, he went back to watching the three men disrobe the giggling dancing girl at one of the tables. She was a shapely little wench, twisting and twirling her voluptuous body, pushing her ample breasts into the faces of the laughing men.

She was naked now, and he tried to get a better look at the dark patch of thick hair between her legs. He sighed, scratching his groin. "Ah, to be young and handsome again!" Then he called out, "Hey, you're upsetting an old man over here. I still have some feelings."

The girl shook her long hair and laughed, sticking out her tongue. One of the three men, a big, bearded brutish-looking individual, slowly emptied a cup of wine into the deep cleft between her breasts and then he proceeded to lap it up with his tongue.

Giggling, the girl rubbed her naked body against him. The other two men laughed and clapped their hands.

"She sure is something," one of them called hoarsely, downing his wine. He noticed the stranger silently watching and staggered across the room, banging a fist on the table. "Hey, you!" he roared. "You haven't said a word since you walked in here. Tirka is dancing for your entertainment also, you know. Show your appreciation!" He steadied himself against the table. "Or don't you like women?"

The stranger threw back the hood, and the man stared at the flood of long black hair spilling out.

"A woman!" he exclaimed, stepping back, "By the three horny devils, a woman!" he peered at her face in the dark, trying to make out her features.

She looked young. He noticed her beautiful face, her full lips and high cheekbones. Long, black eyelashes framed her slightly slanted eyes. She kept them half-lidded, and he could not make out their color.

Her lips formed a mocking, flirty smile. "By the look on your face, one might think you've never seen a woman before," she said softly.

The innkeeper looked in her direction. She had a clear soft voice that carried far, and he detected a slight edge to it. "I want no trouble in here," he called out sharply. "Bork, go back to your entertainment."

The young man staggered back to his companions, who were still busy with the dancing girl. The big, bearded one, and the girl were rolling on the floor, giggling and laughing. He was trying to force himself between her legs, while one of his hands fumbled with his belt.

"Bring me some bread and another pitcher of ale," the strange girl called. He walked over and set the order down in front of her.

"This is a man's place," he said in a low voice. "Women usually don't come in here."

"I can see why," the dark-haired girl said dryly, nodding in the direction of the tangled bodies on the floor. "Are all men in this town like those three?"

The innkeeper looked at her sharply and took a step back involuntarily when he looked into her eyes. With his left hand, he drew a sign in the air.

For a moment, the light from the oil lamp had fallen full into her face and her open eyes.

They were bright blue with slit pupils.

Seeing the look on his face, she hooded her eyes. "I need a room for the night," she said. "Or until the rain stops."

"We are full," he blurted out.

"You're lying," she said. "I know that your rooms are empty."

"But they are not very comfortable," he protested, ringing his pudgy hands.

She laughed. "I've slept on rocks, old man. Have a room readied for me."

He stared at her as she leaned back. Her cape had fallen open, and he glimpsed her full breasts hidden beneath small metal breast cups. She had stretched out her long shapely legs, and he saw that her calves were covered up to her knees with high leather boots. He also noticed the jeweled hilt of a long sword hanging from a belt around her hips.

"All right," he grumbled. "As long as you can pay for the room."

She watched the innkeeper waddle back to his counter and chuckled softly. "Old fool," she murmured. She had sensed the resentment the moment he saw her eyes, his resentment and his fear. She shook her head, a scowl marring her face. Eating the dark bread slowly, she sat watching the three men and the dancing girl.

One of them was just pulling up his pants, while another one fell between her open thighs, his naked buttocks quivering in anticipation.

"Animals," she whispered. "Decadent filthy animals." Shrugging, she emptied her pitcher. It was none of her business how these people entertained themselves. She had seen worse.

After three men finished with the girl, they all staggered over to the counter, dragging the giggling girl between them.

She saw the innkeeper whispering to one of the men. They all looked in her direction. She didn't care what they were discussing; it was not her business.

The men and the girl disappeared through a doorway in the back, and she heard them stumbling up some wooden stairs.

Deciding it was time to retire, she got up and asked for directions to her room.

"Up the stairs, second door on your right," the innkeeper grumbled.

"Thank you." Carrying a large bag made from animal skins, she walked slowly up the creaking stairs and then down the dark corridor. Stopping in front of the second door, she sensed a wrongness and carefully pushed open the door.

The room lay in darkness, but her keen hearing picked up the barely audible breathing of someone behind the door and others across the room. The three from the bar below.

She kicked the solid wooden door wide open and registered with a satisfied smile the heavy thump and a loud curse as it hit the person behind it. Whoever it was didn't know she possessed night vision.

The other two men, hiding in the corner, were clearly visible to her. One held a knife.

She kicked it out of his hand with her right food and sent him sprawling. Her left elbow caught the other one under the chin, knocking him unconscious.

The big, bearded man, who had stood behind the door, approached her from behind, but before he could put his heavily muscled arms around her, she kicked backward, knocking the air from his chest. She turned, moved in closer and rammed the stiffened fingers of her right hand into his solar plexus. When he doubled over, gasping for air, she hit him hard behind the ears.

Without a word, his heavy body crashed to the floor.

She walked out of the door and closed it softly behind her.

Opening the door across the hall, she looked into the room and found it empty. She discovered a heavy wooden bar which she laid across the door, and with a satisfied sigh, she sank onto the hard mattress of the bed. After a while, she removed her clothing and slipped under the thin covers, stretching her slim body. For a long time, she lay, listening to the steady drumming of the rain against the windowpanes. It was good to lie in a bed again, even one as lumpy as this one.

The innkeeper gave her a sour look when she walked up to the counter the next morning.

"You must have made a mistake last night, because the room you told me to use was already occupied," she said sweetly. "So I used the one across the hall. I hope you don't mind."

He said nothing, just swooped up the coins she threw on the counter.

The rain had stopped, and the fiery ball of sun was already

drying up the wet ground. *Stormbringer*, the smallest of the three visible moons, was halfway across the sky on his endless journey.

Her steed, already restless, was pawing the ground around the tree where she had tethered him. She smoothed the smooth flanks and cupped his nostrils. "Getting impatient, my friend?" she whispered softly. "We'll be on our way soon."

After tying down the bag that held her belongings, she unfastened the rope and mounted. Neighing happily, her steed trotted down the trampled dirt road. The town seemed quiet, deserted. She didn't see anyone on the road nor in front of the small houses nestled among shrubs and tall trees. Most of the rough sawn boards and wooden shingles were in need of repair.

When she came to what looked like a marketplace, she discovered the reason why she had met no one. The town's people had assembled to watch a hanging.

They had erected a scaffold with a tall timber in its center. A rope with a noose hung from it. Beside it stood a naked young woman, her hands tied behind her back. She had long, red hair, which hung loosely down her shapely back.

Dismounting, the girl walked over to the watching crowd. "What crime has she committed?" she asked one of the watchers.

"They say she's killed a boy," the man said.

"Has it been proven?"

The man looked at her. "With her kind, you don't have to prove it. She's evil. We burned two of them last season."

Making a quick decision, she walked back to her steed, mounted and forced her way through the crowd toward the large open space around the scaffold. She didn't have much time; the hangman was just lifting the noose to put it around the red-haired girl's neck.

Digging her heels into the steed's soft flanks, she galloped toward the structure, leaned over and grabbed the girl's arm, yanking her off the platform. The rescued red-head clung to the long mane of the steed, desperately trying not to fall, while they forced their way through the surprised crowd.

The watching people parted to get out of the way of the big animal's pounding hoofs. Before anyone realized what had happened, they were galloping down the street, headed for the outskirts of the town.

Angry shouting rose up behind them, accompanied by the noise of running feet.

"I don't know who you are," the red-haired girl said, "but thank you."

"My name is Orola, and you're welcome."

"I am Pira. How about letting me ride behind you? Lying in front of you like a sack of flour is not very comfortable."

Orola laughed. "I believe we're being followed. So, I guess, you'll have to suffer a bit longer."

They had left the town and were racing down a dusty road. Not too far ahead lay a thick stand of trees, and Orola wanted to get them to safety before stopping.

When they reached the tall trees, she reined in and slid to the ground, helping Pira safely off the animal.

"How about untying my hands?" Pira held her arms toward Orola. "They're about to fall off."

Orola unraveled the knot with deft fingers and chuckled. "For someone with such slim hands, you should have been able to slide out of that knot easily."

Rubbing her wrists, Pira shook her long hair out of her face and looked at Orola. Her eyes went wide, and she studied Orola's face. "You're one of us," she said. "Except you have blue eyes."

It was Orola's turn to be surprised. The red-haired girl had yellow eyes with black slit pupils. Her smooth skin was extremely white, like the skin of someone who spent little time in the sun.

Pira looked at the red crystal nestled between Orola's breasts. She touched it and smiled. "A beautiful pendant."

Orola nodded. "Yes, it is beautiful." She knew that this girl did not belong to the *Sisterhood*; otherwise, she would have recognized the *Holy Communicator*. "Did you kill that boy like they said you did?"

Pira laughed. "I guess I got carried away. You know how it is, after not having had any for a while. I was thirsty. I just kept on feeding, and before I knew it, he was dry." She smiled as if Orola would understand her need and approve her actions.

For the first time, Orola noticed her sharp, pointed upper canine teeth.

"Dry?" she asked, already guessing what she meant.

"Yes, dry. I drank every last drop of blood he had in his veins." She smiled sadly. "And he was such a nice boy."

Now Orola understood. This girl was a vampire. She had run into vampires before, but never in human form. "Where do you want me to take you?" she asked, jumping on her mount's back.

Pira climbed behind her and pointed north. "Follow that trail. We live deep in the forest."

They rode for a long time along the narrow path. Sometimes, they had to dismount and go on foot because the branches that crowded the path hung low and thick.

It was already getting dark when they finally arrived at a small cottage built from logs.

"This is my home," the red-haired girl said, jumping to the ground. "Come inside. My family is probably waiting anxiously for my return."

Inside, an elderly woman, another young girl and a young man, both a little older than Pira, greeted them.

The elderly woman, who had had been standing by a stove, cried out and ran toward Pira, taking her into her arms. "I was so worried, girl. What happened?" Still holding Pira, she finally noticed Orola. "Who did you bring and why?"

Pira patted the older woman's hand soothingly. "Don't worry, Mother. I'm fine. Thanks to Orola here. I'll tell you everything, but first, let's have something to eat."

They sat down at a wooden table. The woman brought a loaf of coarse bread, the stew she had been cooking, and a pitcher of wine. The stew was good, but the wine tasted sour. It didn't matter; Orola was hungry and thirsty and consumed the offered food and drink thankfully.

The family listened silently as Pira told her story. Orola noticed the young man watching her from the corners of his eyes. The girl beside him sat listlessly and hardly touched her food. She stared with a dull expression at the tabletop. Only once did she look up. Orola saw that her eyes lacked the slit pupils.

She was not one of them, and she wondered about her presence in this family.

Orola sensed a certain hunger in the young man, and she recognized it for what it was.

"You are not one of us," the mother said, looking into Orola's eyes. "Even though you have the eyes of a night hunter."

"No," the dark-haired girl said. "I am not like you."

She felt the young man's hungry burning eyes on her and knew she must be careful.

After eating, she grew tired and asked where she could sleep.

"You can sleep in my room," Pira said. "I'll sleep with my mother." Grateful, Orola followed the girl into the room and had barely crawled under the covers before she fell asleep.

Orola awoke, unable to move. Reaching out with her mind, she encountered nothing but emptiness.

Her *Holy Communicator* was gone.

Patches of light fell through a small window onto her breasts, and she knew it was dawn. She had slept through the night, without waking once.

Again, she tried to sit up, but her body refused to obey. She was paralyzed from her neck down, only able to move her head.

"So you finally woke up," a mocking voice said beside her.

Turning her head, she saw the young man standing on her left side, her pendant in his hand. "A lovely piece of jewelry," he said. "As red as your blood, which I am going to taste now. But first…" He grinned and yanked the thin covers from her, exposing the rest of her naked body. His fingers followed a trail from her breasts across her belly, down to her black triangle.

Even though she couldn't move her body, she felt the touch of his hands. Her skin seemed to be more sensitive than before. His yellow eyes burned as he moved on top of her.

"What did you do to me?" she asked.

He laughed. "Don't worry about the paralysis. It is not permanent and won't last long. Just a harmless herb in the wine. You won't suffer any aftereffects."

His breathing became heavier and he hissed like an angry serpent. His pale lips drew back to expose his sharp fangs.

Then he sank them into her throat, carefully, almost gently, penetrating her skin.

He erupted with tremendous force, oddly enough climaxing on her chest, while drinking deeply from her veins. After he finished spurting his seed, his member shrank, and he slid off of her.

Grinning, he said, "I give some, and I take some."

Orola looked at him coldly. "Is this how your kind repays a kind gesture?"

A giggle from the door made her turn her head. She saw Pira standing in the doorway, her robe half-open, her red hair disheveled. "So what did you think of her, Nastor?"

He sighed. "She has sweet blood, but not as sweet as yours, my dear cousin."

Laughing, Pira threw off her coarse robe and joined them on the wide bed.

Nastor laughed and slid over Orola and on top of his cousin. Pira giggled and opened her legs wide. She gasped when he plunged his member into her and wrapped her legs around his lean body.

"I am glad you two are having such a great time," Orola said sarcastically, "because I am bored."

They acted like two wild animals. For a long time they pumped and bucked beside Orola, Pira shrieking in ecstasy and Nastor shouting until his throat was hoarse.

Finally, they climaxed and lay in each other's arms.

When Orola looked at them, Pira gave her a warm smile. "We haven't been charged up like this for a long time," she said softly.

"It is nice to see so much love between two cousins," Orola said, her voice dripping with sarcasm.

Nastor stretched, a satisfied smile on his lips. "Yes, we are a loving family."

"Actually, Nastor is my second cousin," Pira said.

"What difference does that make?"

"None, really, we are very close. Necessity sometimes brings out the best in us."

"Or the worst," Orola said. She craned her neck to see if she could find her pendant. She saw it lying on the floor where Nastor had discarded it. If she could only get it to touch her skin, she might have a chance to neutralize the poison in her body. Without the jewel, she was helpless.

A shadow appeared in the doorway, and the other young woman walked into the room. Without smiling, she stood beside the bed, looking down at the three. Her sad eyes looked into Orola's. "I'm sorry," she said. "I thought you were one of them because of your eyes, but I can see I was wrong."

Orola's gaze searched the young woman's face. "What's your name?"

"Marinda."

"Are you a prisoner here, Marinda?"

The girl seemed to hesitate, but she shook her head. "I can't really answer that. Maybe I am a prisoner. Maybe I'm not. I don't know."

"She likes too much what Nastor gives her." Pira laughed.

"Don't you, Marinda? You are a prisoner, but only because you want to be one."

Nastor chuckled and held out a hand. "Come, join us, Marinda. I know you want to."

Shrugging out of her robe, the girl climbed over Orola and slid between Nastor and Pira. Orola watched the trio as they went through all kinds of sexual perversions. Marinda might not have been a vampire, but she certainly liked what they did to her.

When it came to sexual prowess, Nastor was a giant. Orola didn't count the many times he climaxed.

When the older woman stuck her head into the bedroom, Orola almost expected her to climb into bed with them, but the woman just called out, "Sorry to break up your party, but you must all be hungry by now."

"We certainly are," Nastor panted, without missing a stroke.

"I don't think I can take any more," Pira moaned. "My lips must be rags of raw flesh by now. Nastor is like a wild animal this morning."

"Overdoing it as usual," the older woman chided, and walked back into the kitchen.

"Somebody carry me out of here," Nastor said with a weak voice, but he had a satisfied smile on his face.

Pira leaned over and kissed him. "We must do this again some time, my virile cousin." He grinned. "How about tomorrow? Now that she has seen us perform, perhaps our guest will join us then out of her own free will. I'm certain no mere mortal can do what I can." He winked at Orola, who gave him a cold stare.

"I admit you do have certain abilities. If you would not have poisoned me, I might have shown you some of mine."

Only after the older woman assured her that the wine was not drugged did she empty the offered cup and eat the food. Albeit flat on her back.

She was still paralyzed, and she started to worry. They left her alone that night, but she could hear soft moaning sounds and rhythmic creaking of bedsprings from the next room, the room the older woman slept in. From time to time, someone cried out.

Nastor had been correct. This was certainly a loving family. However, she despaired. She might never get out of here alive, even though they seemed to mean her no harm.

In the morning, someone fumbling between her legs awakened Orola. She opened her eyes to stare into Nastor's grinning face.

"Pleasant morning," he said

Before he could slide his organ into Orola, Pira rushed into the room, a terrified look on her face. "They are here!"

"Who is here?" Nastor asked.

"Four men. They must have followed our tracks."

Orola heard shouting outside and the crash of a wooden door being smashed open. Someone screamed, and two figures burst into the room.

"Looks like we found a whole nest of them," said a familiar voice. Orola recognized the big, bearded man from the inn.

Nastor hissed angrily and jumped from the bed, attacking the burly man with his bare hands.

Orola saw Nastor fall to the ground, blood gushing from his mouth.

The big man pulled his sword out of Nastor's chest and wiped it on the bedcovers. "Blood is not good for the metal. Makes it rust," he said, grinning at his companion.

Pira looked aghast at her dead cousin. Screaming, she threw herself at the bearded man, clawing at his face. He hit her across the mouth and sent her staggering back. "Next time I'll kill you, too, Bloodsucker," he rumbled.

The other two men came into the room. Looking at Orola,

one of them broke into a huge, gap-toothed grin. "Hey, isn't that the bitch from the inn?" Turning to his friend, he warned, "You better watch her. She's as fierce as a jungle beast."

Staring at Orola's open legs, his friend laughed. "I think she's inviting us in." He walked over to the bed and put his hand between her legs. When she didn't move, he chuckled. "She likes it."

Orola spit into his face. "Get your claws away from there. Can't you see I am unable to move?"

Wiping the spittle from his face, the man cussed her hard. Grabbing her long hair roughly, he tried to pull her up.

When Orola cried out, he dropped her and looked down at her contorted face. "You are an awfully good-looking wench," he said. "Maybe you're good for something after all." He turned to the others. "There are four of them. Why not have some fun before we leave?"

"I'll take the one on the bed," the big, bearded one said. "I owe her. You can take the redhead, since you like them wild, but let's get rid of him first." He threw the blood-covered lifeless body of Nastor out of the open window, and then he approached the bed. "So soon we meet again. This time it will be my pleasure."

"You'd better kill me," she whispered when he lay down on top of her, "because I will surely kill you."

"I don't think you are in a position to threaten me, bitch."

One of the others dragged Marinda into the room and threw her on the bed beside Orola. The bearded man looked at her and grunted. "I know this girl. She's the daughter of someone I know."

Marinda's eyes grew large. She seemed to recognize him also. "Please, help me," she begged.

"She's with them, isn't she?" the one who had dragged her into the room said.

The big man grunted again. "She means nothing to me. Do as you please."

Marinda whimpered softly.

On the floor, Pira fought and spit like a wild beast, but finally calmed down, almost as if she was going to enjoy what was about to happen. When the man sank down on top of her, she pulled him to her for a kiss then sank her teeth into his throat, drinking his blood.

He didn't seem to notice. He just lay on top of her, moaning softly, until the bearded man kicked him in the side. Swearing, he jumped off the red-haired girl.

"Vampire!" he cursed and hit her.

She laughed and moved quickly out of the way. "You liked it," she said, mocking him. "Everybody does."

The fourth man came out of the other room, pulling up his pants. He had a dreamy look on his face. "She couples like no woman I ever had," he said, looking back and rubbing his neck.

Behind him, the older woman came out, stark naked. She was a little overweight, but her body was in good shape, her legs and buttocks fleshy, yet smooth. Her large breasts were sagging, but more because of their size than from age.

The vampire woman smiled up at him, her sharp fangs gleaming in the light that fell through open window. "I'd stay with you if you wanted me."

"And kill me the first chance you got," said the big man, shaking his head. "The fact is you're not really a woman, you just look like one." He bent down to pick up something from the floor. Holding it, he said, "Look at this beautiful pendant."

Orola watched him hang the jewel around his thick neck. Maybe there was a chance she could get at it after all.

———

They arrived back in town shortly before dusk. Solar, the largest moon, had already begun its journey across the dark sky. Looking at the bright disk, Orola sent a short prayer to her god, hoping he would hear her even without the *Holy Communi-*

cator, but her mind stayed empty, untouched by her god's answer.

During the trip through the forest, she had felt some control coming back to her limbs, but she lay unmoving, lest she betray herself. She had to have full control before she could act.

They had not bothered to tie her up like the others, who sat in front of each of the men. She lay in Bork's arms, and he cursed endlessly because of her dead weight.

When they rode into town, it didn't take long for the news of their arrival to spread, and by the time they reached the marketplace, a large throng of people had assembled to watch the judging of the vampires. In anticipation, some were busy collecting logs and branches and heaping them into four piles with a tall wooden pole in the center of each.

A group of men grabbed the girls and shoved them toward the woodpiles. The older woman shook off the groping hands and walked proudly through the crowd.

Pira kicked and spit at the men and managed to bite one in the arm when he fondled her naked breasts. Marinda walked quietly between her captors, her head hanging down.

Two men carried Orola. She knew she had to escape soon, but still she hesitated. She had no weapons; her *Communicator* hung around the big man's neck and out of reach. She needed it. Without it, she was lost.

When they tied Orola to the stake, the older woman was already engulfed in flames. She died without a sound, much to the disappointment of the watching crowd.

"Let's have some entertainment here!" someone shouted.

"Yeah, those girls are much too pretty to waste their bodies like that!"

The men, who were trying to light the branches around Pira, pulled her down.

As men prepared to mount both women, one turned Marinda around and called out in surprise, "Marinda?"

She looked at him with big eyes and sobbed loudly, trying to hide her face in her hands. "Help me, Shelgard."

Shelgard pushed at the man behind him. "This is my sister, you fools," he shouted. He jumped up, a long knife in his hand. "Where is that spawn of a swamp-viper? I'll kill you, Hirso!" he screamed angrily. "My own sister! I nearly raped my own sister!"

When he spotted the big, bearded man, he lunged for him. Hirso laughed and blocked the knife-hand with his arm. "So she's your sister. You've coupled with whores before."

He stabbed at the young man with his own knife, but Shelgard jumped back, out of reach. "I'll kill you, Hirso," he whispered hoarsely. "I've never liked you. You're an evil man." His arm snapped back then forward, releasing the long knife. It tumbled through the air, and with a loud thud, the heavy hilt struck the bearded man's head. The big man gave a groan of surprise and toppled to the ground, where he lay unmoving.

Marinda grabbed her brother's arm. "Don't kill him, Shelgard," she begged. "If you do, his friends will surely kill you."

He shook off her hand and bent down to pick up his knife. Glaring at the big man, he kicked him in the side. Then he took off his shirt and put it around his sister. They walked away without looking back.

Orola, who had been watching, called out to the dark-haired girl.

"Marinda?"

The girl stopped and looked at Orola.

"Marinda, please, bring me the jewel Hirso is wearing around his neck."

Marinda hesitated. Her brother urged her on. "Come, let's get out of here."

"Please, Marinda," Orola cried. "I must have it. If I die without it I am without honor."

For some reason, nobody had paid any attention to her until that moment, but now a few men turned their heads to look at Orola.

A couple of men jumped on the woodpile and cut her bonds.

114

She kicked one of them in the head with her left foot. The other man jumped back in surprise. She dashed toward the bearded man, who was still out cold on the ground. Ripping open his shirt, she slipped the jewel over the unconscious man's head.

The power of the jewel hit her like a fist and sent her staggering. She put the chain around her neck, letting the *Holy Communicator* fall into the cleft between her breasts, where it hung, pulsing with a bright, red fire.

Power washed through her body. She closed her eyes for a moment and relished the ecstatic feeling as her strength returned.

Some of the men, who looked into her flaming eyes, stepped back involuntarily, exclaiming loudly.

She lifted her eyes toward Solar, searching for the eye of her god. "Thank you, Central Computer, God of the Ancients," she whispered. "Give me strength and endurance so I may defeat my enemies and speak of your Glory."

With one swipe of her arm, she brushed off the groping hands. On the ground, Hirso moved and sat up, groaning. Opening his eyes, his gaze fell on the scene in front of him. "What in the name of the three horny devils is happening?"

"She's a witch, a she-devil," one of the men said. "Look at her eyes, like the fires of Hell."

Hirso drew his sword. "She's a vampire. She can only move at night. During the day, she is paralyzed. I saw it with my own eyes. Just watch how she bleeds."

Orola spotted her steed. The animal must have followed them to town. She whistled and moved out of the big man's way. The point of his sword whistled past her and stabbed the man behind her in the arm.

Orola's foot shot out, kicking the bearded man in the side. Her steed had answered her call and pushed its way through the mob. Before Hirso could regain his balance, she jumped onto her mount's broad back and pulled hard on the reins. The animal reared up on its hind legs, pawing the air.

Pira, who had taken advantage of the confusion, fought her way through the crowd. "Orola," she cried, desperately reaching for the dark-haired girl.

Orola bent and pulled her up. Then she forced the beast through the crowd.

"Don't let her get away," Hirso yelled behind her, but she was already gone.

"You saved me again." Pira sighed and relaxed against Orola. "I don't know why you did."

Orola shook her long hair and shrugged. "Don't thank me yet. We are far from being safe."

Dawn was already breaking when they arrived back at the cottage. Nastor's body was gone. Heavy marks on the ground indicated something had been dragged into the heavy brush.

Pira shrugged. "Probably animals."

"You seem to take everything so lightly," Orola said. "Don't you care? I understood you loved your family so much."

Pira walked back to the cottage. Orola followed her slowly, shaking her head.

Inside, the red-haired girl threw herself on top of the bed. Stretching her naked, dirt-streaked body, she smiled up at Orola. "I love coupling, but last night was too much, even for me." She sighed and touched the swollen lips of her womanhood with the tips of her fingers. "I am quite sore."

Orola had found her sword and clothing and slipped into her leather kilt. Adjusting the small metal cups over her large breasts, she looked down at the vampire girl. "Is that all you think of… coupling?" she asked. "Are you so heartless that the death of your family means nothing to you?"

Lifting her white shoulders, Pira stared into Orola's questing eyes. "They are dead, and I live," she said after a while. She closed her eyes. "I am going to rest now. Maybe you should too."

Orola buckled the sword around her hips and went into the other room, where she lay down on the bed.

She closed her eyes and relaxed her body, her mind in touch with her god. She sensed the gentle pulsing of *Communicator* between her breasts and the reassuring presence of her sword.

The red jewel in its hilt glowed softly and felt warm under her touch.

She was ready. The town's people would come. They knew right where to find Pira and her.

It wasn't a very long wait. She sensed six of them. They tried to walk quietly, having left their mounts back on the trail, but her keen hearing picked up the sucking sounds of their boots in the soft, moist soil and the cracking of the twigs they stepped on.

When the first one crashed through the door, she pierced his heart with one deep thrust. He was dead before he fell. Stepping back to let the second man enter, she cut his throat before he even saw her. His knife clattered to the floor, and his hands tried to still the gushing of blood. Then he slowly sank to his knees and toppled on top of his companion.

Two dead...four to go.

Orola looked back at Pira, who came sleepy-eyed out of her bedroom. When she saw the two bloody corpses on the floor, she cried out, but Orola waved her to silence. "There are more," she said gently. The jewel between her breasts pulsed brightly, and a cold, fierce fire burned in her eyes.

Pira looked at her and shivered. "You are not like me," she whispered, "but neither are you human. I feel a presence around you, which makes my mind still and my body cold. Who and what are you?"

Orola shook her head to clear the long strands of black hair out of her face and cut her glance briefly to Pira before turning back to the door.

"I am Orola from the island Antanakka. A Moon Priestess. I pray to the God Solar."

The bulky figure of Hirso appeared in the doorway. Looking

117

at the dead men, he spat and cursed, "I told the fools to be careful!"

Baring his steel, a long broad-bladed weapon, he stepped into the room. "You won't have it that easy with me," he growled and swung the sword over his head.

Steel clanged against steel when Orola parried his thrusts. She lashed out with her left foot and kicked him in the chest, sending the heavy man reeling into Bork who stood watching just inside the doorway.

An ugly grin spread over the big man's bearded face. "Not bad," he said, respect growing in his eyes.

Another man appeared beside Bork. He was tall and thin, with an ugly scar on his right cheek. When he saw Orola with the bloody sword in her hand, he gasped and stepped back.

"She's a witch," he said. "A Warrior Priestess from the Island of the Witches. I've seen her kind before. She's as fierce as a wild banter and as strong."

"You are right. She is fierce and strong." Hirso laughed. "But she's only a woman."

Anger welled up inside Orola. She lifted her head and thrust out her breasts. "Any man who receives my favors freely experiences pleasures not many men ever experience, and as long as they live, they remember me. Men who displease me and take advantage of me do not live to remember anything at all."

Hirso laughed with a booming sound. "She has fire. I like that."

Without warning, he attacked again.

Orola had sensed the tensing of his body, and she easily knocked his sword away, but stumbled over a small footstool on the floor when she stepped aside.

Bork stabbed at her falling body. She twisted, brought up her right foot and kicked at his sword hand. He cried out and let go of the sword.

She rolled on the floor, away from Hirso's descending weapon. Before he had a chance to lift his sword again, she moved back in. Her slender sword flashed as she sank it into his throat. A gurgling sound escaped his open mouth. His eyes stared unbelieving at what they saw when she pulled out the bloody tip of her sword.

"She's killed Hirso," cursed a voice from the doorway.

She recognized the man. His stubbly face was drawn into an ugly mask of fear.

"She's a demon! I'm leaving," he cried out.

Orola pushed Bork aside and moved swiftly toward the doorway, following the man who was running away.

Lifting her sword, it began to transform. Stretching, it elongated and became a whip. A loud crack split the crisp morning air, and the tip of the lash wrapped itself around the running man's legs, tripping him. He thrashed around to free himself.

Orola withdrew the lash. The whip became a slender sword.

Wide-legged, she stood over the fallen man, a cruel smile playing around her lips, the sharp tip of the sword against his throat.

"Don't kill me," he begged.

"Why should I spare you?" she asked. "You had no mercy when I lay helpless. Now I return the favor."

"Please, please," he whined. "Let me live. I was out of my mind when I…"

Orola removed her sword, stepping back with a disgusted expression on her face. His right hand shot out, up between her legs, and his fingers dug into her pubis.

She let out a cry of surprise and pain. Angered and furious, she pierced his chest with a vicious thrust. He died without another sound; his fingernails scratched the insides of her thigh when he fell back, his feet still kicking.

A scream from inside the cabin made her rush back to find Bork holding Pira in front of him, his knife digging into her breast. "I'll kill her if you make one move against me," he threatened, his eyes bloodshot and full of fear.

A silent command changed the sword in Orola's hand into a

short dagger. In a flurry of motion, her hand whipped back and forward, releasing the dagger. It buried itself in the man's throat.

His mouth opened to scream, but he died without making a sound. Only bloody foam bubbled from his lips when he sank to the ground, his hands clutching at the protruding hilt.

Pira moved away from him, staring at the pumping blood. Then she looked at Orola, who calmly stepped closer and removed the bloody dagger. Changing it back into a sword, she cleaned it on the man's clothing and sheathed it.

"You are cold," Pira whispered, "and you accused me of having no heart."

"I don't enjoy killing," Orola said, "but I am not against it. These men deserved to die."

"One of them is still outside. There were six. You only killed five," Pira said.

Orola shook her head. "No, he is gone. It doesn't matter. He meant nothing to me."

A smile spread across the red-haired girl's pretty face. "So there is still pity within you," she said. "You're a strange creature."

"I am a woman, Pira, just like you. Come on, let's clean up this mess and us."

"In a moment," the vampire girl said. "Suddenly I feel a hunger inside me that must be stilled." She crouched down beside Bork and put her mouth over the bleeding wound in his neck.

Orola heard the barely audible sucking sounds and turned away.

They were of two different species, and Pira couldn't help being what she was. But Orola didn't have to watch.

She went outside and looked at the pale green disk of the moon Solar, the home of her god. She felt his calming presence inside her, felt the gentle, soft vibrations of *His* power emanating from the *Holy Communicator*, bathing her body with strength and confidence.

Lifting her arms, she bent her head and closed her eyes.

"Thank you," she whispered in the sacred ancient tongue. "I knew you would not forsake me. Great is your glory, oh Great Computer."

Orola finished the stew Pira had prepared and washed it down with a cup full of water.

"What will you do now?" she asked the other girl, getting up and reaching for her pack.

Pira ran her fingers through her freshly washed red hair and shrugged. "I don't know. Perhaps I'll leave this place and look for others of my kind. What about you?"

"I must also move on. I am on my way to Guata, a place far away from here."

Pira's yellow eyes glanced at the floor, then back to Orola. "You are lucky, you know," she said. "You travel alone, and yet, you are never truly alone. I have no god to protect me." She pointed at the sword hanging from Orola's hip. "That's a strange weapon you carry. A sword and yet more than that. I've seen it change. How do you do it?"

Orola touched the jeweled hilt of the sword, sensing its passive presence, its potential. "It's an ancient weapon, brought to us from the stars by my ancestors. Only I can change its shape through the power of the Great God Solar."

She fastened the cape around her shoulders. On impulse, she hugged the other girl briefly to her. "Good luck, Pira, and be careful."

Without looking back, she walked out of the door. Outside, her steed stood waiting. She jumped on its broad back and put her heels into the soft flanks. "Let's go." She clucked. "It is still a long journey."

THE SLEDPEOPLE

Topping the hill, a familiar sight greeted the lone rider's watchful eyes. She had come across similar scenes many times.

Bandits, waylaying lonely travelers, but appearances, she knew, could be deceiving.

She counted four of them. Dressed in gray homespun robes, their shaven skulls gleaming in the bright sun, she recognized them at once. Sledpeople.

They were young and wild, laughing and kicking at a man on the ground. One of them had a girl slung over his broad shoulders. She seemed unconscious. Her skimpy clothing was torn and revealed one of her small white breasts.

The watcher clucked, gave her steed a slight kick and raced down the hill toward the group underneath the clumps of broad-leafed Sirptrees.

They looked up and drew long knives when she reined in her mount beside them.

She left her own sword sheathed. There was no need for bloodshed...not yet.

"Who are you?" one of them challenged, leering at her

voluptuous figure. Turning toward the others, he grinned. "She'd be a nice addition to the stable."

She gave him a level stare. She was tall, young, wearing a short warrior's kilt that left her long, slender legs bare. Her high boots were made from soft leather, covered with intricate designs.

A short cape was draped around her shoulders. It had fallen open, but she made no move to pull it together again. The small metal cups that covered her large ample breasts did nothing more than enhance their size.

In the deep hollow between her breasts nestled a large, sparkling jewel. It glowed with a soft, red fire.

Pointing at the unmoving body on the ground, she said, "Four strong men against one unarmed boy! Would you call those favorable odds?"

"Favorable? Sure. For us." The one who carried the girl grinned. "He asked for it."

"Where are you taking her?" the rider asked. She looked at the ugly bruise on the side of the girl's head.

"Home. Where she belongs."

"Where is *home*?"

One of the others pointed east. "In the sleds. She is our sister. Lucky for her, we came in time to rescue her. This filthy little *Son of a Desert-slug* almost raped her. We should have killed him."

They turned away. "Well, we must be going."

The tall girl watched them walking away. The jewel between her breasts was pulsing softly. Something was wrong; she could sense it. They had been lying about something, of that she was certain. Not for the first time, she wished she could read thoughts and not just emotions.

Sliding off her mount, she walked over to the unconscious figure. He was quite young, as she had already seen, dressed in the garb of a corn grower. His wide-brimmed black hat lay beside his bleeding head. He had a nasty cut on his forehead, where he had been hit with a blunt instrument, probably the hilt of a knife.

She walked down to the small stream that flowed nearby and filled her empty canteen with water.

Gently washing the blood from the young man's face, she put the tips of her fingers on his temple. He reacted to the trickle of the healing power and opened his eyes.

When he struggled to get up, she said softly, "Easy, friend." He sat up and looked around. "Where are they?" he cried out.

"And where is Kicki?"

"The girl? They took her back to the sleds?"

"Back to the sleds?" he almost screamed, choking on the words.

"That is what they told me." Something was wrong. She sensed his hysteria and his terror.

He grabbed her shoulders and shook her. "You must get her back," he shouted, sobbing. "You must get my sister back from those monsters!"

She should have known. Silently, she cursed herself for being so stupid and removed his digging fingers.

The girl's hair had been light and her skin as well, just like his. The sledpeople were mostly darks-skinned, even though they sometimes captured other women to bring new blood into their tribes.

That's what had happened here. She had stumbled across a kidnapping and done nothing to stop it.

"Please," the boy begged. "Help me. She is so young and tender. She will die if we don't get her away from them."

She pulled him toward her and held him close, trying to comfort him. "I will do what I can," she promised. Somehow, she felt responsible for the girl's abduction and had to make up for it.

She knew a little about the sledpeople. They lived in giant sandsleds in which they crossed the burning desert. The sandsleds were as old as history. Villages on wheels, moving across the shifting sands, powered by the sun.

Nobody crossed the desert in the Hot Zone. Nobody but the sledpeople.

Ancient machines created cool comfort inside the sleds, providing the people who rode them with everything they needed to survive.

Merchants and travelers who wanted to cross the desert quickly booked passage with the sandsleds.

It took only twenty days to cross the Rhasi-desert from the borders of Rahoz to Horn, a city at the foot of the Darso-mountains, whereas it would take four times as long to travel north through Virgoss. Still desert, but more temperate. Or travelers could choose to join a caravan in Slir, which would take them south through Cish, around Lake Cocrom and then along the river up north to Horn. Again, four times as long, with much more hardship and more dangers.

With the sandsleds, they traveled in comfort and comparative safety, but it was expensive.

She jumped on her mount, a large-hoofed animal with short, sleek dark hair covering its muscular body. Helping the young man climb up behind her, she galloped after the four desert men, hoping to get to the sleds in time.

Studying the tracks made by three-toed splayed feet in the soft turf, the girl shrugged her shoulders.

"They must have had their riding beasts tethered here. By now, they're probably back in their sleds."

"What now?" The boy had calmed down. He looked up at her. She was about half a head taller than him. "Your eyes," he said. "They don't look right."

The girl laughed. "Where I come from, nobody would think so."

HERBERT GROSSHANS

He kept staring at her. "You must come from very far away then. I've never seen a human with eyes like a swamp-tiger." Touching the jeweled hilt of her sword, he asked, "Can you use that thing?"

She laughed again. "I've had occasion to use it."

"A beautiful girl like you should not play with dangerous weapons." He blushed, realizing he was staring at the creamy swell of her ample breasts.

She noticed his embarrassment and pulled his wide-brimmed hat over his eyes. "Put them back into your head," she said, chiding, but smiled. She was used to men staring at her, but he was just a boy, though, obviously, old enough to appreciate a beautiful girl.

He shuffled his feet. "I'm sorry. I never introduced myself. I'm Dirko."

"I am Orola." She pulled her cape together, her face suddenly serious. "I promised to help you with your sister. Since I'm a stranger here, you must help me. Take me to the sleds."

They mounted the steed and followed the tracks, easily visible until they reached the rocky road that lead into town. However, Dirko knew where the sandsleds stood. There really was no need for tracks.

This town was like any other town Orola had seen. The main street was lined with small shops and stores, the sidewalks filled with people.

The town of Slir was located near the desert. Here, the sledpeople came to trade and take on passengers. People from different places came to Slir to trade. Either with the sledpeople or the local merchants. Others came to book passage cross the desert.

And a few came with a purpose only they knew.

Dirko told Orola to stop in front of one of the shops. "My father's friend lives here," he explained. "Perhaps he can help."

As soon as they entered, a short, fat man came waddling toward them. "Dirko," he called out. "May the sun shine upon

126

you. What are you doing here?" He looked at Orola and winked, "And in the company of such a lovely young woman."

"This is Orola…a friend," the boy said, blushing. "We need your help, Uncle Darsell. Kicki has been taken by the sledpeople."

"Oh." The old man sat down heavily on a bench beside his counter. "That is not good. How did it happen?"

"We were on our way home when four of them jumped out of the trees. They knocked me unconscious, then they took Kicki. Lucky for me, Orola came along, or I might be dead now."

The fat man wrung his hands. "How can I help, Dirko? I am an old man and not very good with a weapon. The sledpeople, they are fierce and without mercy. I fear your sister is lost."

"No, no! Don't say that," cried the boy. "Give me a sword, and I will go after them."

Shaking his head, the old man looked at Orola. "I don't know who you are and where you come from, young lady, but if you know anything about the sledpeople, you will tell this young hothead that I am right."

"You may be right," agreed the girl, "but I am willing to try. I promised. Can't you go to the authorities?"

The old man threw up his hands. "The authorities! What authorities? There are a few soldiers in this town, and they break the law more than anyone else. No, I'm afraid we can't expect any help there. And the sledpeople? The moment anyone starts inquiring about a missing girl, they'd rather kill her than admit she was abducted by any of their young men."

"How do I get into one of the sleds?"

"You book passage, that's how, but you still won't be allowed to walk around once inside."

Orola spread her hands. "I can't afford to book passage. My purse is empty."

"The only way for a girl with no funds to travel is to join the stable for the duration of the trip." The old man sighed sadly. "With your good looks, you'd be too busy to do any searching."

"Somehow, I don't like the word *stable*."

"I assume you don't know much about the sledpeople."

"You assume correctly. I know a little but need to know more." She sat down beside him. "Explain."

"The sledpeople..." the old man began, "...have a very rigidly controlled society. There are never more than eighty adults in one of the sleds, in addition to the passengers. The number of children is also kept under control. Once the adults are too old, they retire to one of the stationary sleds by Lake Locrom.

"There are always more men than women, and sometimes they abduct young girls to keep their tribe from inbreeding. Their families consist of one woman to three men. That means the women have a hard time satisfying the sexual appetites of the men.

"To give them relief, they have created the stable. They employ women who entertain the tribesmen and the merchants who feel like having company. For a certain fee, of course."

"In other words...they hire whores."

"If you want to put it that way...yes." The fat man wiped the perspiration from his face. "This heat is killing me," he wheezed. "Sometimes I wish I had been born a woman. I might have looked for employment with the sledpeople. They say it's always cool inside the sleds."

Orola looked at Dirko, who had listened quietly, and winked at him. "I'll find a way."

"Then you'd better hurry," the old man said. "The sleds are scheduled to leave the day after tomorrow."

The sleds were huge. Three stories high and so long an ordinary man would not be able to throw a stone from one end to the other. They always traveled in pairs. It was a long and treacherous way across the desert and if anything happened to a sled, the people inside were surely doomed.

Orola stood in front of one of the sleds, impressed by its sheer size. It must take an awesome power to move such a bulk. The outside hull was pitted by centuries of exposure to sand particles bombarding it; only the top looked smooth. It reflected the sunlight like a huge mirror.

The sledpeople had not built these vehicles. Legends said that the ancient people, who had been like gods, brought them from the stars. The Ancients had known how to tap the very power of the sun, but the knowledge had been lost after the Great War.

They knew many things, the sledpeople, great secrets. They knew how to service the machines that powered the giant sleds, but they could not build new ones.

As soon as Orola entered the small entrance hall, she felt like she had stepped into another world. The air was cool and pleasant, even though it was laced with a strange, unidentifiable scent. The door closed behind her, shutting out the sunlight streaming it, but it did not change the lighting inside. She didn't see any torches. The light fell from tiny suns set into the ceiling.

Ignoring the guards beside the door, she walked toward a desk at the end of the hall.

"I hear you're hiring women," she said to the man behind the desk.

He looked her up and down. She noticed that he had a flat nose and cold, black eyes. He gave her a thin smile. "You heard right.

Have you also heard why we are hiring women?"

"I have."

"Good. Now…remove your clothing."

She put down the leather bag that held her belongings. Hesitating, she slowly undid her cape, let it slip to the floor. Then she unclasped her breast cups, freeing her breasts, then she slipped out of her short leather kilt. Her sword dropped to the floor with a soft clank.

From behind her, she heard the hiss of someone exhaling sharply when she removed the slip of cloth that covered her pubic area.

Proudly she stood, thrusting out her breasts and presenting her round buttocks to the watching guards by the door. She was quite without shame. She knew she had a sensuous, well-formed body with creamy, unblemished light skin.

"You'll do." He pointed to a stairway. "Up the stairs and first door to your right. Don't go anywhere else."

When she bent down to pick up her clothing, he stopped her sharply. "Leave it here. Your boots, too, and your weapon. Everything you need is in your room." He looked at the jewel between her breasts. "That, too."

Orola shook her head, putting her hand over the jewel. She felt the gentle pulsing of it between her fingers. "No," she said. "My religion forbids me to part with it. It must be with me at all times."

"All right," the man said grudgingly. "Keep it then." He waved her off. "You'll be told of your duties."

Walking naked up the stairs, she looked back and saw one of the guards pick up her possessions and put them into a locker behind the desk. The other guard stared after her. His face showed no expression, but she saw the lust in his black eyes. Her mind received his pulses of hot desire, and she knew she'd soon have her first visitor.

At the top of the stairs, she stepped into a long corridor. Another set of stairs led up to the next level. Each side of the corridor was dotted with doors. She knocked on the first one, as instructed.

"It's open," somebody called from the inside of the room.

Carefully, she opened the door and walked in. The room was surprisingly spacious, with partitions dividing it into six smaller cubicles. Each cubicle contained a bed. A curtain could be pulled to shut off the bed from view.

A table in the open part of the room, with some chairs, completed the furnishings, except for a small washbasin in one corner.

Three girls sat around a table, two more were lying on their beds.

"A new one," remarked one of the girls. She was small, with wild red hair.

"The way she looks, we might just get some relief from these sex-driven baldheads," said another one and giggled. She had a pretty face, but an obese body.

"You should complain," said a voice from the one of the beds. Orola looked at her and noticed that she was the only one without clothes. She had thick, golden hair framing a narrow, somewhat coarse face, but her breasts were huge and out of proportion to the rest of her body.

Orola closed the door. "I am Orola," she said, smiling. "I guess I'm your new roommate."

"Welcome to the stable," the redhead said. "The fat one over there is Renta, and this one is Dru," pointing at a tall girl with light hair.

"That skinny, black-skinned one on the bed is Filla. The one with the two monstrous moon globes is Lo, and I am Tamsey."

Orola studied her new companions. None of them was old. All except Lo were dressed in brown, coarse robes. She sat down on one of the empty chairs, removing the robe that was draped over it. "I guess I'll have to wear one of these?"

"When you step out of this room, you will, but in here nobody cares," Lo said, rubbing the nipples of her huge breasts. "I can't stand the feeling of that rough cloth on my soft skin. It makes me itchy all over."

"You're always itching, especially between your legs."

Lo made a face at Dru, who lifted her robe over her hips to

display a hairless pubis and long, slender legs. Her skin was almost white, reminding Orola of Pira, the vampire girl.

All of the girls laughed. Their demeanor conveyed the impression that they were getting along with each other.

Orola looked around the room. "Where do we...ah...entertain the men?" she asked.

Renta laughed, her fat body shaking. "If you're lucky, one of the guests will invite you to his cabin. Otherwise, this is where all the action takes place."

Orola looked thoughtfully at the narrow beds. "Right here?" she repeated, a crooked smile on her lips. It promised to be a very interesting trip.

So far, she didn't have an indication if Kicki was even on this sled. She might be in the other one. "Are there more girls in the stable?" she asked.

Tamsey nodded. "Six more...in the other sled."

"Any new girls join, aside from me?"

"No." Tamsey shook her head and brushed her wild red hair from her face. "Unless one of the others died. It happens, you know."

The other girls laughed again, but Orola saw no humor in that remark and refrained from joining their laughter.

Dru touched the jewel between Orola's breasts. "Pretty stone," she said. "Valuable?"

Orola shrugged. "To me it is. Brings me luck."

"It must have lost its charm when you joined up with the sledpeople." Renta giggled.

Dru pinched Renta's fat belly. "Don't joke about it." She put an arm around Orola's shoulder, casually cupping one of her breasts. "Maybe you should get some rest. Soon you will need all of your energy and more. I hope you're up to it."

"I hope so."

"You have strange eyes," Dru remarked casually.

"All of my people have eyes like mine."

Dru shrugged. "They don't bother me. I've seen stranger things."

Early the next morning, the sleds began to move. It was like being in the bowels of a huge ship. The sled moved steadily with gentle rocking motions across the sand.

One of the girls showed Orola the toilet facilities at the end of the long corridor. Beyond it was a huge room with large transparent windows. When Orola took a peek, she could see the scenery outside moving by. Fascinated, she stared at the swiftly moving sand dunes.

Despite their bulk, the sleds were traveling quite fast. She could hear the slight humming sounds of the machinery below.

When they finished washing up, the girls went into that large room for breakfast. Long tables and benches were set up on one side. The girls had their own table in one corner.

Guards and travelers occupied the other tables. Orola looked for Kicki, but she wasn't there.

If she was on board, she was either below or above, where the sledpeople lived.

After breakfast, they had their first visitor, the young guard Orola had seen when she first entered the sled.

"Take off your robe," he told her, as he licked his lips eagerly.

He took her on one of the beds without bothering to close the curtain. Orola was aware of the other girls watching, but it didn't bother her much. She didn't consider this rape, but a job, and she'd come into the sled of her own accord.

It was over fast. He collapsed between her open thighs and lay on top of her for a while.

"It was great, wasn't it?" he whispered hoarsely into her ear.

She moved under him, trying to dislodge his big body. "You were wonderful," she said. "How about getting off me?"

Reluctantly, he got up. Rearranging his gray robe, he looked at the other girls and grinned. "I had to try her out," he said. "Next time, I'll take one of you again."

"I can't wait for that," Tamsey said. After he left, she thumbed her nose and said softly, "Slug!"

Orola cleaned herself as well as she could with the water from the basin. "It wasn't so bad," she said bravely. "I've had worse."

"He's one of the nicer ones," Filla said, her white teeth contrasted sharply against the black skin of her pretty face. "Most of them are sex-driven beasts, demanding terrible things. Things they are forbidden to do with their own women."

Before long, two other men came in. They chose Dru and Tamsey. The door opened, and four more men entered. Two of them took Renta and Orola. So it went for most of the day. They came in one after the other. By evening, the girls were exhausted and hurting.

She hated them already. This was not really the way she had planned it. If every day were like this, she wouldn't get a chance to look for Kicki.

"How long have you been doing this?" she asked Tamsey.

"This is my third trip."

"How can you stand it?"

Tamsey rolled onto her stomach and propped her head on her elbow. "You get used to it. We have the nights off, unless a guest requires our services. The first day is usually the worst, after that it slows down." She smiled. "It is not so bad, I don't really mind it. It's always cool and nice in here. I eat regularly, which I never did before, and when my contract is finished, I will have enough funds to live well for the rest of my life."

"Contract?" Orola asked.

"Yes, contract. Didn't you know?" Tamsey looked at her sharply.

"When you came aboard, you agreed to stay for ten trips."

"Ten trips?" Orola sat up. "They never told me.

"Poor girl," Renta said. "Like I said yesterday…your good luck piece has lost its charm."

"What if I decide I don't want to stay?"

"Won't help, and if you try to leave, they'll kill you. The first time. There is no second chance."

They went down the hall to the washroom to get cleaned up. The girls stood inside a tiled cubicle that had holes in the ceiling. A spray of water rained down on them and cleansed their bodies.

Orola had never seen anything like it. So many marvels in these sleds!

The toilets were not just holes in the ground, but bowls made from some smooth material. A flush of water took away the waste. No mess, no smell.

Even with all of these wonderful things, Orola couldn't imagine spending her time in this prison. She was already longing for the fresh air and the wide-open spaces she loved so much.

A fierce sandstorm hit the caravan on the fourth day.

The girls had just stopped to have dinner when the sleds came to a halt. Orola looked out of the great window in the front and could barely make out the contours of the second sled. Great masses of sand swirled around the sleds, at times obscuring the other vehicle from sight. Even through the sound-proof walls, the roaring of the storm could be heard.

She counted herself lucky to be inside. No living being could survive the force of this storm.

Studying the other passengers, Orola noticed a tall, handsome man at one of the tables throwing glances in her direction. She looked into his eyes, smiled, and gave him a quick wink.

She needed a change; the days were beginning to drag.

He smiled back, and then he looked away.

She looked for him again at suppertime and found him sitting at the same table. This time, he winked back at her.

After supper, one of the guards came into the stable and told her to get dressed and follow him. He took her to a cabin down the corridor and knocked on the door. When the door opened, he walked away.

In the doorway stood the man she had seen in the dining room. He smiled warmly. "Come in," he said with a pleasant voice, and motioned her through the door.

She entered and was surprised at the luxurious furnishing. The walls were covered with expensive furs; on the floor lay a deep-piled soft rug. The chairs were padded, and the bed was large. Large enough for two.

A small window in one wall allowed a glimpse outside. Of course, there wasn't much to see now, since it was already dark, and the raging storm did not allow for seeing anything but blowing sand.

"Sit down." As she took a seat, he walked over to the bed and sat down.

She sensed his discomfort. "My name is Orola," she volunteered, looking at him from under lowered lids.

He had a strong face with a square chin and deep blue eyes. A thin mustache adorned his upper lip, and he kept his brown hair short.

"I am Torr," he said, smiling apologetically. "I feel somewhat uneasy. This is the first time I require the services of a…"

"A whore?" she finished for him.

He lifted his hand. "Don't say it like that. I'd rather say *professional*."

"Same thing." Orola shrugged off her robe. "Let's not pretend. I know what you want. So here I am."

"I don't want to offend you," he said, getting up and walking to a locker. He took out something and unfolded it. It was a lovely shiny robe.

"Here, put this on. I think it will fit you."

Orola stood up, wondering why he tried so hard not to look at her naked breasts. She took the garment and held it in front of her. "I don't understand," she said. "Most men just want to get me out of my clothes and climb between my legs."

"I am not an animal," he said proudly. "It's a lonesome journey, and I need some company."

She slipped into the robe, enjoying the feeling of the silky material on her skin. "It's beautiful," she said, twirling to see the material float out around her and laughing happily.

"It was made from the silk strands of a leaf-runner and meant to be worn by a beautiful girl. Someone like you. You are beautiful." He studied her. "How can you...I mean, have you been at this for long?"

Looking at him, Orola was undecided for a moment. How far could she trust this man? He seemed honest and sincere. She did not receive any threatening emanations from him, and she could usually rely on her feelings and first impressions.

She watched his face closely when she answered. "This is not what I usually do for a living. I am here for a purpose. I am looking for a young girl who was brought to one of these two sleds, against her will. So far, I haven't had any luck locating her."

He nodded thoughtfully. "You're taking a chance telling me this, and I appreciate it. If the sledpeople knew why you were here, they'd kill you. These people are cruel and without mercy."

Taking a jug from a cabinet, he filled two cups and handed one to Orola. "Here, drink some wine. It is very good."

She accepted it gratefully. "Thank you, Torr. Tell me, what business are you in?"

"I deal in fine clothing, tapestries, jewels."

"You must be quite wealthy since you can afford to travel in such luxury."

He smiled. "I can't complain. Actually, I haven't been doing this for a long time...alone, I mean. I inherited this business from my father, who passed away last season. He was a very shrewd but honest merchant. I hope I can live up to his reputation."

They talked for a long time. Torr told her little anecdotes from his travels. He had a way with words. She liked his warm humor and tried to listen attentively, but after a while, she began to tire and started to yawn.

He noticed and tilted his head to one side, as if undecided whether to be offended or not. "I seem to bore you with my stories."

Orola touched his hand. "No, I love to hear you talk, but it has been a long day. If you want to have sex with me, we shouldn't wait too much longer."

She lifted the garment over her head and slipped into his bed, leaving the cover open so he could look at her nude body. "Come on," she said, her arms open.

He took off his clothing and joined her on the bed. Kissing her gently on the forehead, he lay back and pulled the covers over them.

"I want you, but I wouldn't feel right. Let's just sleep together tonight, and maybe tomorrow you can spend the whole day with me. I will make arrangements first thing in the morning."

She kissed him, pressing her body against his, her naked breasts touching his chest. She could feel him responding, but he just held her close, and they fell asleep in each other's arms.

When she awoke in the morning, he was already up. He stood in front of the window, staring at the swirling sand. Hearing her stir, he turned. "This is the worst storm yet," he said. "They're turning down the lights to conserve energy. It will probably get warmer in the sled, because they can't run the air-conditioning machines continuously."

She yawned, stretching her lithe body. He looked at her exposed breasts and sighed. "This trip is going to take longer than expected. By the way, I already talked to the Sledmaster, and it's arranged. You can stay with me for today."

"That is nice," she said, giving him a sly look. "Since there is nothing to do, why not come back to bed? I am well rested."

He chuckled and removed his robe. "I am glad you asked."

He had soft, gentle hands. Exploring every part of her body with his hands and his tongue, both were highly excited in a short time and when he entered her welcoming sheath, she did not hold back, unlike when she entertained the men of the sledpeople.

She had many talents and making love to a man was only one of them. She knew how to excite a man, knew secret pressure points and positions to keep him from reaching his climax too soon.

The jewel glowed red, pulsing softly and steadily between her breasts as Torr moved rhythmically between her clutching open thighs. He took a long time before he finally shuddered in her embrace, and she felt him erupt inside her. She pushed upward to meet his thrust. Pulling up her knees and digging her heels into his quivering buttocks, she gave in to her own desire, dousing his throbbing penis with her own hot discharge.

Outside, the sandstorm still howled, its fury not yet abated, rocking the huge sled and obscuring the sky. Orola and Torr spent most of the day in bed, leaving the room only to get something to eat.

She stayed the night, but early next morning she went back to the stable.

The storm calmed down during the day, and the sled began moving again. In their stable, the girls were busy as usual. Not much had changed.

At night, Orola went to Torr's suite. He was surprised, because he hadn't sent for her, but he seemed happy to see her. When she left in the morning, hurrying down the corridor, she almost collided with one of the sledpeople. He gave her a strange look and walked on. She didn't know if he had seen her leaving Torr's suite or not.

When she walked into the stable, she had already one customer waiting. Shortly after she finished with him, a big, husky man came in and told her to follow him.

She had never seen him before.

"Trouble," whispered Tamsey. "Watch yourself."

She followed the man up the stairs to the next level. She had never been up there before; only the sledpeople were allowed on this level.

They walked down the corridor and through the dining hall, which also served as living area for the sledpeople. A few of them sat on couches, looking out the window. For the first time, she saw the women.

Most of them were dark-skinned. Their black hair was clipped short, flat against their skulls. Only two of the ten she saw had a light complexion.

The faces of the eight dark-skinned women were broad, with flat noses, their eyes slightly slanted, like hers.

Orola and her guard hardly received any glances when then walked past the tables and couches. They headed for a door at the end of the huge hall. The guard knocked and they entered the other room.

He pushed her into the center of the room.

It was nearly as large as the dining hall and lavishly furnished.

She guessed that these were the living quarters of the Sled-masters.

There were four. Three men and one woman, all of them old. They were garbed in red robes.

"So this is the female you saw coming out of the merchant's room?" one of the men said.

"Yes, it is," said someone behind her.

Orola turned to see the young man she had almost bumped into in the corridor.

The old Sledmaster stared at her with cold eyes. "You went to a passenger's suite without permission." His voice sounded flat and emotionless. "You will be punished. Take off your robe!"

She complied, already knowing what to expect. She had seen the whip in the guard's hand.

The whip cracked ten times, each time leaving an angry welt on her naked back and buttocks. The sledman was an expert with the whip, obviously enjoying what he did.

With expressionless faces, the Sledmasters watched the flogging.

When it was done, Orola bowed her head to hide the anger flashing in her eyes. She didn't cry out. She was too proud to show any weakness, but she swore to take vengeance.

"Remember this lesson. Next time, you may not walk out of here. Go now so we can attend to more important matters!"

She put her robe on her burning back and walked ahead of the guard who had one of his hands clamped around her left arm.

When they walked down the stairs, he whispered into her ear, "I am not allowed to come to the stable because I am too big." He chuckled. "You know where."

"I can guess," Orola said coldly. "But don't try to impress me."

He chuckled evilly. "Seeing you naked has given me an idea."

They walked down the second flight of stairs to the first level. The corridor was empty. He urged her to walk to the end of the corridor and then through a small door into a storage room.

Grinning, he ripped off her robe and shrugged out of his own. He was powerfully built, with huge, bulging muscles, but the biggest attraction hung between his legs.

The largest male organ she had ever seen, and it was coming to life, swelling even larger.

She had no intentions of having that thing shoved into her.

Concentrating on the jewel between her breasts, she fell into a fighting stance. He laughed and reached for her.

Pushing aside his arms with her left, she hit him in the stomach with the stiffened fingers of her right hand. Taken by surprise, he doubled over. She brought up her knee, mashing it into his face. He cried out, tumbling back. She followed, grabbed his arm and threw him into a pile of stacked up boxes, which fell on top of him.

He tried to get up, but she pushed him down with one foot and stood over him, her legs spread, giving him a good view of the thing he had desired so much.

"Let this be a lesson to you, friend," she said, smiling sweetly. "Next time *you* may not walk away…alive."

He just groaned, staring at her with unbelieving eyes. His nose bled, and his lips were split.

She picked up her robe, feeling better already. When she walked down the corridor, she was smiling. He wouldn't talk, she was certain of that. How could he explain what had happened to him?

A powerful man of his stature beaten up by a mere girl? It wouldn't do much for his reputation.

However, she knew she had to watch herself from now on. She had made an enemy. Given the chance, he would kill her.

The other girls were all busy with men when she entered the room. She noticed Drum was not there, and she felt a stab of envy.

She was probably entertaining a male passenger in his suite.

Renta was the first one finished. She joined Orola at the table.

"Tomorrow we'll get some rest. We should reach the Oasis before nightfall. We usually stay there one day to breathe fresh air, even if it's hot. After that, we get transferred to the other sled."

"Oh?" Orola was suddenly interested. "You mean we *stay* in the other sled?"

"Yes, we switch places with the girls in that stable." She giggled. "We'll get some new pieces of meat to play with."

"Yes, it will be a change," Orola agreed. She knew the girl Kicki was not on this sled because none of the men who had come to the stable had looked familiar.

Not really looking forward to the first day in the other sled, she was nevertheless pleased with the turn of events.

She kept her robe on for the rest of the day. Only two men visited her, and they didn't care if she was naked or dressed. At night, she healed her wounds.

The Oasis was a welcome relief. The girls were allowed to leave the sled and go swimming in the small, deep lake. Orola enjoyed the cool water as well as the trees and shrubs framing the lake. All of the passengers from both sleds and some of the sledpeople were in the water, but she didn't see Kicki.

A hot wind from the south blew across the lake. Orola looked at the mounds of sand surrounding the small oasis and stared into the cloudless sky. The sun was burning down on them. It would nearly be impossible to spend much time outside of the water.

Even if she found Kicki now, she'd have to stay with the sled until they arrived in Horn. Nobody on foot could survive a long trek through this wasteland. Without water and protection from the fiery sun, a traveler would be dead before a day was over.

Orola swam away from shore, gliding easily through the water. It was good to get some exercise and fresh air, even if it was hot air. Looking back, she noticed somebody else breaking away from the crowd, heading toward her.

She recognized Torr.

He smiled when he came closer. "I've missed you," he said. "Where have you been?"

"I had some problems. Somebody saw me coming out of your door after my unscheduled visit."

His expression became grim. "Did they hurt you?"

She smiled when she saw his face. "Thank you for your concern, but there is nothing you can do. I...ah...got even."

He swam close to her and touched her breast. "Will you come to see me tonight?"

She shook her head. "I'm sorry, Torr. Tonight, we are being transferred to the other sled."

"Too bad. I was beginning to...to like you. Is there a chance we could get together in Horn?"

"Maybe. I can't promise. Let's swim back. I think we're being watched."

They swam slowly back to the noisy crowd. Before they parted again, Orola took Torr's hand and held it briefly. "You're a fine man, Torr. I like you, too, but I can't get involved. There is much you don't know about me, and it is best you don't find out. Take care, friend."

She turned quickly and swam away. On the shore, beneath the trees, she saw a large figure in a gray robe watching her. She pretended not to notice and joined the other girls.

"Don't fraternize too much with the other passengers," Tamsey warned her. "You'll only invite trouble."

Orola laughed and splashed her with a spray of water. "Don't worry, I can take care of myself."

"You wouldn't last long if they decide to evict you from the safety of the sled," Tamsey said. "And nobody would know." In the evening, they boarded the second sled.

The room was almost identical. As expected, the next day brought the same frantic action they had experienced the first day on the other sled. Except for the faces, the men were the same...beasts.

There was one change. Orola recognized four of the faces, and she knew she was on the right track. They, however, did not recognize her.

When one of them came back the next day, she gave him a special treat, made him last longer than he probably ever had with any girl. He was the one who had carried off Kicki.

Having spent himself in a tremendous climax, he lay panting in her arms.

"How is your sister?" she asked him.

He lifted his bald head. "My sister? I don..." Suddenly, he seemed to remember her. Pushing up, he said, "I know you. You're the one who surprised us by the river."

She pulled him back down, smiling. "Small world." Nibbling his ear, she whispered. "I like you, and I liked the way you took care of your sister. You're such a man!"

He puffed up his chest proudly, then kissed her roughly. "I noticed that I drove you wild. I will come back tomorrow."

From behind them, somebody called, "Are you finally finished, Voir. Sure took you long enough. Something wrong?"

The youth turned, grinning. "She's an old friend, Tan. Don't wear her out." He strode out, swaggering.

The next day, he came back, eager to mount her. "Not so fast," she whispered, stroking his erect penis. "You will enjoy it much more when you take it slow." She fondled him again as she gazed into his eyes. "And so will I."

He moaned, ready to explode. "You have strange eyes," he said hoarsely. "I've never seen a human with such eyes."

She captured his member between her thighs. "Maybe I'm not human."

He pried her legs open and entered her. "You're probably a swamp-demon come to torture me," he groaned.

"You're such a love-machine," she moaned, feigning ecstasy. "I've never met a man who could fuck like you."

She milked him with her inner muscles and decided she might as well enjoy it. He was not a bad looking youth, and it didn't make much sense to waste her efforts. He was probably the last today, anyway.

"You are so different," she said. "Most of the others are just animals, but you...you make me enjoy it." Her finger traveled down his belly. "I'd like to visit you in your cabin so we can spend some time together away from watching eyes. I would be more relaxed just being with you. Do you live alone, or does your sister live with you?"

"My sister? Oh, you mean...?" He sat up and stared at her, but she just smiled innocently.

"It's not possible," he answered, falling back. "I'm not alone. I live with four younger brothers and my...sister."

"What cabin are you in?"

"The last one on the left, top level." He got up and stretched. "I have to go. I'm not allowed to wander around during the sleep period."

Orola gave him an adoring grin, satisfied with her progress.

The rest of the journey went by uneventfully. Voir came every day; he was hooked on Orola. She was like a drug to him, and he couldn't stay away. Even the other girls noticed it, and they made their usual jokes.

Orola didn't let it bother her. She had a reason to carry on the way she did.

They arrived in Horn late in the evening. Nobody was allowed to leave until morning.

Orola decided it was time to act. When everybody was asleep, she stole quietly out of the cabin and walked up the stairs to the next level. The corridor was empty, with no guards in sight.

She reached the last door and stood outside, listening. Everything seemed quiet. Carefully, she tried the lock and discovered it open. Pushing against the door, she slipped inside. It was dark, but her night vision let her see the sleeping shapes clearly.

There were six bunks, three at the bottom, three at the top. In the corner bunk, at the bottom, she spied the light hair of the girl she was searching for. Kneeling beside the sleeping girl, she put her hand over the girl's mouth, gently shaking her. The girl's eyes fluttered open. She clutched at Orola's arm and tried to push her away. She would have screamed had Orola not covered her mouth.

"Shh..." Orola whispered. "I'm a friend. Your brother Dirko sent me. I'm here to get you out." She removed her hand.

"Who are you?" the girl whispered, her eyes frightened. She couldn't see anything because of the darkness.

"Later. Come now, let's get out of here."

The girl slipped out of her bed. She stopped when she heard one of the sleepers stir and mumble something. Orola took her hand and headed for the door.

The girl followed without making a sound.

Outside in the corridor, she stood, looking helplessly at Orola.

"What now? Where do we go?"

"I'll hide you in my cabin. We leave as soon as the sun rises."

The girl clung to Orola. "If they find me in your cabin, I will be beaten, and you may be killed. These people are so cruel."

Orola gave her an encouraging smile "Don't worry, Kicki. I'll get us out of here. Are you all right? Did they hurt you in any way?"

Kicki sobbed, but managed to smile bravely. "No." She shook her head. "They didn't touch me...yet. I was supposed to be joined into the family once we arrived in Horn."

Orola stroked the young girl's hair. She was very pretty, just past puberty. Her small breasts were clearly visible under her thin nightgown. Orola couldn't help but notice her beautiful green eyes.

"Wait a moment, Kicki. You can't walk around like this." She went back into the cabin, looked around and found a gray robe. Closing the door softly behind her, she took Kicki's arm. "Come, before someone sees us."

The other girls were not happy to find a strange girl in their room.

"We're in trouble," Dru said, "unless you get her out of here fast."

"We will be out soon enough," Orola informed them. "This is where my contract will be terminated."

"You're crazy," Lo said. "You'll never leave the sled alive."

"We…"

The door flew open, and two burly sledmen pushed their way into the room. Behind the two men stood Voir.

"There she is," he said, pointing at Kicki.

One of the sledmen advanced toward the girl. Orola stepped in front of her. He lifted an arm to push her aside.

She grabbed his arm, twisted him around and threw him into the other sledman.

A couple of the girls cried out.

"You can't fight them," Renta called. "They will surely kill you."

Orola didn't answer. She had followed the sledmen who had fallen backward into the corridor. As the first one got up, he pulled a long knife from his belt. She kicked him in the face with her right foot. He went down, sprawling on top of Voir, who had stepped into his way. Before the second man stood up, she hit him behind the ear with a short chop.

She whirled when she heard the girl's screams, but it was too late.

Kicki had run down the corridor, right into the arms of another sledman. He held a knife to her throat, calling to Orola, "Stop right there, or your friend will die."

Orola knew he meant it and stood still. From behind her, two gray-robed men grabbed her arms and tied them behind her back. They led her quietly down the stairs to the level below and pushed her into a small room.

Then they pushed Kicki in and locked the door behind them.

It was dark inside, and even with her night vision, she couldn't see much.

Kicki cowered on the ground where she had fallen, afraid to move. "It's so dark here," she sobbed. "I'm afraid of the dark."

"Don't be scared," Orola said soothingly. She tried her bonds and found they were not very strong. One good yank and she was free.

"What are they going to do with us?"

"I don't know, girl. Probably kill us."

Kicki's head jerked up. "Kill us?"

Sorry she had said that, Orola sat down beside the young girl and put an arm around her thin shoulders. "If I can help it, they won't hurt you."

"I saw you fight, but not even you can defeat a whole sled full of these people. There are just too many." Her hand groped for Orola's.

"What is your name?"

"I am Orola."

Kicki smiled in the darkness. "That's a nice name. You said my brother sent you?"

"I was there when you were abducted, but I didn't know who you were. I might have been able to prevent it. I promised your brother I would bring you back."

"Thank you for trying. I am only sorry I dragged you into this mess."

"It was my choice, Kicki."

They sat without talking for a long time. It was silent in their small prison, except for the hiss of the air blowing from the air ducts.

"The passengers must be leaving the sleds now," Orola said after a while. "I don't believe anything is going to happen for quite some time. So let us get some sleep."

She lay back, her eyes closed, concentrating on the jewel resting on her chest.

Slowly, she went into a deep trance, meditating and praying to the moon Solar, her god.

Orola woke when she heard somebody turning the lock. She sat up as the door opened.

She counted six sledmen standing in the corridor. They waited with drawn knifes.

"Just walk quietly," said one of them and grabbed her arm. "One hostile move and both of you are dead."

It was dark outside. Only two of the three visible moons stood in the night sky. The largest, Solar, hung high above them, flooding the land with its pale green light.

Six sandsleds were drawn up in a huge circle. The occupants of the sleds sat or stood inside the space created by the sleds, leaving a large area empty. Many held torches in their hands.

They led Orola and Kicki into the empty area. A tall figure, dressed in a red cloak, stepped out of the silently watching crowd. One of the Masters.

"We know what you are," he addressed Orola, fixing the gaze of his dark, cold eyes on her.

"You do?" Orola lifted her head and stared back at him. "What am I?"

"You are a Moon Priestess from the island Antanakka," the Sled Master said. "We know what you can do, but we are not impressed. When you entered our service, you entered into a contract with us. You violated that contract, and now you will be punished, according to our laws." He turned to one of the men behind him. "Bring the *Hound*!"

The man he spoke to disappeared into the crowd and came back moments later leading a huge black creature. It walked on short powerful hind legs, its long arms trailing on the ground. It growled softly when it reached the Sled Master.

"Easy, my beauty," the old Master said, caressing the creature's head. "You will be happy tonight."

The thick lips of the creature parted to reveal a row of large teeth. "Happy," it said with a deep, rumbling voice.

The master chuckled, his gaze on Orola. "You have been heard calling our men *beasts*. Since you do not mind coupling with beasts, you shall truly do so tonight. Take off your clothes and get on your knees!" he commanded.

"Stop!" Orola commanded, her voice sharp and clear.

The sledmen who held Kicki stepped back involuntarily when they looked into her eyes.

"I am Orola, Moon Priestess of the God Solar," she said. "I command you to release the girl."

Avoiding her burning eyes, the old Sled Master lifted a hand, holding a smooth, metallic object. "The first time I saw your slit pupils, I knew who you were. I know of your powers, but they cannot stand against the powers I command. You will watch the humiliation of your friend and then you will submit to the beast Gorgas." He chuckled. "He has an enormous appetite. I will let you experience his release and then you will die!"

Orola recognized the thing he held. It was a weapon as ancient as the sleds.

It could hurtle deadly lightning bolts at the wielder's command.

Her muscles tensed, and then she moved with lightning speed. Striking the Sled Master's arm a terrible blow, she heard the crack of breaking bones. The weapon fell from the useless hand, and she caught it before it dropped to the ground.

Not realizing what happened, the Sled Master's beast Gorgas moved toward Kicki.

Orola's foot caught him under the chin, flinging him away from the young girl. He lay unmoving on the ground, his head twisted in an impossible angle.

Sensing movement beside her, her hand shot out, plucking the thrown knife out of the air, scarcely a handbreadth from her breast. Then, with a savage thrust, she sent the long knife into Gorgas's throat.

She heard a growl behind her and turned to see the massive body of the *Hound* leaping at her, jaws wide open and clawed hands ready to tear her apart. The beastly half-man fell on top of her, teeth reaching for her white throat.

Dropping the strange weapon, she grabbed the shaggy head and twisted with all her strength. It cracked horribly when the Hound's thick neck broke. Lifting the kicking body high into the air, she threw it into the silently watching sledmen.

They moved back in horror, staring at her with fear in their dark eyes.

She could feel the heat of the throbbing crystal between her breasts and knew that her eyes must be like flaming stars. Bending down, she picked up the weapon again, fingering its metallic grip.

"I should teach you a lesson. You people are less than the beast I just slew. It paid for what it did to me, but it was only a stupid beastman, barely intelligent enough to speak a few words. You claim to be civilized, you and your sophisticated sleds." She spit into the sand. "You are nothing but arrogant savages!"

Spotting Voir in the watching crowd, she pointed at him. "You, bring my possessions and a riding beast so I can get away from here as fast as possible!"

While she waited, she watched the crowd, but nobody made a move against her. Only faint whisperings reached her ears.

"She's a witch. A demon come to punish us."

Finally, she reached for Kicki's hand. "Come on, girl, let's get out of here."

Stuffing a piece of succulent meat between her gleaming teeth, Kicki giggled merrily. Orola grinned and downed her cup of wine.

"It's good to be free again," she said, wiping her mouth with the back of her hand. She looked at the man across from her. "Thank you for what you did, Torr. I don't know how I can repay you."

Torr took her hand and held it. "No need to thank me, Orola. I enjoyed it. How could any man let two beautiful girls walk around hungry and tired?" His face grew serious. "Are you certain you want to go on alone? You could accompany me to Flass, and then we could travel back to Slir together. The Sled-people would not dare to touch you if you were in my protection."

Orola shook her head, giving him a warm smile. "No, Torr. I must travel north to Guata. I only wish Kicki would change her mind and go with you, but she seems to be set on staying with me."

Kicki brushed her golden hair out of her face and bit heartily into a round, juicy fruit. She was bubbling over with happiness, still not believing that she was finally free. "I want to stay with you, Orola. I'll never set foot into one of those sleds again."

"It will be a long and dangerous journey, Kicki, but you are welcome to accompany me."

CHILDREN OF THE GROUND

"Get up, slut. It's your turn on the block."

The girl opened her eyes and winced, shrinking back from the heavy boot that had kicked her in the side. Her head was humming and ready to explode into a million fragments.

A loud crack split the air, and she cried out in pain as the tip of the lash was laid across her naked back, leaving behind an angry welt.

"Move, I said!"

She glared at the fat man, her eyes narrow slits, hiding the anger behind them.

Shakily, she rose to her feet and stood swaying. She was tall and slim, her light-skinned body almost voluptuous. Long black hair spilled over her shoulders.

The fat man stared at her large breasts, and then his gaze wondered to the fuzzy black triangle between her legs. Grinning, he reached out, his pudgy fingers kneading one of her bare breasts.

"You should bring me a good price," he said with a reedy voice. He spat onto the dust-covered floor and moved away. "Probably some spoiled son of the rich lords is going to have that lovely body of yours." He sighed. "I wish I could try you out first, but I am not allowed. Mustn't spoil the merchandise."

He cracked his whip again. The girl flinched, but he didn't touch her anymore.

"Get going," he told her. "We don't have all day."

She stumbled out of the doorway and blinked when the blinding light of the midday sun fell into her eyes.

Dazed, she looked at the people standing around the raised platform onto which she had been pushed.

A soft moaning went through the men in the crowd when she stepped into the open. The girl moved as if drugged. Through the fog that enveloped her brain, she heard the voice of another man. "How much am I bid for this fine specimen of a female?"

A rough hand grabbed her long hair and cruelly whipped back her head.

"Look at those magnificent breasts, how they stand like two ripe *larps*. Notice her belly, flat and smooth, and look at this!"

She cried out sharply when a hand thrust between her legs, forcing them apart. "Her legs are long enough to reach around even your fat belly, Nirkus."

Laughter erupted from the crowd, and somebody called, "She doesn't look that lively to me. I like my women to have some fire between their legs, and I don't care if they are long or short." More laughter.

The girl shook her head. The buzzing inside her head seemed to fade slowly.

What happened?

She stared at the red crystal hanging around the auctioneer's scrawny neck. There was something about that crystal, but she didn't remember what.

"Twenty pieces of gilds."

"Thirty."

"Fifty."

"Seventy pieces, and I want that amulet you've got around your neck."

The auctioneer called something to the man who had brought out the girl. After a few moments, the fat man came waddling out and handed him an item.

A slender sword with a jeweled hilt.

"One hundred pieces of gilds for the girl, the amulet and her sword."

"I'll give you thirty pieces for the sword, and you can keep the bitch," a fat woman garbed in a long flowing gown shouted.

Everybody laughed.

"I'll give you one hundred pieces," said a quiet voice from behind the crowd.

They all turned to look at the speaker and an excited whisper ran through the watchers. The man who had spoken was tall and well built, with wide shoulders, clad only in a short kilt and a leather harness that covered his deep chest. His bare arms and legs were thick and heavily muscled. A long broadsword hung down his broad back.

The crowd parted when he pushed his way through to the platform.

"Ah, Captain Horgan." The auctioneer smiled. "Did the last girl you bought satisfy your needs?

"Don't be concerned about the last girl."

Lifting his hands, the auctioneer said, "I'm not. I don't care what you do with them. Are you buying this one for yourself or for the Lady Geisa?" His voice carried a slight sneer, and some of the onlookers snickered.

The big man stared at him coldly and threw him a purse. "Here, Slaver," he said, contempt in his voice. "There are a hundred pieces of gilds in there. Count them if you must."

"Oh, I trust you, Captain." The little man shoved the purse into his tunic, a greedy look in his eyes. "Perhaps you'd be interested in another excellent buy. There was a second girl with this one. She is young, not much meat on her yet, but she shows promise. Her body is strong, and she has nice looking breasts."

He grinned, indicating the girl beside him. "Not like hers, but then this one is an exceptionally well-formed specimen."

Captain Horgan climbed onto the platform, took the sword and the amulet, grabbed the girl's hand and turned away, pulling her behind him. "No, thanks," he said. "I need only one."

He stepped off the platform, but he stopped and looked back when he heard the wailing cry of the other girl.

She was small, barely past puberty. Her long, light hair hung matted and filthy around her naked shoulders. The slaver had been right; she did have nice breasts, although a little small. Her face was pretty. He saw the dark streaks where tears had run down her cheeks.

She stood, looking sullenly out of large, green eyes.

He shrugged and turned away again.

"Fifty pieces of gilds and you can have her, Captain. A bargain."

When the big man kept walking, the slave trader cried, "She is a virgin, and I'll let her go for forty."

"A virgin?" someone called out of the crowd.

"You sold me a virgin once. It turned out she had brought more action into the barracks than all the king's mercenaries ever found on the battlefields…"

An uproarious laughter swallowed the rest of what the man said.

The trader waved him off angrily. "I've checked this one out myself." To which everybody laughed again.

The young girl seemed to come out of her stupor. Her gaze fell upon the tall girl beside the captain.

"Orola," she cried out.

At the sound of the plaintive cry, the tall girl stopped and turned around.

The captain looked at her tortured face and then at the girl back on the auction block. He seemed to consider.

"Thirty pieces and I'll take her."

A wide grin split the ugly face of the trader. "She's yours,

Captain." He shoved the girl forward. Then he bent down and picked up the thrown coins.

The fair-haired girl stumbled toward her new owner and clung to the tall girl's arm.

"Let's go," grumbled the big man. He headed for a hunting wagon parked nearby.

Before he reached it, a small boy came running and thrust a bundle into his hands.

"This belongs to the slaves."

The banter, a vicious scaly beast, screamed in defiance when the captain removed the leather hood from its eyes. Jumping onto the hunting wagon, the big man cracked his whip, and the beast moved forward, pulling the wagon behind.

The road was paved with stones, and the vehicle jumped dangerously as the captain drove the banter to reckless speed.

Looking back at the houses and clay huts, Orola hugged the young girl close to her, gently stroking her hair.

"I am scared, Orola," said the young girl, shivering, in spite of the sun's rays burning hot on her naked skin.

Orola shook her head. Her thoughts were clear again, and her memory seemed to be coming back, but her limbs still felt weak.

They must have shot my system full of poisons.

She turned to look at the big man in the driver's seat. If she could only get her sword...But they were moving too fast. The best thing she could do was to hang on tight and hope the wagon wouldn't overturn. Her time would come; they had to stop at some time.

After what seemed like an eternity, the vehicle slowed somewhat and stopped jumping. They had left the main road and were traveling on a dirt-packed narrow trail. Breathing became difficult because of the cloud of dry dust whirling around them.

On one side of the trail, high cliffs loomed into the sky, and on the other side, she saw nothing but emptiness.

Orola hesitated to think what would happen should the hunting wagon begin swinging again and leave the narrow trail.

The cloud of dust finally disappeared, and Orola saw that they were high in the mountains. Below them stretched the valley they had left. Gnarled trees and low shrubs had replaced the tall timbers and lush vegetation of the valley, some of them already without leaves, signaling the coming of winter.

Now the air seemed cold. Heavy dark clouds obscured the sun, and white flakes of snow fell on them, gently at first but heavier as the wagon climbed higher.

Then the wind started to blow.

The girls crawled under the thick furs, their naked bodies pressed together for warmth.

After a while, the wagon slowed and came to a halt. Orola stuck her head from under the furs to see why they had stopped. An icy blast washed over her face. Shielding her eyes against the harsh wind and blowing sleet, she stared in surprise at the heavy blanket of snow covering the road.

She couldn't see far, her vision blurred by the thickly falling snow.

"It's a storm out there!" she exclaimed, her hopes of freedom dashed. No sense in trying to escape now, naked as they were. They'd freeze in a short time. As it was, her skin was turning blue from the cold.

She turned to look for the driver. She could barely make out his shadowy form moving beside the banter.

"Hey!" she called. "We're freezing. How about finding us some shelter?"

The big man fought his way around the wagon. He had thrown a heavy fur around his wide shoulders. Covered with snow, he looked like a monstrous snow-beast.

"Stay under the furs," he advised, bending close to her.

"There is an abandoned castle nearby. I'll try to get there before you freeze to death. It's not far."

He stomped through the snow to the front of the wagon and grabbed the beast's reins.

"Come on, my scaly friend," he coaxed the banter, pulling forward and leading the way. "We'll be in a warm place soon."

It was not an easy journey. Many times the vehicle stopped, and the girls could hear the captain cursing as he tried to free the wheels from the deep snow.

Underneath the furs, the girls clung to each other, shivering.

"My feet are like clumps of ice," the younger one complained. "I wish I had my mocs."

"Hush, Kicki." Orola ran her hands down the young girl's back. "We'll be warm soon."

"I'll never be warm again," Kicki wailed. Leaning her head against Orola's breast, she sobbed, "It's all my fault, Orola. I should never have asked you to let me accompany you."

"Don't blame yourself, girl. It was my choice."

And maybe partly my fault we are in this predicament. I should have been more cautious when we stopped to rest.

That night by the quiet creek, so safe and peaceful looking. The memory of the sharp sting on her naked buttocks just before she plunged into the cool water was still fresh in her mind.

She could have sworn she felt the fast action poison entering her bloodstream. Losing consciousness just before she hit the water, she was lucky she hadn't drowned.

The next thing she remembered was staring into the greedy little eyes of the fat slave trader, her hands and feet bound.

At least nobody took advantage of my helpless body, she thought with a touch of grim humor.

When the rocking of the hunting wagon suddenly stopped and she heard the voice of the captain, she sat up.

"Come on out, unless you want to spend the night out here in the cold."

He pulled the furs away, and she stared into his snow-covered face. He helped her off the wagon then he lifted Kicki out and stomped away, carrying her in his arms.

Orola grabbed one of the furs and wrapped it around herself. Then she took another one and followed the captain, who had already disappeared into the shadows. His footsteps in the snow were already filling in again.

Her bare feet were going numb so she hurried after him. When she reached a narrow opening in a wall built from large stones, she slipped through. In the darkness, she could hear the sounds of the man's heavy boots on the cold stone floor. Her eyes adjusted to the darkness, and she saw his shadow at the end of the room she had entered. He disappeared through another doorway.

That bastard! Leaving me behind like this. He knows damn well I would never try to get away without Kicki.

She sighed and walked into the other room. It was smaller than the first one. The captain was busy collection scraps of wood strewn across the floor and piling them in the fireplace in a corner.

Kicki stood shivering in the middle of the room, her arms wrapped around her naked body.

Orola put the fur she had brought around the girl's thin shoulders.

"Oh, Orola," Kicki cried. "Is this the warm shelter you promised? I'll be frozen by morning."

Captain Horgan laughed softly. "I'll get a fire going, and you'll be warm soon. Besides…" He grinned. "There are many ways we could warm up together."

Orola shot him a cold look. "Don't touch her! She's just a child." She put a protecting arm around Kicki.

The big man laughed, but somehow she didn't detect any menace in his laughter. She watched him as he produced a flask filled with liquid from his pouch and preceded to pour some of it onto the pile of wool in the fireplace. Then he struck a piece of flint against his knife, sending sparks flying into the liquid-drenched wood. Small flames began to lick over the scraps of wood, and soon the fire burned brightly.

"See if you can find some more wood," he instructed Orola. "I'm going outside to get the banter. He'll be a lot happier in the protection of the castle walls."

She could clearly see broken pieces of furniture lying around so began collecting some.

Then she squatted in front of the fireplace, enjoying the warmth of the crackling fire.

***

Orola watched the captain's handsome face in the flickering light of the flames, wondering what plans he had for her and Kicki.

He looked up and stared at her. "You have strange eyes. Like the eyes of a night-hunter. Where do you come from?"

"From the island *Antanakka*."

"The Island of Witches." He gave her a sharp look. "Are you a witch?"

Orola shrugged and gave him a smile. "I have been called that and other things. You have heard of my people?"

He shrugged his wide shoulders. "I have, but what I've heard is probably just nonsense. You look like an ordinary woman to me." He paused and leered at her partly exposed breast. "Maybe not so ordinary. Your beauty is…ah…quite disturbing."

She let her fur fall open wider, exposing her creamy breasts fully. Giving him a calculating look, she said, "What would our freedom be worth to you?"

"Are you trying to tempt me by selling your body?" He chuckled. "I've bought you already, but you don't belong to me. The money I paid for you was not mine. You should know, though, that I am not one who takes advantage of a situation such as this."

Pulling the fur closer around her shoulders again, Orola asked, "Where are you taking us?"

"You'll find out," he said curtly, getting up to throw some more wood on the fire. He sat down again and yawned.

"This place is giving me the shivers," Kicki said. "What is it anyway?"

"It is an old castle. I don't know much about it. Rumors have it that the owner and his family disappeared without a trace. Apparently, demons took them away." The captain stretched his large frame. "Let's get some sleep. I am tired."

He made himself comfortable, his back against the wall, his big sword beside him. "Don't even think about escaping," he warned. "There is no place for you to go. Also, I am an easy sleeper." He closed his eyes and slept soundly a few moments later.

"He didn't even give us anything to eat," Kicki complained. "I am hungry and thirsty." She looked at the snoring man. "Let's take the hunting wagon and be on our way. He'll never find us in the morning."

"And we'll get hopelessly lost out there." Orola shook her head. "No, Kicki. We'll have to stay here tonight. Maybe tomorrow. I am still quite weak from the poison. Let's wait for more favorable conditions."

Wrapping up in the warm fur, she lay down to sleep. The stone floor was hard, but she was too tired to care. She was warm, and that was all that counted for the moment.

The sound of the howling wind outside and the softly spitting fire made her drowsy, lulled her senses. There was no danger from the captain, and this place seemed to be safe enough…except for the demons.

She awoke to discover she was being dragged across the floor.

Someone screamed her name.

Kicki.

It was still dark, but her eyes adjusted quickly to night vision.

Her captors were Dorbs.

The Children of the Ground.

She had run into them before, but she had never been captured by them. They were vicious, cruel and stupid, not much more than animals. Grotesque beings, their large hands and feet out of proportion to their short bodies. The tallest one reached barely up to her navel.

Their high-pitched voices and cackling laughter filled the room.

"Good catch," one said beside her ear.

"Yes, yes, yes. Good catch," repeated another one. "King be pleased."

"Yes. Good. Good."

She tried to get free but was unable to do so. There were too many of them. Their size belied their strength. They were incredibly strong.

Her hands and feet were tied together. The air felt cold on her skin and her fur was gone. Turning her head to see what had happened to the captain, she saw him being carried like so much dead meat. Either they'd knocked him out or he had been drugged. Maybe he was dead.

They lowered her through an opening in the floor into a dark tunnel. Even her night vision didn't help her much. The Dorbs became shadows moving in a dark black sea.

The air around her wasn't quite as cold anymore but smelled musky and humid. Lower and lower they moved, down narrow and dark tunnels. After a while, they entered a large cavern. Containers with burning oil were spaced at irregular intervals along the walls, throwing a dim light across the empty space.

In the center of the cavern, a large fire burned inside an enormous pit.

She saw a group of Dorbs butchering a carcass. When she came closer, she realized it was the banter. The Dorbs were obviously getting ready for a feast.

I am glad it is the beast and not us.

Why had she not searched for her amulet when she had the chance? Without the *Holy Communicator*, she was helpless.

The Dorbs dumped their captives unceremoniously onto the cold floor.

"Orola," Kicki cried beside her. "What are they going to do with us?"

"I don't know, girl." She craned her neck to look at the captain.

He was still out cold.

"I hope he is not dead," she murmured. "He seemed very nice."

A big, fat Dorb, wearing a filthy cape that had once been white, came waddling over. He gave her a gap-toothed grin and with a thick, knobby finger, he poked her breast.

"Me King," he announced with a surprisingly deep voice.

"If you do this, you will pay for this. No man enters my body without a price. Remember that, king!"

He looked into her glowing eyes, taking a step away from her.

"You not hurt me," he said hoarsely. Then he bent and slapped her face. "Me King. Take you again and again."

He walked away, over to the fire and ripped out a large chunk of meat from the sizzling carcass of the banter.

"Me big hungry." He bit into the half-raw meat.

The other Dorbs cheered and began ripping off their own pieces. They drank from large crocks, dancing and singing in a strange language.

"Bring treasure!" the king called.

A group of Dorb-females, their breasts skinny strips of skin hanging down to their hairy bellies, brought the furs and the bundle that contained the girls' clothing.

One of the females carried Orola's sword.

They threw everything into an untidy heap. Then one of them put Orola's amulet onto the top of the heap.

Longingly, she looked at it, her mind reaching out and trying to make contact, but it didn't respond. It could only be activated when it touched her skin.

The Dorb-king picked it up and hung it around his fat neck. Proudly, he displayed it by parading around the fire, his hairy chest inflated. Grabbing a clay bucket filled with liquid, he stepped in front of Orola and poured the liquid into his mouth, spilling most of it over himself.

Belching noisily, he babbled, "Me big thirsty." He fondled his penis. "Me big all over," he boasted.

Orola just looked at him, her eyes riveted to the jewel around his neck. If she could only get her hands on it!

The king stumbled away and ripped another chunk of meat from the charred body of the banter.

She heard groaning sounds behind her, and she knew that the captain was finally regaining his consciousness.

"What in the name of the *Triple-headed Demon* happened? Where are we?"

Orola wanted to laugh at his oath, but the humor was not in the situation. "We are prisoners of one-headed demons. Short and ugly ones, but extremely dangerous nonetheless."

"What are they eating?" he yelled. "That looks like..."

"It is," Orola said. "That is the bad news, but there is a positive side to that. It could have been us."

Most of the Dorbs were lying on the ground, either copulating or sleeping in a drunken stupor.

She saw the king lying on his back, his mouth slack, snoring noisily. His thick flabby lips fluttered like the wings of a dying small bird with every breath he took. In his hand, he clutched the jewel.

Something touched Orola's hands.

"It's me," Kicki whispered behind her. "I managed to loosen my bonds." She began working on the rope that held Orola's hands together. It didn't take her long to untie the knot, and Orola was free.

Rubbing her wrists to return the circulation into her hands, she walked over to the king. She kicked him in his fat stomach, making him moan in his sleep, though he did not wake. Then she bent and pried the jewel from his hand.

Sighing, she hung the leather straps around her neck, letting the jewel nestle between her breasts. As soon as it touched her skin, it began to glow with a bright fire.

She stood, her eyes closed, relishing the feeling of power that flowed through her. Forgotten was her pain, forgotten the clammy air on her naked skin.

She opened her eyes, picked up her clothing and dressed slowly, first slipping into her high boots. Then she tied a strip of cloth between her legs and fastened the short leather kilt over it. Finally, she covered her breasts with the small metal cups and hung her cape loosely around her shoulders.

Then she picked up her sword and hung it onto the belt around her hips.

Walking over to the captain, who had been watching her, she stood over him, her legs spread wide.

"Well?" he demanded. "Are you going to free me, or are just going to stare at me?"

She chuckled and cut his bonds with the tip of her slender sword. The jewel in its hilt glowed as brightly as the jewel between her breasts.

"You *are* a witch," he said, getting to his feet. "Maybe the rumors I've heard are true after all." He stared at the shining jewel hanging from her neck. "It has something to do with that stone, doesn't it?"

She nodded. "Through the *Holy Communicator* I am in touch with my god, who lends me his strength. Without it, I am a mere mortal." Turning toward Kicki, who had finished putting on her clothes, she asked, "Ready to go?"

Captain Horgan pointed to the furs. "Let's take those along, or we'll freeze to death. With our transportation gone, it's going to be a long walk across the mountain."

Looking over the mass of sleeping Dorbs, Orola's gaze fell on the snoring king. She walked over to him and gave him a harder, vicious kick. His eyes fluttered open, and he sat up, holding his side.

Staring at Orola's boots, he lifted his eyes to look at her. Seeing the cold look in her eyes and the naked sword in her hand, he cowered and rolled into a ball.

"Not hurt," he whimpered. "Me King."

"Get up, you ugly, fat ravisher. Now you pay the price for trying to harm us."

Her sword flicked twice, and the king stared at the two bloody things hanging from his scrotum. Clutching himself, he began to howl terribly.

Other Dorbs started to wake up from the noise and discovering the freed prisoner, they closed in on them, brandishing clubs and long knives.

"Kill! Kill!" screamed the king.

One of them carried the captain's big sword, and he came at Orola, swinging the heavy blade over his head.

Orola lifted her own sword. It began to change, elongated, became a whip. With one flick of her wrist, she sent the tip of the lash flying toward the Dorb and wrapped it around his wrist.

She yanked hard. The ugly creature stumbled, fell, and dropped the weapon.

Captain Horgan, moved in, gave him a mighty kick and picked up his sword.

The whip in Orola's hand changed back into a sword and, standing side by side, the big man and the tall warrior girl met their attackers head-on. Their swords flashed in the flickering light of the torches, and they laid heavy carnage upon the screaming horde.

The howl and moans of the dying Dorbs echoed through the

169

cavern, and the awful stench of spilled intestines filled the already dank air.

That had been an unlucky day for the *Children of the Ground*, the day when they captured Orola, the Moon Priestess, a member of the fierce warrior clan from the island Antanakka.

Unluckiest of the all was the Dorb-king, who managed to survive the carnage but lost his manhood, of which he had been so proud.

When the battle was over, half the tribe of little people lay dead or dying. The other half fled into the darkness of the tunnels.

Bleeding from a dozen wounds, none of them life threatening, Captain Horgan turned toward the tall girl, who stood silent now, her eyes gazing over the grisly scene.

"The rumors I've heard were just that, only rumors," he said with a tired grin. "Your strength and courage are mightier than that of any man I've ever known. I'm glad I am on your side."

She looked at him, a smile tugging at the corners of her full lips. "Are you really on my side, Captain?" she said mockingly. "I thought we were your prisoners."

"I wouldn't dare hold you prisoner." He laughed dryly. "If my life depended on it."

"You have that right, Captain Horgan. Your life depends on it." Orola's eyes still glowed like the flames of a burning fire, and the jewel between her breasts matched that blaze.

He watched that fire slowly subside and relaxed, lowering his broad sword.

"Can we go now?" a voice piped up behind them.

Both of them turned to look at Kicki cowering on the ground. "Yes, girl," Orola said gently. "It's time to get out of here."

Dawn glowed when they emerged from the ruins of the castle. The storm had died down, and only a few gentle snowflakes still fell from the clearing sky.

Solar, the largest of the three moons, was still high above the horizon.

Orola went down on her knees and gave thanks to the moon-god. She felt his presence inside her, flooding her tired body with his unfailing power. Soon her full strength returned.

They found the hunting wagon where they had left it the night before, useless to them now without the banter to pull it.

After brushing the snow off the driver's seat, the Captain opened the lid that covered the compartment under it and took out a bow and some arrows.

"Not a very dangerous weapon in a fight." He shrugged apologetically. "But it might help get us some food for our empty bellies."

The girls went back into the castle and collected more wood for the fire, while the Captain went hunting. When he came back with a small furry animal, they already had a good fire going. Soon the skinned and cleaned carcass was sizzling on a wooden stake.

They sat huddled in their furs in front of the fire and watched the flames lick over the broiling meat.

"I guess our roads will part soon," the captain said. "Where are you headed?"

"I was on my way to Guata." Orola glanced at Kicky. "But I was side-tracked."

"Guata? Where would that be?"

"A long journey away from here. It is north of the Gibli-desert, deep in the jungle. I am looking for one of my sisters who is advisor to the queen of Mirr. We haven't heard from her in a long time."

The big man gave her a curious look. "If that place is so far away, how can she communicate with you?"

"We have our ways." Orola said, smiling mysteriously.

Outside, the wind seemed to pick up again.

"It looks like we'll be stuck here for another night." The captain looked at Kicki, who had fallen asleep, and said remorsefully, "Now that you are free, I have nothing to show for the money I spent."

Orola laughed gaily, giving him a knowing look. She spread the fur on the ground and unhooked her breast cups. Her arms reaching out for him, she smiled. "Come here, and I'll show you some of the other things I'm good at."

Grinning hugely, the big man sank into her arms. Very gently, he removed her kilt and then his own.

His hands roamed over her naked body, cupped her breasts, stroked her round buttocks.

"You must have read my mind," he said as they slipped together.

"Perhaps I did." She sighed and moved lazily underneath him.

"But then it wasn't hard to read."

THE POWER OF SOLAR

"So, then it's settled." Lady Geisa leaned back in her wooden chair, smiling gently at Kicki, who sat beside her. "The caravan will come through here in perhaps eighteen or twenty days. Until then, the girl will be quite safe with us."

Orola pursed her lips thoughtfully. "But will she be safe with the caravan?"

Lady Geisa laughed, waving a jeweled hand. "Old Balsir, who is the Caravan Master, has been a good friend of mine for more years than I care to remember. I can assure you, Kicki will be in good hands."

"How about his people?"

"They can all be trusted. A bunch of roughnecks and thieves they may be, but they would never hurt a young girl who has been put under their protection. Their honor would not permit it."

Orola, dressed in a short leather kilt, high boots, her large breasts only covered by metal cups, stood and shook her long black hair out of her face. "I trust you, Lady Geisa. You have been more than generous. How can I ever repay your kindness? I don't have any money."

The old woman spread her hands. "What is the value of

money? I have more than I will ever need. You saved my captain's life, and that is more than enough. He has been with me since he was a little boy, and he is almost like a son to me."

"But you paid money for us at the slave market!" Orola shook her head in wonderment.

Smiling sadly, the old woman nodded. "From time to time, I send Captain Horgan across the mountains to buy slaves, but not to keep them as slaves. I let them work off their debt, and then I give them a choice. They are free to leave or stay with me. They are welcome to do so as free men or women. I have no love for slave traders."

"You are a remarkable woman, Lady Geisa," Orola said. "I am glad we have met."

Clapping her hands, the old woman called one of the serving girls to the table. "Bring us some more wine, please, and tell the captain to join us."

The young girl bowed slightly. "Yes, my lady." Humming, she ran light-footed to do as requested.

Orola watched her as she disappeared through the entrance to the hall. She had to agree. From what she had seen, there were no unhappy servants here. She had sensed the feeling of peace and happiness as soon as they had entered the castle.

She smiled tenderly at the big man who came walking into the room. Narrow of hip and wide of shoulder, he moved almost silently across the stone covered floor.

"Good evening, my lady," he said, nodding toward the old woman. Then he took Orola's hand in his and led her to the table. "Come, sit beside me," he said. He sounded cheerful, but she sensed the sadness in his voice.

The serving girl brought wine, and she accepted a cup. While they sipped the sweet wine, nobody spoke. Manners dictated that no one speak until the second cup was served.

When she had finished her wine, Lady Geisa rose. "I am quite tired. I think I will go to my chambers." She put her hand on Orola's shoulder. "I will see you in the morning. Please, don't leave without saying goodbye."

"I won't, my lady," Orola said, clasping the old woman's hand.

Kicki, who had said nothing all this time, gave Orola a shy smile. "Thank you for everything, Orola. Maybe some day…" She didn't finish the sentence and rushed out of the door.

Orola had seen the tears in the young girl's eyes. They had grown fond of each other, but now it was time they parted ways. Looking at the man beside her, she said, "I am tired myself." With that, she rose and headed for the door.

Before she walked through it, she turned and, reaching out with one hand, she said, "Are you coming?"

The captain chuckled. "I thought you'd never ask."

They walked down the corridor in silence, his strong arm around her waist. The cold stonewalls were covered with price-less tapestries. Lady Geisa had told Orola the truth; she didn't need any more money.

She already possessed an enormous amount of wealth.

"She is a wonderful woman," Orola said. "You are a lucky man."

"Indeed I am," agreed the captain, "but I am even luckier to know you. I just wish…"

Orola put her finger on his lips. "Please, don't say it. You know I have to move on. I can never belong to a man. Since I have been a child, I was raised and trained to be a Warrior Priestess. My duty lies with my sisters, but let's not speak more of that."

They had arrived at the door that led into her room.

"Once more, I will share with you some of the secrets I have been taught," she whispered. "Just accept what I give you and remember me as someone pleasant who came your way."

She closed the door softly behind her. Slipping out of her clothes, she stood naked in front of him.

He drew in a sharp breath as he stared at her lovely form.

"You are so beautiful," he breathed. "I can never get enough of you."

She threw back her head and laughed, thrusting out her round, creamy breasts. "Look at me, then. It gives me pleasure to have a man like you admire me."

Turning, she bent her knees slightly and pushed out her rear, letting him admire the curve of her back, the roundness of her smooth buttocks.

He groaned and began unlacing his leather shirt and kilt with flying fingers. "I can't wait any longer," he said hoarsely, reaching for her. They tumbled to the floor, on top of a soft, deep carpet.

She spread her strong, slender legs, exposing her black, fuzzy triangle. Stroking his erect member with her hands, she guided him gently into her moist cleft. "Easy, my love," she whispered. "We have all night."

He tried to control his movements, but his control was slipping fast. For a while, she let him move on top of her, but when she sensed his climax approaching, she applied pressure at certain parts of his body, and he calmed down.

When he began to tire, he lay on his back, and she straddled him. Riding him, her body gyrated sensually above him. The jewel between her breasts glowed brightly as she drew power from her god.

Joining with a man she liked was part of a religious ritual, and her god fully approved. She could feel *His* invisible presence inside her, giving her the strength and endurance she needed. Some of the power even leaked to the man, letting him experience greater pleasure than he would with another woman.

Her eyes locked with his. He had his hands clamped around her hips, and his strong fingers dug deep into her soft flesh. It was almost time.

This time, she let him reach his goal. When he lunged upward with a deep shout, she pushed down hard, her inner muscles milking him gently. His hot discharge flooded her insides, and she cried out when her own pleasure surged through her body.

As the intense pleasure slowly subsided, she stretched out on top of him, her soft breasts flattening against his deep chest.

"You couple like no other woman I have ever met." He let out a sad sigh. "From now on, I will always compare. It will be pure torture."

She kissed him deeply. "You will forget. Soon, I will be nothing but a fond memory."

The hot wind had been blowing across the burning desert since early dawn, covering the lone rider with fine sand.

For three days, Orola had ridden her steed, a gift from Lady Geisa, through the shifting sand dunes. So far, she had met no one on her trek north. According to an old map, she should reach the mountains by nightfall, unless the storm made it impossible to move on.

Already, the banter was restless and stopped every so often, refusing to move, unless she got off and walked in front of the animal for a while.

"You're not going to give up now?" Orola coaxed, stroking the beast's soft belly. The banter hissed softly. She ran a hand over the scaly flank. "I am tired, too, my friend, but it would be better for both of us if we camped in the protection of the mountains tonight."

She removed the heavy water bag from the beast's back and poured a little water into a flat container. "Here, drink this. It will make you feel better."

After drinking, the animal seemed more amiable, and she climbed on its broad back. She pulled her hood tighter around her head and slid the dust mask over her face.

The captain had warned her back at the castle about the desert and the sandstorms. She wouldn't be able to find any water or shelter until she reached the mountains. Even then, it would be next to impossible to find water. The banter was very much at home in the dry desert and could go without liquids for a long time.

Orola, with the help of her god, possessed more endurance than other individuals did, and she had waved off their well-meaning warnings. Circumstances didn't leave her much choice. She could have waited for the caravan and joined it to cross the Rhasi desert back to Rahoz. From there, she would have had to book passage with the Sledpeople to get to Gmaly.

She had no desire to meet again with the Sledpeople. Even if she could afford the cost of the voyage, they'd probable kill her on sight, given the chance. Time was the other reason. It would take too long to take that route, time she didn't want to waste in an attempt to find her missing sister.

Once in the mountains, she would stay close to them, crossing into Virgoss. In six or seven days, she should reach the River Gma. If she could rely on her map, there was a lake at the edge of the desert long before she reached the river. With any luck, she'd be there in three days.

Food and water were no problem. She had enough to last until she came to the lake, even if it took longer than expected. After that, traveling should be easier.

She had overcome larger obstacles.

The storm didn't let up for the rest of the day. Then suddenly, when she had already resigned to spending another night in the desert, she passed into the mountains, surrounded by high cliffs, on a narrow, natural path, probably an old riverbed.

The cliffs rose high on both sides, cutting off the wind and the drifting sand.

Darkness was coming fast, and she decided to set up camp. Sliding off the banter, she jumped to the dry, hard ground. She had seen a break in the cliffs. When she headed for it, she discovered it was a small cave, large enough to give her and her steed protection for the night. The banter lay down, hissing and snorting. She didn't worry about the animal wandering away; it would stay close to her. After drinking some water and eating sparingly from her rations, she unrolled a sleeping bag and crawled inside. It would be nice to wake without being covered by a blanket of drifting sand.

Through the entrance to the cave, she could see the moon Solar in the dark sky. Partly obscured by clouds, the *Eye* of her god was still clearly visible, watching the world below. None of the other moons was in sight.

She closed her eyes. This was a good time to make a report. Concentrating on the jewel nestling between her breasts, she evoked a soft pulsing, like a tiny heartbeat.

When nothing but the steady drumming of the *Holy Communicator* filled her being, she sent her message. It would be received by her god, the *Great Computer*, and relayed to the *Watchers* on the island Antanakka. Her sisters would know that she was still alive and well.

Every time she communicated, she was filled with wonder. How awesome the powers of the Ancients must have been.

According to the legends, the Ancients had come to this world a long time ago, from far away, arriving there after a great war among the gods who lived amid the stars, those shiny lights in the night sky.

After the war, only one of their metal cities that traveled between the worlds was left. Their enemies, the fathers of the dragon people who lived in the swamps, had come one day in one of their star vehicles. Shooting at each other with terrible weapons, both metal cities crashed.

From that day on, people on this world were stranded here, forever forgotten by the gods.

A few of the Ancients had been living on Solar, where they built the *Great Computer*. The builders had been Orola's ancestors. After finishing their mission, they came down to this world in a small metal vessel and founded the *Order of the Moon Priestesses*.

Through the *Great Computer*, they commanded great powers

that set them apart from the other inhabitants. Some day they might be able to rejoin their brothers and sisters who resided on other worlds. Until that day, their duty was to teach each new generation and be prepared for that great event.

Of course, much of this was only legend, and unfortunately, so much knowledge had already been lost, but she knew her god was real. She could feel *His* presence.

Most sisters agreed, though, that the legends had to be wrong on at least one account. It seemed almost blasphemy to believe that the Ancients had built the Great Computer. Someday, the doctrine would have to be changed to *And then the Great Computer created the first Sisters and Brothers and sent them down to the world below.*

Maybe someday. Either way, she didn't really care. The power of Solar was there when she needed it, as long as she wore the jewel, the *Holy Communicator.*

The sky was clear when she awoke the next morning. She crawled out of her sleeping bag and stretched her lithe body, breathing deeply.

The wind had shifted over night, and a pleasant cool breeze blew from the north through the canyon.

To get the kinks out of her body, she stripped and went through a series of exercises. Then, with a moist cloth, she scrubbed clean and tied a fresh strip of cloth between her legs. Slipping into her short kilt, she left her breasts bare, enjoying the cool air on her naked skin.

Feeling rested and full of energy, she settled down to a meager breakfast of dried strips of meat, some hard wafers, dried fruit, and a cup of warm water. Not exactly a meal fit for a queen or a king, but providing her with needed nourishment.

The banter had made no move to rise, but it was watching her with lazy interest. Usually a vicious beast, this one was remarkably docile and friendly. When it was time to move on, the animal reluctantly stood, shaking its long neck and narrow head. Orola tied her packs down and jumped onto its scaly back.

For most of the morning, she followed the old riverbed, covering a lot of distance. At midday, when the fiery sun stood high, the canyon made a sharp turn east. She rode on for a time, hoping that it would turn north again, but when she saw the straight line going on and on, she realized she had to leave the riverbed and take to the mountains.

She removed her cape from her pack and threw it around her shoulders to protect her fair skin against the burning rays of the sun. Already, she could feel her skin tingle.

Up the slope, she went toward the top of the riverbank. The banter with its broad splayed feet was used to climbing rocks.

The ground was rough. Many times she had to turn back and try a different route when large boulders barred her way or when steep cliffs made it impossible to move on.

For a long time, they traveled on a narrow ledge until it ended abruptly. A long jump to a flat rock on the other side of the deep crevice was the only way to go on.

With a lot of coaxing and stroking, the beast finally jumped across, but Orola had doubts that the animal would do her bidding again. They barely made it, and only because the rock they landed on was below the ledge. She looked back into the crevice and shuddered. It was a long way down. Even if the banter would jump again, she wouldn't.

So far, she had seen no signs of life, except for the odd small reptile-type sandfish scurrying away.

Early in the afternoon, after stopping for a drink of water, Orola heard a strange wailing sound ahead on the trail. She slipped off her mount and, cautious not to make any noise, she crept over the next rise.

The sight before her raised her anger instantly. Her lips narrowed and her fists clinched. She had never seen them before, but from her teachings, she recognized the creature below her as one belonging to the dragon people. A large male, his crest rising above his scaly head and down his spine, he was in the process of killing another creature.

A foot on top of his victim's chest, he brought up a short-bladed knife, and with a vicious cut, he slashed the exposed throat.

Uttering a savage battle cry, Orola stood up and drew her own sword.

The reptilian turned, surprised at first, but after seeing the puny human female walking toward him, he roared, "Who are you who dares to stand up against a prince of the People?"

"I am Orola, a priestess of the god Solar, and you are a murderer of helpless women and infants!"

Looking down at his slain victim, the reptilian showed his teeth. "Only a useless female. Good enough only for food, that's all." He sheathed his knife, bent to pick up a large bow, and reached for an arrow. "Prepare to die, Priestess," he said, grinning.

The jewel between Orola's breasts began to glow brightly, as did the jewel in the hilt of her sword. The sword changed, became thin and long. Orola flipped it backward and with an explosive crack, the tip flew toward the reptilian, wrapping around the bow, and wrenched it from his grip.

She took off her cape and moved toward her huge adversary. The whip in her hand shortened, became a sword again.

"Witchery!" the reptilian hissed, drawing his knife.

"The power of Solar," Orola said quietly, falling into a fighting stance. "You may be large and strong, dragon man, but I am not afraid of you."

"You may be a witch, but I am a prince and invincible. You can't hurt me with that plaything of yours!" Roaring angrily, he charged her, his knife in front of him.

Orola sidestepped him, turned and kicked him in the side.

Kicking him was like kicking a rock.

"Are you trying to tickle me to death?" He laughed.

Spreading his muscled arms, he advanced again. "Come into my embrace, soft human female, and let me crush you to death," he taunted.

She studied the heavy scales covering his broad chest. Even her sword couldn't pierce that, unless she managed to slip it between the plates. Looking into his glittering, black eyes, she knew she faced a dangerous foe, one who could match even her extraordinary strength. He towered over her at least by two heads, and his body was wide and massive.

She had one advantage over him; he obviously underestimated her and didn't realize the powers she possessed.

When he reached for her with his long arms, she easily evaded his grasp. Dancing backward, she flicked her sword across his armored chest, testing his reflexes. He parried with his knife, nearly knocking the sword from her hand. He was fast.

"I hear human females are always in heat," he said, his teeth glinting in the sun. "Too bad I am not, otherwise I might just see if there is truth to those rumors."

"You've heard only half-truths, dragon man. It takes a strong male to get a human female into the mood to copulate. Aside from that, I am not really human."

"But you have swollen mammary." He grinned, inflating his chest. "I am a strong male. Do I get you into the...mood?"

"Hardly," Orola answered coldly. "I don't couple with animals."

Without warning, she lunged, aiming for a spot on the inside of his right arm. She felt the tip of her sword enter soft meat. He roared, his left arm swung around, but she dropped to the ground and rolled away from him.

He picked up his knife, which had fallen from the fingers of his injured arm, with his left hand. Then he let out a piercing cry.

Orola heard it answered as a huge lizard-like creature came bounding over the rise behind them. The reptilian swung onto the giant lizard's back.

"We'll meet again," he called, turned the beast around and sped away.

Orola walked over to the still figure on the ground.

One of the cloud people. A whorll female.

Her chest was a bloody mess from the reptilian's clawed foot, her throat cut. Blood covered her black skin, and the membranes of her wings had been cut to shreds.

Beside her lay a male child, an arrow in his chest.

Hearing a rustling, she swung around. On a ledge above her, crouched a small winged girl, staring at her with huge, fearful eyes.

With one hand, Orola reached out. "Come, little one. Don't be afraid."

Then she heard another sound. The flapping of many wings. Looking up, she saw a flock of the winged people. Males, all of them, their black bodies painted with bright colors.

Hunters.

They dropped down all around her, the tips of their long spears almost touching her.

One of them grabbed her arm. "Killer!" he spat, lifting a long, thin knife.

Her hands and feet bound and suspended from long ropes, Orola was carried by four of the winged men. They flew high above the ground, heading west.

The flight was short. They dropped her unceremoniously on a wide ledge, high up on the side of a cliff. She saw dark holes in the rock, probably entrances to caves.

The dwellings of the cloud people.

The one who had threatened her with the knife landed beside her and cut the ropes on her legs. "You're not going anywhere from here," he said, glaring at her.

"I have no such intentions." She returned his stare. "Not until this matter is cleared."

"There is nothing to clear. You are guilty. Answer me only this: Why did you murder them?"

Orola shook her head, getting angry. "I told you before. I did not kill them."

"The bloody sword was in your hand. The bow you used to kill an innocent child lay beside you on the ground, the arrow in the boy's chest!" the whorll shouted. "Had we not come along, you would have slain little Wa-eina."

He turned away, putting a hand over his eyes. "My daughter." With a savage cry, he grabbed her and shook her. "You murdered my woman and my son. My only son! And for that, you will die!"

"Let her go," said another voice, causing the whorll to release her.

Orola looked at the newcomer. He was old, his black skin wrinkled and his once muscular frame thin, but she saw strength and wisdom in his eyes.

She gave him a quick, thankful smile. Maybe he would listen.

"The Elders will decide her fate." He waved two strong looking males over. "Take her down to the *Resting Place* and put her into the cage."

The two grabbed the ropes and lifted her up again. They carried her down into a small valley. Orola saw water bubbling out of the ground, creating a small creek and spilling into a large pond. Shrubs and short trees grew around the creek and pond and even some grass.

Huts, built from rocks, branches, and dried grass, stood on the other side of the creek.

A number of people came to greet them when they landed. Most of them were very old, their wings drooping. A lot of them were small children. She also saw a few with only one wing or none at all.

This was the place for the old, those who couldn't fly

anymore and the very young, who still had to learn how to fly. And the crippled.

Their excited chatter stopped when they learned the reason for Orola's presence, and they threw hateful glances at her, some of them shaking angry fists. They put her inside a wooden cage that stood in the center of a cleared area.

She could have broken her bonds easily, and a wooden cage would not hold her, but she knew that these people were not evil. They were gentle and peaceful, and under different circumstances, would have offered her their hospitality.

Orola sensed the fear of a terrible threat overshadowing their existence, something that made them hostile and wary of strangers.

It was getting dark, so she settled down for the night. Before she lay down, she freed her hands. There were no ropes strong enough to keep a Moon Priestess with full powers bound.

In the morning, the sound of something rattling against the wooden bars awakened her. She opened her eyes to stare into the yellow eyes of a small group of children.

She smiled at them, but their solemn faces didn't smile back. When she stood, they retreated away from the cage. Some ran away, flapping their underdeveloped wings.

"They must take me for some kind of monster," she mumbled, combing her hair with her fingers. "I wish I had some water and a shiny surface so I could see myself. I must look awful."

When none of the children was looking, she squatted down in a corner and followed nature's call. "This is terrible. I feel like an animal."

She had almost decided to break free when she heard the flapping of wings, followed by the footsteps of a number of people approaching the cage.

Three sides of the cage were made from solid branches. Thick wooden bars closed off the front.

A group of the winged people stepped into sight, one of

them the old man she had seen on the ledge the day before. He opened the door and beckoned her to come out. She followed his order and walked out of the door, hoping that finally she would be able to explain her role in the murder of that female and her child.

They marched her to a large building. Inside, on wooden benches, sat five old men and three women. While the younger men and women had only small cloths draped around their hips, the elders wore coarse robes.

In front of the Elders lay the bow and arrow and her sword.

Orola stood in the center of the room, facing them. Her guards watched her warily from the entrance.

"Wingless One, you are accused of murdering in cold blood one of our women and her child." The speaker, an old man with one of his wings in shreds, pointed a long, bony finger at her.

Orola gave him a level stare. "I am not guilty of that crime. They were slain by one of the dragon men. When I came upon the scene, it was already too late. I fought with the killer, and after I wounded him, he fled. I tried to explain that to your hunters when they found me standing over the dead female, but they wouldn't listen."

After talking at length in hushed voices with the other Elders, the speaker turned to her again. "You say you wounded the dragon man? You...a mere woman?"

"Yes, I did."

"You are lying. The dragon people are invincible. Their armor cannot be penetrated. All the evidence is against you. You may think us barbarians. We are not, but we have no choice. We sentence you to die. You will be executed tomorrow. The manner of your death will be left to the man whose woman and son you murdered!"

Orola looked at him, not quite believing her ears. "I am Orola, a Moon Priestess. It is obvious you have never heard of my people. You shall know that I never lie, and I am quite capable of defending myself against any mortal foe. Even one of the dragon men."

The Elder just shook his head. "Please, do not take us for fools." He turned toward the guards. "Take her back to her prison!"

Orola looked at her sword, debating if she should make her break now, but decided against it. She would have to kill some of the whorll, a thing she could not do. She still believed they were not evil.

She would wait until nightfall and then escape. Too bad she would have to leave without clearing her name.

Back in the cage, she watched the whorll children at play. The older ones would flap their wings, even lift into the air for a short span, while the little ones just ran around, chasing each other.

One of the older ones took to the air, circled a few rounds, and landed beside the cage. She put her face between the bars and looked at Orola. She recognized the girl she had rescued.

"You know I didn't kill your mother," Orola said gently. "Why don't you tell them?"

The girl just looked at her for a while, and then she ran away and into the arms of a grownup...her father. The girl gestured and pointed at Orola.

He stroked her hair and said, "It's all right, Wa-eina. Tomorrow she will be punished."

The little girl banged her fists against his chest. He hugged her tightly and put her down. "Go, play. I have to speak to the Elders."

Orola watched him walk away, the tips of his great wings trailing on the ground.

Suddenly, he stopped, looked around wildly and drew his knife.

Then he stumbled away, an arrow piercing his shoulder.

She saw them then.

Dragon men.

There were only six. They strutted arrogantly into the village, carrying their large bows and long, broad-bladed knifes strapped across their huge, armored chests.

———

Orola watched in horror as they grabbed screaming children and knocked them unconscious with their bare fists. Two young women who stepped in front of the children to protect them had their throats slit by one of the dragon men.

His right arm was wrapped with ropes. She saw blood and she knew he was the one she had fought.

Before she could act, he glanced toward the cage. A huge grin spread over his scaly face. "I told you we'd meet again," he roared and charged the cage.

With one mighty swipe of his good left arm, he smashed the wooden bars and reached for her.

Orola stepped back, but not fast enough. His clawed hand hooked the leather strap that held the jewel and ripped it off her neck. She clutched at the empty spot between her breasts, feeling her powers already ebbing away. Falling into a fighting stance, she brought up her right foot and kicked her attacker in the face.

With an angry bellow, he swung his fist and knocked her on the side of the head. Stunned, she lost her balance and fell. He pounced on her and put his blade to her throat, but then he seemed to change his mind, sheathed his knife, and pulled her up by her hair.

"Our god will be pleased," he said, pushing her out of the cage.

They bound and tossed her to the ground like a captured treegoat.

Helplessly, she had to watch the winged people fall from the sky, their chests or wings pierced by arrows.

The winged warriors finally gave up and flew back to the safety of their caves high up on the cliffs. It was an uneven battle.

Their spears could not penetrate the heavy armor of the dragon men.

The old people wailed and hid in their huts, watching the reptilians toss some of the dead and wounded and a few children on top of their mounts.

They draped Orola across the broad neck of one of the giant lizards. The rider, who sat behind her, gave her an ugly grin. She closed her eyes, tried to reach her god but could not feel his powerful presence. Without the jewel, she was cut off the communications grid. Without the *Holy Communicator*, she was alone…and scared.

The lizards moved easily across the rocky ground. They traveled east, toward the swamps on the other side of the mountains.

Orola was surprised to find them this deep in the mountains, so far away from their homes.

By late evening, they rode into a deep canyon, which seemed to be their destination. The walls were pockmarked with large holes leading into the cavern inside the mountain.

She saw one gaping hole in the ground from which a red glow radiated, lighting up the immediate area around it.

The captives and the dead were taken into one of the caves, through dark tunnels lit up by torches in the walls, down rough-hewn steps into a larger cavern. Others of the dragon people came to meet them, three females and a number of young ones. The young reptilians hissed excitedly when they saw the slain whorll. One of the adults spoke in a hissing, guttural language, and they began dragging the carcasses away.

They dumped Orola and the living whorll into a small, dark cave, removed their bindings, and allowed them to walk around freely in the cave. Two of the dragon men stayed to guard them; the others left.

Tired and weak, Orola slid to the ground and relaxed, her back against the damp wall. Having had nothing to eat and drink since the day before, a gnawing hunger ate at her stomach.

"I am sorry I brought you into this," a weak voice said beside her. She looked at the winged man who had spoken, recognizing him. Even though there was not much light in the cave, her ability to see in the dark showed her the suffering he endured. His shoulder wound was still trickling blood, and his face looked gray. She could tell he was dying.

She reached out to touch his hand. "You did what you thought was right. I don't blame you."

"I should have believed you," he protested. "I should have listened to my daughter. She was trying to tell me, but I was too angry in my grief." He stopped, coughed. "I saw the wound on the prince's arm. You must have fought him well. Too bad you did not kill him."

"Yes, that is too bad." She smiled. "I tried my best. Tell me, for how long have you been fighting these dragon men?"

"We have no quarrel with them, and we can't fight them. The cycle of seasons has not been completed yet since they raided us the first time. Since then they've come many times, killing and capturing our people. Usually, they take only a few, but this time they took many."

"Why do they hunt you?"

"You ask me why?" The winged man tried to laugh. Wincing from the pain it caused him, he winced. "We are meat to them."

"I should have guessed." Orola sat quietly, hugging her knees to her bare breasts. "I wish I had my cape," she said after a while. "It is chilly and damp in here." She remembered the caves of the Dorbs, those ugly little people, and the battle when she and Captain Horgan had killed half the tribe. She had been lucky then, because the Dorbs were stupid, but now her luck seemed to have run out.

She was alone, her link to her god severed by the loss of her jewel, and no hope of ever getting it back.

Relaxing, she meditated and prayed, but there was no answering surge of power.

Her thoughts wandered to Kicki, and she was glad the young girl stayed behind in the castle. Lady Geisa would take good care of her until she joined the caravan that would take her home.

Orola tried to sleep. She managed to doze for a short time, but the loud moaning of the wounded kept waking her up. The man beside her lay in an uneasy slumber, his eyes closed, his breathing rapid and rattling in his throat and his body shaken by shivers. His wound had stopped bleeding. Maybe he'd be lucky, but it didn't really matter.

They were all dead anyway.

She felt so helpless. She could do nothing for him.

When morning came, one of the wounded had died from his injuries. The other four sat with their leathery wings curled around them, staring into empty space.

The stench of blood and feces was strong in the confinement of the cave.

Orola stood up when she heard the sounds of clawed feet on the stony floor.

They were coming.

"Hear us, Great Nameless One. Hear your children. Enjoy the offering we bring you. A few morsels to fill your never-ending appetite."

Orola watched in fascination as the dragon men threw the bodies of the dead winged people into the moving tendrils of the giant Koldra. The mass of tendrils wrapped around the bodies and pulled them into the gaping maw.

She had recognized the Koldra immediately when they had entered the pit through one of the tunnels.

It was an enormous meat-eating, half-sentient plant. She had seen its smaller cousins many times. Something in the crater must have stimulated this plant to grow to such immense proportions.

It was hot and humid in the pit. The plant grew around a

deep hole from which a red glow threw an eerie light against the walls of the crater. She had seen the red glow from above when they arrived the night before, and she knew there was fiery liquid far below.

She lay naked and spread-eagled on top of a stone slab. A living sacrifice for their god. After tying her down, they forced a strong tasting liquid down her throat, which made her feel light-headed and strange.

***

She awoke to discover that she was lying stark naked on a cold, smooth stone surface. When she tried to sit up, stabs of pain shot through her body and she sank back. Her whole body felt sore and a terrible pain left her weak and sick.

She didn't know how long she had slept, but it was dark above—only the crater was lit up by the red glow from the pit. The Koldra lay in silence; just the tips of its tendrils weaved slowly as if moved by a soft breeze.

A fluttering noise from above made Orola crane her neck to look into the night sky. In the dim light of the two visible moons, she saw the silhouette of a small, winged figure dropping into the crater. Circling slowly, whoever it was had seen Orola and headed straight for her, landing moments later beside her.

"Wa-eina," Orola exclaimed, her hand reaching for the small-winged girl.

The girl grabbed her hand and put something into it. Sobbing with pleasure, Orola's hand closed over the precious item. Then she laid it between her breasts and closed her eyes.

The jewel seemed like a conflagration on her naked skin as she made contact with her god. Healing power surged through her, removing the pain, lending her tired limbs and body the strength she needed to escape her captivity.

She lay for a long time, absorbing the much-needed energy. When the pain was gone, she opened her eyes and sat up.

The little girl had been watching her silently, and when Orola sat up, she smiled and held up the other item she had been carrying.

Her sword.

Orola slid off the stone and hugged the little girl. "How did you know where to find me?" she asked.

Wa-eina shook her head and pointed to her throat. Orola saw the deep scars and understood.

The little girl couldn't talk. That's why she couldn't tell them about Orola's innocence.

She stroked the girl's hair. "Listen, Wa-eina. I am still a little weak, and I will need much more time to get back my full strength. You'd better fly up and hide until tomorrow. I will try to get your father out of here."

The girl nodded and took to the air. Orola watched her as she disappeared through the crater entrance.

What a brave little girl! It must have taken a lot of courage to fly through the mountains, following the dragon men, always staying out of sight.

The most astounding thing was the fact that she had the intuition to bring the jewel and the sword!

Orola moved into the shadows and lay down. Closing her eyes, she went into a deep trance. What she had to do in the morning required more strength than she had ever needed before. She meditated and prayed until morning, absorbing and storing as much energy as she possibly could.

When the first rays of the sun strayed into the crater, she was ready.

She stood, filled with the power of Solar, and walked confidently toward the altar and lay down to wait.

The jewel lay warm on her chest, glowing with a soft, red fire. Her sword lay beside her, the jeweled hilt resting easy in her right hand.

She sensed the dragon men coming toward her, and when

they were close, she stood up slowly and looked at them with luminous eyes.

"You have violated a priestess of the god Solar," she said with a loud, clear voice, pointing an accusing finger at them. "Now you must answer for that!"

The giant leaves of the Koldra had opened at the break of day, and the huge maw was opening and closing slowly, waiting to be fed during the dragon people's sacrificial ceremony. Creepers and moving tendrils began to spread all over the rocky floor of the pit.

Orola estimated close to a hundred dragon people had assembled to witness the ceremony. She smiled without humor.

There would be a great sacrifice today, but not the one they had been expecting.

"Oh, great peril!" cried an old male, his gray crest drooping and his scales covered with scars. "She is a Moon Priestess from the Island of the Witches. A demon with terrible powers. Powers as great as our ancient enemy possessed. We are doomed!"

"Nonsense, Old One. She is only a puny human," bellowed the warrior she had wounded.

"No, no, you are wrong," wailed the old male. "She is not human. She only appears to be. I have heard stories…"

"Ah, stories!" laughed the young warrior. He drew his broad blade and pushed through the parting crowd. "I have fought her before. Watch me dispatch her."

Orola jumped off the altar to meet him. The other dragon people backed away hastily, creating an empty space in front of the huge block of stone.

The young reptilian stepped forward confidently. He carried the blade in his left hand, but his right arm was without a bandage.

He grinned. "It will give me great pleasure to slay you, Witch! Even your trickery will not help you now."

He lunged for her, his broad blade flashing, but she easily

stepped to one side and parried his thrust. With his long arms, he had a greater reach than she and he was very fast, but she kept him at bay, playing with him. She had wounded him once, and she knew he was not invincible, as he so falsely believed. This time, her strength was double that of the last time they had done battle.

The clashing of their swords echoed from the high walls of the crater. His broad blade had been fashioned by master artisans in the smelters of Rahoz. Orola recognized the great workmanship.

Her own sword had been handed down to her through generations. Only members of the warrior cast received them. Made by the Ancients so long ago from an alloy unknown to anyone in the present, it was superior to even the excellent steel they used in Rahoz. Her sword's ability to change shape at her command was more proof of the knowledge and powers the Ancients possessed.

She pivoted to meet another one of his attacks, dropped to the ground, somersaulted past him, turned and kicked him in the head from the back.

He swiveled around, hissing and spitting angrily, lashing out with his clawed foot. Just out of reach, she grabbed his foot and heaved. Caught off balance, he crashed heavily to the ground, hitting his head on the hard rocks.

Receiving her silent command, her sword changed shape, became a whip, and with a flip of her wrist, she sent the lash around his sword, pulling it out of his hand.

He came up roaring, his clawed hands opening and closing as he advanced. "You've made me angry, Witch! I am through playing."

She saw the touch of respect and fear in his eyes. Laughing, she cracked her whip, flicking it across his face. Enraged, he charged her, but she moved like the wind, always a step ahead of him, her whip lashing at his body.

Finally, she grew tired of the game. Shortening the whip and metamorphosing it into a short sharp-bladed knife, she stepped into his embrace. With a savage thrust, she pushed the keen blade into his eye, driving it deep into his brain.

Before his massive arms could close around her with a deadly lock, she slipped out of their embrace and stepped back.

His heavy body slumped to the ground. He was dead; his heart still, while only his arms and legs still twitched.

She bent over him and grabbed the jeweled hilt of her knife. It changed as she pulled it out of his head, became a slender sword.

"Your prince is dead," she announced, the naked, bloody sword in her hand.

―――――――

She stood proud and erect, her long legs spread slightly apart. Her long black hair spilled over her shoulders, down her chest, partially covering her thrusting breasts. Breathing more rapidly than usual, the muscles of her flat belly rippling, she was suddenly bathed in the bright rays of the sun creeping over the crater.

To watching humans, she might have looked like a sensual warrior goddess, but to the dragon people she presented a terrifying figure.

Screaming and hissing, they tried to back away from the terrible angel of death.

"Stop!" she called with a ringing voice. "My wrath has just begun!"

―――――――

The giant Koldra seemed to sense what was going to happen. Its huge leaves twitched, and the mass of tendrils whipped back and forth.

Orola pointed her sword. "Look at your god! It's only a plant, nothing more. All it does is eat and eat. The god Solar is very angry to find you worshipping a plant. He is also angry that you have been murdering the whorll, a race of gentle people who have done nothing to provoke you. To show you the powers of my god, there will be a lesson!"

Her head thrown back, she lifted her arms. In the zenith, the largest moon Solar was still visible, even with the bright sun moving up into the sky.

"Hear me, oh Great Computer," she called above the hissing and screaming crowd. "Justice must be done. Show your mighty powers. Show your terrible anger." To evoke the awesome powers of the god Solar was nothing to be taken lightly. Only extreme conditions warranted her doing so, but she felt it was necessary now.

Looking at the living plant, she uttered the sacred ancient words. *Target within vision. Fifty-five meters. Activate lasers...now. Destruct!*

For a long time, nothing happened. Then suddenly, the very air seemed to come alive, crackling and spitting millions of exploding sparks. The acrid stench of burning plant fibers filled the crater.

Where the main body of the giant Koldra had been, nothing remained but an ugly black hole.

"Mighty is the Great Moon god Solar," Orola cried, arms lifted, her naked body bathed by the light of the sun. The powers she commanded elated her, and when the gaze of her burning eyes swept the horrified dragon people, they sank to the ground, begging for mercy.

"No more shall you kill any of the cloud people," she commanded them. "You shall leave these mountains and go back to your swamplands, never to return!"

Tired and ready to move on, she jumped off the altar. She walked over to one of the cowering dragon females and said, "Take me to the prisoners." Following the old female, she was close to collapsing. *I have to get some food. I've burned up all of my energy.* "I need my clothing," she told the female. "And food."

The old one nodded and took her to a cave they used for storage. After putting on her kilt, she wolfed down the strips of dried meat the dragon woman gave her. While she ate, she relaxed as much as possible and made contact with her god. Slowly, her body recovered some of her strength. It would have to do until she could take a good rest.

Arriving in the cave where the captives were held, she found Waeina's father unconscious, but still alive.

"Go!" she told the female. "Leave us alone."

She squatted down beside the whorll man and ran her hands over his body, her mind in contact with Solar. She put one hand on his wound and the other on his forehead. A slight tingling in her fingertips told her that the unconscious man accepted the power of healing.

He lay propped up against a wall in an awkward position. Pulling him away from the wall, she laid him on his back, taking care not to damage his wings. Then she removed her kilt and lay on top of him. Cradling him in her arms, she pressed her lips on his mouth.

Having achieved maximum physical contact with his body, she began the healing.

Her concentration on the man under her, she heard the surprised exclamations of the other four captives, but she had no time for explaining her actions.

Her soft breasts pressing into his chest, the jewel between them sent waves of pulsating heat through her body into his, wherever their skin made contact. Waves of heat and healing.

The greatest concentration of transfer, however, occurred where their bodies were joined. The last thing on her mind had been to have sexual intercourse with a mortally wounded man, but this was the fastest way to speed up his healing.

She could feel his body responding. His hips lifted slightly off the ground to thrust deeper into her.

Then he opened his eyes, and his body stiffened. He tried to push her off, but she held him down. Removing her lips from his, she said gently, "This is not exactly what it appears to be."

"What are you doing?" he blurted. "Has captivity clouded your mind that you must rape a dying man?"

"You are not dying," she said and smiled. Snapping her hips, she milked him softly.

"I feel so strange," he moaned. "I know this is wrong, the position is wrong, but I can't help myself. The pleasure is nearly unbearable."

"Don't worry about it," she told him, kissing him deeply. "I like to finish what I started." When it was over, she rolled off him.

He sat up, touching his wound. "I don't quite understand what has transpired here, but I am healed," he said, shaking his head.

Spreading his leathery wings, he stretched and reached toward the ceiling. "What did you do to me?" he asked. "I feel so elated."

"I shared something with you that few men have the privilege of receiving," she said. She dressed and turned to the other prisoners.

"You are free," she told them. "The dragon people will bother you no more."

The whorll had accompanied her to the outskirts of the mountains and shown her a safe way out. She had found the banter close to the place where she had been captured. She planned to reach the small lake before nightfall, camp there, then follow the river north to Gmaly.

Watching the winged people disappear into the clouds, Orola clucked her tongue and turned her steed toward north.

REVELATION

Solar, the largest of the three visible moons, hung low in the night sky, its weak green light almost non-existent beneath the tall Kappa-trees. A lone traveler riding a black-skinned beast moved silently along the narrow trail that wound its way through the jungle.

The beast suddenly lifted its scaly head and hissed softly.

"Hush." The rider patted the steed's flanks. "You're trying to tell me we're not alone, but I know that already."

The road ended abruptly; high walls loomed darkly against the sky.

"Stop right there," a voice sounded from the shadows.

From a niche in the wall, a helmeted guard stepped into the rider's path, a long spear pointing threateningly. "Who are you, and what is your purpose?" he demanded with a harsh voice.

"If I didn't lose my way, then this must be Guata. I seek audience with the queen. If this isn't Guata, then I ask for shelter to spend the night. The insects are killing me."

The man with the spear uttered a sound of surprise. "By the wizard's tail!" he exclaimed, "You sound like..." He turned and spoke to someone behind him, "Bring me a light."

Another guard came out of the wall, carrying a lantern. He lifted it to shine into the traveler's face.

"I knew it," said the first one, a wide grin spreading across his unshaven face. "A girl."

His companion laughed and moved the lantern up and down. "A gift from the jungle demons to play with. She can't be real. No sane woman would dress like a warrior and go riding alone at night in the jungle." He grabbed her naked thigh and squeezed it. "She's real." Grinning, he tried to pull her off her steed.

The girl lashed out with her booted foot and kicked him below the ribs. "Take your paws off me, you clumsy *gurs*," she hissed, her eyes flashing angrily. "I feel filthy enough from the dust and my own sweat. I don't need to wallow in the dirt under your stinking body."

"She's got the fire of a hell-dragon," laughed the sentry with the spear.

"And she kicks like a neutered banter," the other guard cursed, clutching his chest.

The girl slid off her mount and stepped back carefully. She carried her slim, lithe body proudly and stood nearly as tall as the two men. The warrior's kilt around her hips barely covered her buttocks and exposed long, smooth, yet muscular legs.

The helmeted sentry pointed his spear at her full, high breasts. Her cape had fallen open, exposing them to his view. Breast cups, held together in the front by leather straps, didn't do much to hide their size. His eyes lingered for a moment on her breasts and on the large, red crystal nestled between them, and then they dropped to the slender sword at her hip.

She pulled the cape close. Fully aware of the impact she had on the men, she gave them an ironic smile. "Did you see enough?"

"Not really." Grinning, the guard reached for her.

With a swift movement, the girl whipped out her sword. It sang as it came free from its sheath; the red crystal in its hilt

202

glowed with a bright fire. Pushing the quivering tip into the sentry's throat, she smiled sweetly and said with a demanding voice, "Will I see the queen now, or do I let my sword drink your blood?"

"The queen is dead," the guard blurted out, surprised by the girl's speed.

His companion, still holding his chest, made no attempt to help him. "She's a demon," he murmured. "No mortal moves that fast."

"The queen is dead?" repeated the girl, not believing. "When?"

Before the man could answer, another guard stepped out of the narrow gate in the wall. "What goes on here?" he demanded.

"Someone to see the queen," the helmeted guard answered.

The newcomer looked at the girl for an instant. Then he nodded. "Put down your weapon and come with me."

Without so much as a backward glance, she followed him through the gate.

Her steed disappeared silently into the darkness of the jungle.

They walked silently down the narrow, unpaved street. The low houses on each side were strangely quiet, the windows dark holes in the wooden walls. Only the three moons above created eerie triple shadows on the trampled dirt.

The girl shivered inside her cape, and it was not the chill in the air that caused it. She wondered why she had this feeling of dread.

The windows should be lit. She should be hearing the sound of laughter coming through open doors. There should be people on the street.

Guata was the capital of Mirr, a small country north of

Virgoss and east of Sabatorra. Lake Gmaly bordered it to the south, and the north consisted of unexplored deep jungle.

About three thousand inhabitants called Guata home, most of them hunters and fishermen. Fish were plentiful in the river Gris, which ran through the town, and there was an abundance of game in the lush valleys to the south of the capital.

She knew of a few smaller settlements throughout Mirr, but most of the people preferred the safety of a larger town, because of the tribes of wild men coming out of the jungle occasionally, killing, looting and kidnapping young girls.

Guata was protected against these wild men by a high wall that surrounded the whole town.

"What is your name?" her guide asked suddenly, breaking the silence.

"Orola," the girl answered.

"Orola?" the guide repeated. "We do not get many travelers, so we are not prepared to host anyone. You must be tired."

"I am," Orola agreed. "I have come a long way to see the queen."

"The queen is dead, but we have a king now. He will be interested in listening to your stories from far places, but he…" He hesitated and stopped abruptly.

The feeling of dread inside her became stronger. The red crystal between her breasts pulsed softly, alerting her senses. "What about the king?" she asked.

"Nothing," the guide said, his voice now emotionless.

When he looked at her, she noticed his young face.

"You're beautiful," he said gravely. "Be careful." His voice carried a clear warning.

"Be careful of what?"

He stayed silent, began walking again. They came to another gate. Beyond it, she could see a well-lit courtyard, at the end a large structure. The palace.

A guard stepped out of a small tower beside the gate. "This is Orola, a traveler," her guide said. "She wants to see the king."

The guard looked her up and down; his eyes lingered on her smooth, naked legs. Then he grinned. "Go in."

"This is where we part," her guide said. He pointed at the large carved door leading into the palace. "Just climb up those steps and walk right in." He turned and walked away.

"What is your name?" Orola called after him.

He turned and gave her a tight smile. "Should we meet again, I am Bran."

Orola crossed the courtyard with long, sure strides, well aware of the guard's leering stare on her backside. Being female did have certain advantages. Most men were fools; they usually tended to underestimate her. She kept her body trim and firm; her female attributes were more than generous, and she used them shamelessly.

When she reached the top of the stairs, she stood for a moment in front of the huge double doors, studying the crude carvings in the woodwork. Then she looked up at the large moon Solar and touched the star-crystal between her breasts. Her thoughts linked with the passive presence of *Communicator*, and she sent a silent prayer to the moon-god in the ancient tongue.

"Oh, Central Computer, God of the Ancients, much danger lies behind these doors. Give me strength and speed and endurance so I may defeat my enemies and speak of your Glory."

She felt the power flowing through her body and knew her prayer had been answered. *He* was always there.

With one powerful arm, she pushed open the door and walked boldly past the two guards standing on either side of the doorway. Her cool gaze swept across the court as she walked toward the center of the huge room.

Soldiers and noblemen with their ladies, as well as a few peasants were eating, drinking and shouting. All seemed to be in good spirits, but Orola sensed the unease beneath the noisy merriment. Something gloomy and sinister.

The king sat on a throne made from stone, or rather he sprawled on top of the pillows covering the throne.

He was fat and ugly, with a large bald head. A group of plump, young men with painted lips and eyes, dressed in colorful clothes, sat at the foot of the throne, laughing and giggling.

Looking around, Orola saw a small pond close to the throne. Inside it sat a creature, its upper body above the water. Orola recognized the species. One of the sea-people who lived in the ocean south of Cish. A young female, her breasts shapely but small.

Orola felt the searching tendrils of a mind touch and, looking into the large black eyes that looked out of the fine elfin face of the seagirl, she acknowledged the girl.

Beware, stranger, whispered the silent voice. *There is much evil here.* As quickly as the contact came, it broke off.

A hand closed on Orola's breast and a hairy arm closed around Orola's breasts from behind.

The alcohol-reeking breath caught in the man's throat before he could utter any suggestions, when she jabbed her elbow sharply into his belly. Then she whirled and kicked him in the face with her booted foot.

The man, a big brute with a large eye patch covering part of his bearded face, staggered back and shook his shaggy head. "You filthy little *She-Thirp!*" he roared, trying to grab her again, but a sharp voice stopped him.

"Leave her be!"

Her would-be assailant glared at the speaker. Then he growled and turned away.

Orola looked at her rescuer, not quite sure if she had made a better trade. He was bigger than the other man, disfigured by a large scar running across the right side of a face that had never been handsome.

His grin was huge as he touched his left breast in a mock salute. "Welcome to our fair city, wary traveler. Let me introduce you to my king. I am Nargos, Captain of the Royal Guards."

Orola decided she didn't like him. Even without touching his mind, she knew he was not to be trusted.

As they approached the throne, the king looked at them sleepily. His fat lips formed a smile, and he beckoned her to come closer. "A visitor. How delightful," he boomed in a surprisingly strong voice. "And at such a late hour. You must be absolutely fatigued."

"You are correct. I am quite tired, my lord." Orola studied the man who called himself King. She wished she could read his mind, but since she was not a natural telepath, like the sea people, she could not enter another mind. She could only sense emotions and hear other minds, but not read thoughts.

"What brings you to this part of the world, so far from what your people call civilization?"

Orola watched him closely when she answered. "I seek one of my sisters. She was an advisor to the former queen. I am surprised to find a king in the queen's place." Her voice had taken on a slight edge when she spoke, and she sensed the captain of the guards start moving toward her.

"Mind your voice when you speak to the king," he said sharply.

The king smiled and lifted a pudgy hand. "It is all right, Captain Nargos. She is young and full of courage, and I forgive her. One might say she is very beautiful, but then…" With a tender smile, he looked affectionately at the young men with their painted faces, "…my tastes are somewhat different." He bent down and tickled one under the chin.

Turning his attention back to the girl, he said, "Tell me, where are you from?"

"My home is on the island Antanakka," Orola said, waiting for the king's reaction.

"Ah, the Island of the Witches." The King nodded. "Then you're a witch, but why the sword? I understood you people are peaceful."

"There exists the secret cast of the Moon Priestesses, my lord," said a man in a dark cloak.

The king's sorcerer.

"They are said to be fierce and dangerous warriors," the sorcerer continued. "Supposedly, they possess strange powers and are as strong as ten ordinary men."

"She doesn't look very dangerous to me," laughed Nargos. He put down the large pitcher he had been drinking from and wiped his mouth with a hairy hand. "I claim this wench," he roared drunkenly. "I'll teach her some fierce tricks of my own."

Orola sighed. Her first impression of the man had proved correct. She touched the hilt of her sword.

The captain laughed and pulled out his own. "The wench wants to play. This should be interesting. Let's see how good you are with that toy."

"I am not in the mood for games," Orola said loudly.

"This is no game." He staggered forward.

Orola lifted her sword from its jeweled sheath. It sang with a chiming sound as it was freed. Shimmering brightly, it lengthened and changed into a whip. With a loud crack, it wrapped around the captain's sword hand, pulling the sword from his grasp.

As it clattered to the ground, Orola let the tip of her whip flicker across the big man's forehead, drawing a trickle of blood.

Nargos roared angrily and charged her. The whip shortened, became a club and when he was close, Orola moved slightly, lifted the club and brought it down sharply behind the man's ear, felling him like a tree. Without a sound, the big man collapsed on the floor.

The club changed back into a slender sword, and she slid it back into its resting place. She was still smiling, but her cat-like eyes glowed as brightly as the jewel in the sword hilt.

The spectators who had witnessed this let out gasping sounds. "Magic. Witch," they whispered.

"Nonsense!" the sorcerer said with a loud voice. "There is no magic. Just cheap tricks." He stepped forward, bowing to the king. "My lord, may I show you some of my magic?"

"Yes, yes." The king waved a hand. "I have seen your so-called magic too many times already, but if you must satisfy your ego…go ahead."

"Thank you, my lord." The sorcerer bowed again, and then he performed a few simple tricks, but didn't inspire much enthusiasm from the watching crowd.

Then, with a malicious smile, he stepped toward Orola, reached under her kilt and seemingly pulled out a long, writhing object.

"Look at what the witch hides between her legs," he called out triumphantly, holding it between his thumb and finger. "A swamp viper. Its bite fatal almost instantly. One never knows what one finds under a female's skirt."

Some of the people laughed. The closest ones pulled back in horror.

With a flick of his hand, he threw the serpent toward Orola. It landed in front of her, hissing and striking immediately.

Her hand became a blur as she snatched the sword from her side, but none of the watchers' eyes could follow her movements any further. One moment the deadly viper struck at the girl's legs, the next its severed head flew through the air, landing at the sorcerer's feet, jaws still snapping angrily and dripping venom.

The sword was back in its sheath as Orola stood smiling confidently, arms crossed in front of her chest.

"This confirms it. She is a Moon Priestess," the sorcerer said to the king. "I know of no other mortal creature that can move so fast." He bent down and whispered something into the king's ears.

The king nodded slowly. Clapping his hands together, he called to one of the serving girls. "Bring Royal Wine for our distinguished guest." Turning to Orola, he said, "Please, join my people in their celebration and accept a cup of my finest wine."

Orola took the cup from the girl and nodded toward the

king. "Thank you, my lord, but you haven't answered my question. What happened to the queen?"

The king stared at her for a moment. Then he sighed and rolled his eyes upward, apparently bored with this whole thing. "You are an impertinent creature, but to answer your question, our beloved queen died of some unknown disease. Since there was no one here to take her place, I graciously gave my services to these wonderful people of Mirr, who have taken me into their midst and into their hearts."

"What about her advisor, the woman I'm seeking? My sister."

"I don't know anything about her whereabouts." The king shrugged. "She left before the queen died."

Orola knew he was lying. She had seen the jeweled ring on his left finger. The ring with its star crystal, the ring that her sister wore. Without it on her body, her sister was powerless, the link between her and the mind-net severed.

The king turned away, his interest in her gone. "All this excitement has made me tired." He waved to one of the young men at his feet. "Bring the sea girl to my quarters. I'll need her services tonight."

The presence of the sea girl had puzzled her at first, but no longer. The sea people raised their young by carrying their eggs in their mouths until the tiny young hatched, usually just one, but occasionally two or even three.

The mouth of a female could stretch considerably to accommodate the growing offspring. Since the eggs and young had to be kept from getting diseased while inside the cavity of the mouth, the tongue of a female was in constant motion to keep the water inside germfree.

Because of the mobility of their tongues, certain males of the land-based species searched out the females of the sea people.

Orola felt suddenly tired and sleepy. The day's travel and her exertions in the king's court finally caught up with Orola; weariness crept over her like night over the land. She called to the serving girl who had brought the wine, "Tell me, is there a place here where I can rest? It's been a long, hot day, and I am quite exhausted."

The girl, a young thing dressed in a flimsy, almost transparent garment that revealed more than hid, grabbed her hand and pulled her through the crowd. "Come, follow me. You can sleep in my bed. I'll be busy in here for the rest of the night."

Orola let herself be dragged through bare corridors, until they finally stopped in front of a wooden door. The girl fumbled with a key, and when the door opened, she pushed Orola through and whispered, "You should be safe in here. Lock the door behind you. Don't open to anyone but me."

Something inside her screamed *Wake up, Wake up*, but she couldn't clear the fog from her brain. She tried to move, push the weight from her body, but she felt so sluggish.

Drugged. The wine must have been drugged.

She opened her eyes and stared into the scarred, ugly face of Nargos, the captain of the royal guards who perched over her body, prepared to enter her. When he saw her open eyes, he grinned, exposing large stained teeth.

"So, you're awake, witch," he said hoarsely.

His hot, fetid breath washed over her, and she almost gagged. She tried to move her arms, but couldn't. Something pinned her against the floor. Then she saw the two grinning faces on either side of her.

One of them wore an eye patch.

"Hurry up, Nargos," the one-eyed one said.

"Yes," said the other one, his breathing coming fast. "I can't wait much longer."

"Shut up, both of you!" roared the captain. "She is mine."

Orola tried to sit up, but the captain's weight held her prisoner. She looked past him to her sword standing in the corner. The jewel in its hilt was dull. She tried to contact it with her mind, but she encountered only emptiness.

When she saw the red pendant around the neck of the man with the eye patch, she knew the reason.

The star-crystal. They had taken the *Holy Communicator* from her. Once again, she was powerless.

However, she knew her time would come. So she waited and let her mind wander; what happened to her body did not matter. She only needed a few more minutes to entice eye-patch man to come to her.

Finally, she held out her arms and shot him a hot look when he came to her. "Let me feel your naked, muscular chest against my breasts."

He released his grip on her and, slowly, she gathered him into her arms, pulling him toward her. As his chest touched her body, the crystal fell between her naked breasts.

When the familiar vibrations of the star-crystal surged through her body, she lay unmoving for a few seconds. She almost sobbed, relishing the build-up of power inside her.

Before the man could spill his seed into her, she made her move. Her mind reached out, made contact and the sword was in her hand, except a sword no longer. It had changed into a short and keen-edged blade.

She slit his throat from ear to ear, felt his blood gushing all over her breasts. She pulled the star-crystal over his head and heaved. His body flew through the air and crashed into Nargos.

Her silent command changed the knife back into a sword, and with one fluid motion, she whipped it sideways, slicing through the thick neck of the other guard. The man's heavy body toppled slowly to the ground and the bearded head rolled into the corner.

Then she spun around to face the captain. His ugly face contorted, showing hate and fear, but mostly surprise. She had moved so fast, he probably still couldn't fully comprehend what had transpired.

She pointed the tip of her sword at his heart, her white teeth flashing in her bloodstained face.

"Take a good look, Captain Nargos," she said, thrusting her blood covered breasts toward him. She could feel the blood running down her belly.

He cursed hoarsely, staring at her nude body. "You are not human. You are a witch!"

She laughed. "Maybe so, but I'm all woman. We are trained in many things. Killing is only one of them. If you had been different, I would have given free what you wanted to take by force. But now you will never find out what you've missed."

With a roar, he threw himself forward. Without moving the sword, she ran it right through him. His eyes stared unbelieving at the hilt in his chest, and then with a great sigh, his big hairy body slumped to the floor.

He was dead before he fell.

Orola wiped the blood from her sword and looked down at her blood-spattered body. In the sudden silence, she heard a soft whimper. It came from a small niche in the wall. With her sword drawn, she walked toward the sound and stared at the nude form of the serving girl huddling in the corner.

"Please, don't kill me," the girl pleaded, tears rolling down her face. "They forced me to do it. They are animals."

"They are dead now and will never hurt you again." Orola held out a hand to the terrified girl and pulled her up. "Don't be afraid," she said, smiling gently. "I won't harm you."

She looked around the room at the dead bodies and the blood on the furs. "Sorry about the mess. I'll help you clean up."

The girl started sobbing uncontrollably and wrapped her arms around Orola. "This is a terrible place," she said between sobs. "I wish I could leave. Ever since our queen was imprisoned, we have been living in a nightmare."

Orola stroked the girl's soft black hair and made crooning

sounds. "Maybe things will change again." Then she stopped abruptly. "Did you say *imprisoned*? I was told the queen is dead."

"No, no." The girl brushed the tears from her face. "Everyone believes the queen is dead, but I know different. She is in the caves beneath the palace, chained to a wall like an animal and treated like a…"

She put her face between her hands. "The king is mad, you know. I've heard rumors. He has a son, who must be the spawn of one of his strange couplings. He lives down in the caves, guarding the prisoners. The king gave him the queen as a present, to do with as he pleases."

"I don't even know your name," Orola said as she finished drying off with the small towel the girl had given her.

"I am sorry." The girl gave her an apologizing smile. "How ignorant of me. I am Mirki." She held up her torn garment. "Look at this. It is ruined beyond repair." She threw it into a corner.

A sharp knock against the door made both look at each other. Orola picked up her sword, but Mirki held her back. "That's probably my brother."

"Mirki?" a voice called softly. "Are you in there?"

The girl rushed to the door and opened it quickly. "Come in, Bran," she said and pulled him in, locking the door behind him.

The young man stopped short when he saw Orola standing in the middle of the room, her hand on the sword. His bright blue eyes brightened when he looked over her nude body, and then he grinned, his eyes still staring at her ripe breasts. "Well, well. Is this an invitation to a party?"

Orola looked at the young man, making no move to cover herself. She had never bothered with modesty. "It could have been under different circumstances." She smiled warmly, because under his jesting tone, she had detected great concern.

Bran looked at his sister, serious now, noticing the bruises on her body. "What happened to you, Mirki?"

She pointed toward the corner. Bran stared at the bloody furs, and then he saw the corpses. He nodded, but stayed silent. When he looked back at Orola, his eyes bore a strange expression. "I am glad to see you unharmed," he said slowly. "I pitied you when you walked into the palace, but I can see it was unfounded. You know how to protect yourself."

He gave the body of Nargos a vicious kick. "Many times I swore I would kill him for what he did to my sister, and I can't say I am sorry that he is dead, but you are in great danger now. He has many friends."

"I came here expecting trouble. This is only the beginning. Mirki tells me the queen is imprisoned in the dungeons below the palace. What do you know about it?"

Bran threw a quick glance at his sister. "It is only a rumor," he said, hesitating. "Nobody knows for certain."

"I know because I've seen her," Mirki said hotly, "but you never believe anything I tell you." She burst into tears.

The young man pulled her close and held her tightly, stroking her back. Then he lifted her face and kissed her gently on the forehead. "Don't cry, little sister. I believe you, but you must admit, sometimes your imagination runs wild, like when you told me the king has a son who is half animal."

The girl pushed him away angrily. "Even that is true, Bran. I've seen that monster when he assaulted the queen. I can still hear her screams."

Bran looked at Orola with an apologetic expression. "I know that the king is somewhat...ah...peculiar, but I can't believe many of the things they say about him. Men like Nargos make life miserable for us."

"Nargos, pah!" His sister spat at the mention of the captain's name. "He was one of the men who came with the king. So how can the king be different?"

Orola held up her hand. "Please, don't argue. From what I've seen, things don't seem quite right here. For one thing, I know the king lied when he said he had never heard of my sister, who was advisor to the queen. I am inclined to believe Mirki if she says the queen still lives. Because, if the queen is alive, there is a good chance my sister might also be alive."

The two prison guards leered at Orola. One of them pulled down her breast cup and fondled her breast. His fingers dug into the soft flesh, kneading it and then squeezing the nipple. "You are certain you don't need help with this prisoner?" he asked.

Bran grinned and pulled on the chain that was attached to the collar around Orola's neck. "When I need your help, I'll call you." He turned toward Mirki who stood behind him, carrying a pail filled with water and a large bundle. "Come on, come on. I don't have all day." They walked down the dark stairs that led into the caves.

As soon as they were at the bottom of the stairs, Bran produced a key and unlocked the collar. "That part was easy, but how are we going to get you out again?"

"Let us not worry about that now." Orola took the bundle from Mirki's hands and unwrapped her sword. Mirki pulled her cloak closer around her slim shoulders. "It stinks down here, and it is cold," she complained, shivering.

They started walking down the long tunnel. The walls were covered with a moist film of condensation, and the air was filled with a musty smell. The torches on the rough walls sputtered as a sudden gush of dank air brushed over them.

The two girls and the young man hid within a small niche in the wall when they heard footsteps coming from one of the tunnels that connected to the one they occupied. Two burly guards came into view; they dragged a prisoner between them. Orola recognized him as one of the pudgy young men she had seen among the king's favorites.

His hands were tied behind his back, and his naked body was covered with bruises. He stumbled and fell when the guards pulled on the chains. One of them kicked him in the head. "Get up, pretty boy," he taunted. "No more favors from the king, hey?"

The other guard laughed. "Why don't you speak to us? I guess you didn't come up to the king's expectations, so he had your tongue removed."

"Only a fast tongue pleases the king," they both said in unison and laughed again, pulling the prisoner to his feet. The young man tried to say something, but only croaking unintelligible sounds came from his bloody mouth. The three turned into another tunnel, and soon their muffled voices disappeared in the distance.

"Now you've seen the king's evil work," Mirki said, turning to her brother. "That was one of his favorite lovers."

Bran was silent and stepped back into the tunnel. A grim expression darkened his handsome face. "Let's follow them. Maybe they will lead us to where we want to go."

They walked briskly but tried not to make any noise for fear other guards might hear them. Finally, they heard the noisy laughter of the two guards they had been following and slowed down. Carefully, they walked on.

By now, it was nearly pitch-black, since there were no torches in the walls, but they saw light ahead, just around the next corner. They had almost reached it, when they heard approaching footsteps, and then the two guards suddenly stood in front of them.

One carried a torch. "Hey, where are you going?" He held up the torch and squinted at Bran.

"Just bringing another prisoner," Bran said, trying to move out of the way.

"Which one is the prisoner?" The other guard suddenly drew his sword. "These two are women, and they are not even chained. One of them is armed!" he cursed.

Bran jumped back as the one with the torch closed in on him. He pushed Mirki behind him and faced his attacker, fencing off the first blow of the guard's sword with the shield-ring he wore around his forearm. Then he drove his sword into his opponent's chest.

Meanwhile, Orola had engaged the second guard. He was no match for her agility and her skill with the sword. After their weapons clashed together a few times, she pierced his heart with one forceful stroke.

"You are quick with your sword," she said to Bran.

The young man wiped the sweat from his brow. "Not as fast or skillful as you. We surprised them, and that was in our favor," he said flippantly, but couldn't hide a proud smile.

They walked on until they stepped into a large cavern. It was well lit from torches attached to rings in the walls. Orola felt a slight breeze and noticed the fresh air.

There must be an air duct somewhere, she thought, and looked around. She found it in the ceiling, but it was out of reach and too small, in case they needed a quick escape route.

She spied an entrance to another tunnel at the end of the cavern, barred by a heavy iron gate. However, she noticed that it stood open, and there didn't seem to be any guards in sight.

Silently, with swords drawn, Orola and Bran padded toward the gate. Mirki followed close behind them. She had taken a sword from one of the dead guards, but she carried it awkwardly.

Muffled screams came from the tunnel. They entered it and walked toward the terrible sounds. As they came closer, they heard other sounds, none of them pleasant. Moaning, whimpering, and sometimes hysterical laughter told horrid stories.

The noises came from small caves on either side of the corridor. Thick wooden doors closed the entrances to the caves. Sometimes, a face, almost unrecognizable as belonging to a human being, peered through small window slits in the doors.

The screams were louder now. At last they stood before of an open door, looking aghast at the scene in front of them.

Inside the cave stood a huge naked creature, half man, half animal, as tall as two men. Its skin was as white as snow with a sickly-looking sheen to it. A white naked tail sprouted from between its two huge buttocks, reaching down to the floor. A filthy rag of hair adorned its tip.

The face of the creature could almost have been called human, had it not been for the large red eyes and the heavy jaw with its two long canines protruding over its upper lip. A brush of bristly hair ran down the length of its spine, starting at the base of its bald head.

Before him stood a woman, her hands up, fear visible in her expression, fear of what was to come in the clutches of the monster. The terrible screams came from her lips.

Bran stood, his face an icy mask, watching the scene for a moment, then he let out a hoarse shout and jumped forward, his sword aiming for one of the giant's thick thighs.

The creature turned its grotesque head. The red eyes stared at the little man who dared to disturb it. It lashed out with the long tail, catching Bran in the chest with such force that he was thrown across the cave. The young man hit the wall hard and slid to the filthy floor, where he lay dazed and bleeding from a head wound.

The red eyes fastened their gaze on the two girls. Mirki started to whimper and rushed over to her brother, cradling his bleeding head in her lap.

Orola met the giant's gaze without fear. The crystal between her breasts pulsed bright red, and the jewel in the hilt of her sword burned like a hot flame.

As she watched the monster approach the poor woman, whom she assumed was the queen, she gathered the power of her god inside her body. The molecules of her cells rearranged themselves, changed the tissue of her flesh, her skin, her bones.

She knew the creature couldn't be reasoned with, but it was

vicious and might physically prove to be a match for her. She also knew that this was the king's son.

A monster. Half man, half beast, he must possess a certain intelligence. She could not be careless or underestimate him.

Without taking his eyes off Orola, the giant man-beast roared and pushed the woman he had grabbed down onto the filthy straw, where she lay crumpled like a used rag, sobbing and moaning loudly.

The half-man grinned, the long canines gleaming in the dim light of the lanterns.

"Me mad," he said with a harsh, guttural voice. "You make me hurry. Me mad. Me like nobody watch. Me like go on for long time. Feel good long time. Now no good. Me mad." Then he laughed with a hollow, ugly sound and advanced toward Orola.

The limpid, white pole between his legs started to rise again. "I take you. You make feel good. You young, not old like she." He pointed to the whimpering woman on the ground.

Orola backed out of the cave into the tunnel. She needed more space to dart back and forth.

"You want play?" The giant picked up a large double-bladed axe and swung it over his head. "Me like play." Moving purposefully toward Orola, the half-man tried to catch her with one of his huge paws, but she deftly moved out of his grasp and slipped through the trunk-like legs.

She quickly turned and, with a defying shout, she brought down her sword arm and sliced off half the tail. Picking up the cut-off piece, she bounced out of the giant's reach.

His howl of pain echoed through the caves as the mad half-man grabbed the bloody tail stump, trying to stop the bleeding. Then he roared savagely and swung the huge axe. It crashed into one of the closed wooden doors, reducing the hard wood into a pile of splinters.

While the giant man was trying to free the axe, Orola dashed back in and, with two deft strokes, she castrated the screaming creature.

"This is for the queen," she shouted, dancing back again.

In a terrible rage and excruciating pain now, the howling monstrous man brought down his weapon again and again, but Orola moved like a swift shadow. One moment she was in front of the raging giant, the next behind him, and every time she danced by, she left her mark.

The half-man moved with a speed Orola would never have thought possible of someone with such great bulk. Had she been a mere human, the fight would have been over in moments, but she was a Moon Priestess, the power of the Ancient God was in her, and even this savage creature could not match her strength.

The giant was bleeding from many wounds, and Orola wanted to bring the fight to an end. She did not believe in torturing an enemy, even a loathsome creature such as this one.

She silently uttered one short prayer to her god, felt the surge of power raging through her body then moved in for the kill. She was only a blur as she jumped into the air. The keen edge of her sword sliced through muscle tissue, cut off the terrible roar of the enraged giant, cut through the vertebrae that held the strands of nerves that carried the messages from the small brain to the huge body and cut off the blood supply feeding that brain.

Orola already stood at a safe distant when the grotesque head fell to the ground with a heavy thud.

The hugely muscled arms flayed helplessly as the headless body walked on, and then the battered, bleeding body of the giant sank to the filthy tunnel floor, blood pumping from the severed neck.

Orola looked down at the fallen giant, almost feeling pity. As evil as this creature had behaved, it had not been an evil thing, just a tormented creature, not human and not animal. The real evil lay within the man who, in an unholy union, had spawned this monster.

Sheathing her sword, she slowly walked back into the queen's prison. Bran stood by the entrance, holding his head. A trickle of blood ran down the side of his face, but he was smiling.

Impulsively, he reached out, pulled her into his embrace, and gave her a hug. She relaxed against him for a moment, enjoying the strong arms of a man around her, a feeling she did not experience too often. Most men, after seeing her in action, were afraid of her, did not trust her. Even her voluptuous body could not hide the fact that she was not a mere human woman, but something else, a creature, a thing to be feared.

She freed herself gently. "How is the queen?" she asked.

"I will be all right," a soft voice came from the back of the cave. "Thank you for what you did."

It surprised Orola to see the queen standing. She was a large woman, with wide shoulders and a solid body. It was hard to judge her age. Her breasts were sagging slightly, but they still had a nice shape to them, which meant she couldn't be very old.

Even though still big, her body showed signs of having lost some weight. Her ribs were showing, and her face looked haggard, with sunken cheeks and large dark rings under her eyes.

She stood erect, and her green eyes looked defiantly. Even the time in this filthy cave had not broken her spirit, but she did cast her eyes down for a moment. When she looked at Orola, she seemed somewhat subdued. "I am ashamed you had to witness my humiliation," she said. "I wish we could have met under different circumstances."

Mirki removed her cloak and offered it to the queen, who draped it around her naked body, giving the girl a grateful smile.

"I came to find my sister," Orola said. "She was your advisor."

"Sirla. The poor woman," the queen said sadly. "She was dear friend. I have not seen her since I was imprisoned in this dungeon."

A commotion in the tunnel outside made them turn to see a man stumble into the cave. Bran drew his sword partly from its sheath but stopped when he recognized the young man they had seen earlier with the two prison guards. He carried something in his hand and offered it to Orola, who took it from him.

It was a ring.

"This is Sirla's ring. Where did you get it?" Orola asked.

The young man just grunted and motioned for her to follow him. Then he turned and stumbled out of the door.

Orola noticed that most of the doors to the other cells stood now open and fearful faces were peering into the tunnel. Some of the people had already ventured out of their prisons and were excitedly gesturing at the headless body of the giant.

Orola followed the pudgy young man, who was almost running now. He stopped in front of a closed door. He gestured wildly as he opened it.

Cautiously, Orola entered and gaped at the grimy creature sitting on the straw, staring at her with large, wild eyes. Her tangled hair was filthy, and her bones showed through her naked, pallid skin.

"Sirla?" Orola cried, rushing into the room to sink down beside the older woman.

"Orola," the woman sobbed and buried her face on the girl's shoulder. "I am so glad to see you. I never gave up hope, because I knew the Sisterhood would not forget me, but I was so lost without my star-crystal, so alone. I tried to speak to my god, but without the *Holy Communicator*, he did not hear me. There was no answer."

Orola stroked the older woman's hair, her own tears running freely. "You're not alone anymore," she said softly, handing her the ring.

With shaking hands, Sirla accepted the ring and pushed it on her finger. As soon as it touched her skin, the jewel glowed brightly and, sighing, Sirla sank back, her eyes closed.

Orola watched silently as the power of the ancient god *Central Computer* flowed through the other woman's system, building up her strength, mentally and physically.

After a while, Sirla stirred and sat up. Her black eyes

sparkled, her face took on a more youthful appearance with her smile, and her whole posture had changed. She was still emaciated; it would take some time to fill out flesh and muscles, but her strength had returned. So had her spirit.

"Where is the queen?" she asked, rising to her feet. "I must go to her."

"She is fine," Orola said, mentally reaching for her sister's mind. Only through the mind-net could they communicate without words, much faster and more complete than any other way.

Their minds touched, merged, became almost one. Orola related events of her journey, and Sirla transferred her own story into the younger woman's consciousness.

Sirla shuddered when she saw the body of the half-man on the floor and re-lived the battle through Orola's mind. She was not a trained warrior like the younger woman, only an advisor. Her mind had been expanded and prepared to absorb knowledge and to teach this knowledge, unlike Orola, who was born into the cast of the Moon Priestesses and was trained to do battle.

The prisoners were a poor sight, most of them undernourished, their bodies and their hair filthy from neglect. All showed signs of being beaten and abused. Some had their tongues cut out; some had been blinded. One man's penis had been cut off, and a few had been castrated. The women had been abused by the monstrous half-man.

They were all angry and ready for revenge. When they saw the dead body of their guard lying in his own blood on the floor and finally realized they were free, they cheered and began moving toward the exit.

Two guards who came running to check what the commotion was all about were literally torn to pieces. Orola and her little group followed slowly behind the raging mob.

When they reached the main gate at the top of the stairs, a number of guards, on the alert upon hearing the screaming prisoners, rushed up the stairs to meet them.

They had managed to close the iron gate, but one of the prisoners, a big one-eyed man, smashed open the lock with the giant's battleaxe. The guards fought for their lives as the mad prisoners attacked them with iron bars, chains, wooden clubs and bare hands and feet.

"Let's get out of here as fast as we can before more guards come. We are not really needed here," Orola said to her companions. They followed her quickly up the rest of the stairway.

They came out in a small guardhouse where only one guard stood sentry. Orola carefully pushed open the gate.

"What's all the…?" he began to say when he heard the small grating sound. Seeing that the one entering was not another guard coming up the stairs, he drew his sword.

Before he could clear steel, Orola kicked him in the head with her foot, knocking him out.

"Don't kill him," she said to Bran, who had his weapon in his hand. "He seems so young. Give him a chance."

They didn't see anyone in the courtyard when they stepped out of the guardhouse. The air felt brisk, and the sun was barely visible beyond the rooftops. It was still early morning. Orola looked into the cloudless sky and sighed in pleasure. The beginning of a beautiful day.

A good day for a prison break.

The queen lifted her arms above her head, breathing deeply, her eyes squinting against the bright light. "It is good to feel fresh air on my skin and to see the sun again," she said, tears streaming down her sunken cheeks. Then she wiped the tears off her face and lifted her chin.

"I must not cry. My people must not see me weak." She

began walking toward the palace. "Let's go. I am ready to take back my crown."

They walked across the empty yard, up the wide steps, and stopped in front of the huge wooden doors. The two guards standing on either side of the entrance turned away sleepily when they recognized Bran.

"The party is over," one of them said, pointing at the people sleeping on the furs.

Bran glared at him furiously. "Mind your manners when you're in the presence of your queen!" he snapped, stepping aside to let the queen pass.

When the guard saw the regal figure walking past Bran, he dropped to his knees and blurted out, "You are alive, your Highness? We were told you are dead."

The queen stopped and smiled with royal confidence at the man. "I am very much alive," she said, "and I am happy to see one of my royal subjects." Then she turned and looked at the other guard, who stared as if seeing a ghost.

He also dropped to his knees and reached for the queen's hand. "Forgive me, my Queen. I can't believe it, but it is you." He kissed her hand and stood up, looking into her eyes. He was still a young man with clear eyes and a large, square chin. "I am yours to command, my Queen. Death to all who oppose you!"

The queen nodded and turned, slowly walking toward the throne.

It was empty.

When she reached it, she stood silent for a moment, and then she sat down, her eyes roving disapprovingly over the sleepers. The two guards had followed her and taken up positions on either side of the throne.

The queen beckoned to Mirki. "Bring me my robe, child."

As Mirki disappeared through some curtains, the queen shook her head and turned to Bran. "Wake up these people and let them know their queen is back."

Orola had been watching the doorways leading into the throne room. She didn't like any of this. It had been too easy.

Her mind reached toward Sirla.

I hope the queen is not so foolish as to believe she is back in power.

She is not, sister. She knows she is in mortal danger, but she has to start somewhere.

Shouting voices could be heard from the outside, just before the doors were pushed open, and the escaped prisoners poured into the room, accompanied by other town's people.

"The queen is alive," they shouted, falling to their knees when they spotted her sitting on the throne.

Some of the sleepers were rudely awakened when the throng of people pushed them out of the way.

The clamor of weapons from behind the curtains made Orola turn. The curtains were pushed aside, and a score of armed guards with drawn swords burst into the room. The fat usurper king stepped through, the dark-robed figure of the wizard close behind.

When the queen saw the pretender king, she stood, pointing an angry finger at him. "Your days are numbered, traitor," she called in a loud voice. "We took you in as a friend, trusted you, but you misused that trust. You not only mistreated me, but my people as well." Her sweeping hand took in the freed prisoners. "I will let them judge you."

A howling went through the assembled people, and they surged forward, but the imposter king lifted his hand, an evil sneer on his fat lips.

"Stop!" he roared, his voice like rolling thunder. "You hurt me and the queen dies."

Without anyone noticing, the sorcerer had slipped behind the throne. He held a knife in his hand, its sharp edge pressed against the queen's throat.

Orola decided to end this farce, but before she could move, a strange power descended over her and paralyzed every limb in her body.

227

So you thought you could defeat me, Moon Priestess? a voice said inside her head. *I knew from the moment you approached the throne who and what you were.* Waves like laughter rippled through her mind. *Poor little creature. Playing with powers, you don't even understand.*

Orola tried to fight the paralysis but was helpless in its grasp.

What kind of creature are you, and what are you doing to me? From where are you getting your powers? she asked.

Again this insane laughter. *I do naturally what you do with the help of an electronic device, one that you don't even understand.*

Orola saw the king walking toward her. He stopped in front of her; his pudgy hand reached out and removed the jeweled sword from her belt.

"A very useful device, this transmuter," he said aloud. "If not somewhat outdated. I have never seen it used like this before."

Orola tried to command her sword, but her efforts proved useless. *What are you doing to me?* she asked mentally, because her vocal cords would not obey her; for some reason, she could communicate with this kind through mind speech.

Doing to you? Not much, Cat's Eyes. I just took over that part of your brain that controls your body. Nothing too complicated.

Orola sensed the spidery fingers of another mind inside her and tried to push it out.

Who are you? What kind of demon has spawned you? You are not of this world.

This time, the king laughed out loud, but his eyes stayed cold. *I am not a demon, but you are correct. I am not from this world. Unfortunately, I am stuck here and so must make the best of the situation.*

Suddenly, a change seemed to come over the king. His face fell, and the blood drained out of it. Orola felt the power that held her slip away, and she was free to move. She turned to face the queen, but a curious sight met her eyes.

In front of the queen stood two human figures. One was dressed in blue, the other one in silver.

The silver one was a woman, evident by her ample breasts and the tight-fitting clothing. Her long black hair was tied behind her head. Her eyes were large and blue, with slit pupils. The other one was a man. Tall, well built, with almost impossibly wide shoulders, handsome face, dark-skin and curly, blond hair cropped close to his skull. Both carried strange looking weapons in their hands.

The man in blue said something in a foreign language, and the woman answered back, laughing. They looked around the room, shaking their heads. Then they looked at the cowering king who had slunk back, fear in his eyes.

Orola sensed a sudden release of power reaching from him toward the two strangers, and she knew instinctively that he was mentally attacking them. She also felt the counterattack and staggered, caught unaware between the two clashing mind forces. She had never been taught how to defend herself against an invading mind.

The battle was over in moments. The fat body of the usurper king lay writhing on the floor. One of the king's soldiers let out a loud yell and ran at the two strangers, his sword held in front of him, but the blue-clad man lifted his odd weapon and pointed it at the attacker.

A blinding flash reached out toward the soldier and he fell to the floor, his lifeless body blackened and charred. Upon seeing their comrade felled this easily, the other soldiers threw down their weapons and fell to their knees.

Orola noticed that the king's sorcerer had also slumped to the ground, his knife still clutched tightly in his hand. The queen seemed unhurt.

The strange man turned toward Orola. He said something in that foreign language, but she shook her head. "I don't under-stand you. What are you? Are you gods?"

Now the woman looked at her, first at the jewel between her breasts and then into her eyes.

Again, Orola felt the searching touch of another mind.

Don't be afraid, a voice said inside her mind. *I am Dreen. This is Markow, and you are Orola, I perceive.*

Yes, my name is Orola. But who are you? She formulated the words inside her mind, hoping they could understand her.

We come from another world. We are members of an intergalactic police force, and we have been searching for this man for a long time. She pointed at the fallen king. *He is a criminal and has to be punished. From what we see here, he has added much to his list of offences.*

Orola tried to grasp what the other woman was saying but had trouble understanding most of it.

Dreen saw her predicament and touched her hand. *I know you don't understand. This planet is so far away from the regular trade routes and forgotten in the archives. We would never have found Cales if it hadn't been for the beacon-computer on…Solar. When Cales crash-landed on your planet, his ship sent out an automatic distress signal, which was picked up by the beacon-computer and relayed to the nearest Search-and-Rescue computer. It was quite some time before we were notified.* She nodded and smiled. *You know, bureaucracy…and since we were busy with more important cases…*

Her smile vanished. *I am sorry to turn your whole world upside down. Your computer is not a god, only a very sophisticated electronic device. You and I, we belong to the same race. Your ancestors must have come to this planet centuries ago. They were probably members of a police force, judging from the way you are linked to the computer. Here, I will give you a crash course in intergalactic history.*

Orola felt her mind being opened. Very gently, the other mind merged with hers, and a flood of staggering information entered her consciousness.

She saw the vast emptiness of space, millions of stars, which were suns like her own, and the thousands upon thousands of inhabited planets circling those suns. She saw strange creatures, strangers than she could ever have imagined. And she saw the invisible lines connecting all of those wonderful worlds.

She saw this and much more. The woman in silver also poured in assurance, the better for Orola to accept the knowledge she had been given. At first, she didn't want to believe, but in her heart, she knew this was the truth.

Suddenly, she understood her strange powers. She also knew that she didn't need the computer anymore.

It wasn't a god. It had no power at all. The power was inside her; the computer only released it.

Dreen withdrew and turned toward the dark man.

"She is one of us now," she said. "She has great potential. Her powers equal my own, but she needs training."

She spoke *Intergalactic*, and Orola understood. She had learned much in a short time.

The man chuckled and held out a hand. "Welcome to the Galaxy," he said, his teeth flashing white in his tanned face. "I hope you won't be disappointed."

The End

Don't miss out on your next favorite book!
Join the Melange Books mailing list at
www.melange-books.com/mail.html

THANK YOU FOR READING

Did you enjoy this book?

We invite you to leave a review at your favorite book site, such as Goodreads, Amazon, Barnes & Noble, etc.

DID YOU KNOW THAT LEAVING A REVIEW...

- Helps other readers find books they may enjoy.
- Gives you a chance to let your voice be heard.
- Gives authors recognition for their hard work.
- Doesn't have to be long. A sentence or two about why you liked the book will do.

ABOUT THE AUTHOR

Herbert Grosshans lives near Winnipeg, Canada. He spends his free time spinning tales about imaginary worlds and the strange creatures inhabiting them. His frst published story `Te Anniversary Gift' appeared in `Sweet Revenge' published by Midnight Showcase. Even though he writes in other genres, his love is Science Fiction. He enjoys building alien worlds and societies. Most of his stories contain an element of Erotica. All of his books are available from Melange Books.

www.fctitioustales.weebly.com
hegro.blogspot.com
hergros.blogspot.com
hegro@shaw.ca

Also by Herbert Grosshans

Novels

Bullet of Revenge

A Matter of Justice

Mark of the Cobra

Orola, Warrior Priestess

Orion

Operation Stargate Series

Codename Salamander

Seeds of Chaos Duology

Eden's Gate

Hell's Gate

Stardogs Duology

Return to Redsky

Redemption

Stars in Chains Duology

Slave

Liberator

Stonewall Chronicles

Outpost Epsilon

A New Dawn